FATE'S SHADOW

MATTHEW LEDREW

FATE'S SHADOW

THE XANDER DREW SERIES

Published in Canada by Engen Books, St. John's, NL.

Library and Archives Canada Cataloguing in Publication

Title: Fate's shadow / Matthew LeDrew.
Names: LeDrew, Matthew, 1984- author.
Description: Series statement: The Xander Drew series ; 5
Identifiers: Canadiana (print) 20200253883 | Canadiana (ebook) 20200253905 |
ISBN 9781989473535
  (softcover) | ISBN 9781989473542 (PDF)
Classification: LCC PS8623.E424 F38 2020 | DDC C813/.6—dc23

Distributed by:
Engen Books
www.engenbooks.com
submissions@engenbooks.com

First mass market paperback printing: May 2020

Cover Image: Ellen Curtis

For
Ellen

CHAPTER ONE

Breakfast at the Horton household typically consisted of plain toast and instant oatmeal, but today was an exception. As Thomas Horton sat at his kitchen table, munching on a long strip of heavily buttered toast, a bowl of freshly made Cream of Wheat slid into his vision, accompanied by the slow sound of the bowl dragging across the table.

He had been reading a faded sheet of paper that was broken into four columns, each one taking up roughly a quarter of the page. Each quadrant had been their own page at some point, but in the evidence collection process had been scaled down for reproduction. Horton was against this process. He preferred to work with text that had been enlarged for further detail, and there was a Post-it pressed to the page reminding him to make an appointment at Records to do just that. The one he had been currently reading had been in the top-left quadrant: a providence list of the tenant building formally located at 668 Hart Avenue.

Horton was a lanky man in his forties that looked to have lost a considerable amount of weight, the skin that had previously been stretched tight now hanging loose on the bones of his face. His hair was full but thinning, the slightest wisps of grey scattered throughout the rusty brown.

His pupils twitched when the bowl came into view, shifting focus from the page to the white curds of cream that rested in the bed of the charcoal black bowl it had been served in. There were four strawberries in the bowl, cut in half lengthwise and arranged with their innards pointing up at him like eight hearts... or, his mind connected but he did not say, like a buxom bride on her wedding night.

He looked at it for a moment as though expecting it to do something other than sit there and emit steam into the atmosphere, and a single spoon was slid into his peripheral vision until it was next to the bowl. The entire affair now looked like a Kellogg's ad taken right from 90s Saturday morning television.

Martha stood on the opposite side of their kitchen table, smiling at him from behind cheeks dragged with laugh lines and freckled flesh. She'd been letting her hair grow and now her grayish curls touched either side of her chin for the first time since her twenties. Her hands were clasped in front of her as she smiled at him with that perfect smile of hers, a picture of the perfectly perfect servile wife that she had never been, and that Thomas Horton had never desired.

"Thank you," he said, nodding slightly. He didn't touch or look at the bowl, keeping his attention focused on Martha's every nuanced movement.

She tilted her head and separated her hands only slightly. The combination of the two somehow created the most minimal approximation of a curtsey possible, although he wasn't sure how. The intricacies and subtleties of human movement communication was something he was constantly studying but never adept in. He wasn't sure anyone could be.

"What's the occasion?" he asked. He placed a single finger on the rim of the bowl and brought it closer. The steam brought the sweet scent of the strawberries to his nostrils, tickling and teasing him, but he did not turn his attention away from his wife.

She laughed at him, not her usual laugh. It was genuine and yet wrong, the sound of it coming from her mouth registering in his ears as something uncanny. 'Uncanny Valley' was a term he'd learned and would have put to good use in this situation if he'd been asked: she was acting so much like his wife that her few differences were highlighted all the more.

He raised an eyebrow at her, then turned and cast a glance over the rest of his kitchen.

It was as small as it could possibly have been for the appliances and furniture packed into it. It was so cramped that the porch door could not open all the way without slamming into the back of the chair closest to it, which had many battle scars in its eggshell finish to prove just that. Most of the kitchen was taken up by the table in fact, to the point that even the skinniest occupant had to suck in their stomach to squeeze between the chairs and the countertop.

All appliances had been sunk into the walls to try and save as much room as possible, including the stovetop that had been installed separately from the oven, operating instead as a part of the counter. The oven was on the other wall and had been built into the cupboard, opening like an old-fashioned laundry shoot. Even though everything in the room was new, its cramped, claustrophobic nature gave it the feeling of early twentieth century homes.

The trash can was missing, he realized. There was a faded round-cornered rectangle of floor that was just slightly darker than the floor around it, having been spared the bleaching effect of the sun. The splotch of floor was in the small amount of space between the doorframe and the countertop.

But that wasn't the only thing missing.

He smiled wanly and nodded, then picked up his spoon and dipped it into his cream of wheat. He was careful to scoop up one of the strawberry halves, and now it sat in the centre of his utensil, outlined in white lumps of sugary delight.

Martha picked up her own bowl from the counter, which she had chosen to adorn with fresh blueberries, and sat down at the chair across from him. The uncanny smile she'd been wearing faded, becoming the normal Martha smile he'd become accustomed to over two decades of marriage.

He took the mouthful of cereal, swallowed it, then took another and did the same. When she had also taken two spoonfuls and had the third (plump with blueberries) in her mouth, he put down his spoon and asked, "So where is it?"

She stopped and met his eye, the metal arm of the spoon sticking comically out from between her thin lips. He laced his fingers together in front of his face and rested his elbows on the table, forming a triangle with his arms and the table itself. She'd pictured him doing this several times, but had never seen it. She swallowed, put the spoon down, then squinted at him with a playful smile. "Did you just entrap me?"

He paused, his head bobbing back and forth as he considered that. "Maybe, yes."

"Kudos."

He laughed, a more honest laugh than she'd had a moment ago, and the facade of the interrogator fell away, his hands retreating to their place on either side of his bowl. She had that power over him: the ability to pick the exact right single-word sentence to retaliate against his seriousness and make him break into spontaneous and unexpected levity.

She went back to eating her breakfast.

"No, but where is it?" he asked again, when his laughter had subsided. "There must be something bad in it this time. I can't remember the last time you hid it."

"Election day," she said flatly, between bites.

"Right," he said, nodding dramatically. "Yeah, that was a fun day."

She bobbed her eyebrows but continued to eat. He watched her, and after a moment he wasn't waiting for his wife of twenty-plus years to stop toying with him; he was watching the same young woman eat soup on their first date. He'd been so nervous he'd placed absorbent towels under each of his armpits, but when he'd watched her eat her soup that had gone away. She had been careful not to slurp or spill anything, so careful that she barely got any broth in each spoonful. She had been just as nervous as he'd been, he realized, and the evening had gone well from that point on.

He smiled at her. "Are you meeting Gwen tonight?"

She gave him a sly smile. "Yes. We're seeing a movie at the cheap theatre."

"Anything I'd want to see?"

"You never come to see them."

"...No," he smiled. "I'm trying to gauge if I'll regret that or not."

Martha rolled her eyes at her husband. She did this at least once a day, but the first time of each was always special to her. "I'm not even sure what it is. The latest superhero thing."

"Ugh," he said, waving a hand in front of his face as if the genre were a smell that offended him. "Keep it to yourself when you get back."

She grinned, then nodded.

They ate the rest of their breakfast in peace. He enjoyed the Cream of Wheat so much that he scraped the bottom of the bowl. When she mentioned that there was still some in the pot, he made the uncomfortable journey around the cramped table to the stovetop and took another half bowl, added a small pat of butter, then brought it back to his chair and ate that until the bowl was clean as well.

They went to their downstairs washroom and stood at adjacent sinks and brushed their teeth together. They both sat down on their comfortable middle-income couch and watched the late night comedy shows they'd DVR'd from the night before, laughing in mostly the same places. Martha laughed at both the wordplay and the sight gags, curled up next to her husband, when he only laughed at the jokes he heard. While he was listening, the red file folder he'd had at the table was resting on the arm of the couch, and he was continuing to glance over providence forms and images of what could have been at its best called a comprehensive blaze. One photo showed 668 Hart Avenue both before and after the fire: one showing a cheap building that packed its residents in tight, the other showing a building lain to waste except for two load-bearing pillars that had survived the devastation. Chlorine trifluoride had been used as an accelerant he'd discovered later.

At one point, Martha had looked up when her husband had failed to laugh at a particularly salient political joke she knew was of his sort and found him to be staring at a picture of a young boy, no more than six months old.

Her smile faded and she watched him for a long moment, before turning back to her program and letting it distract her.

When the programs were over, she went upstairs to change. When she came back down, he was sitting at the kitchen table with the file open in front of him. A tablet computer was propped up in front of him, open to a tab full of text. Every so often he would scroll up on it and compare the text on the screen to something he was reading, then turn back to the page.

"You should finish that novel Clark lent you," she said as she was slipping on her shoes.

He turned and looked up from his notes. "Hn?"

"Clark. He lent you his John Land novels; you should read them."

He warbled, his mouth moving back and forth. "I don't know. The plot was good at first, but it started to get silly towards the middle. Too many things started to pile up, it didn't seem like it made sense."

"Did you finish it?"

"...No."

"Then you can't know if it all makes sense or not. You never know if it all makes sense until the end."

He paused, nodded, then turned back to his notes. "I sincerely hope that's true."

She sighed, then stepped forward and gave him a kiss. "I want some reading time tonight. *Novel* reading. I want to dig into that Janet Evonovich and I want you to read something too. Something *fictional*."

He smiled and nodded. They kissed again, and she walked out through their back door.

He watched her go, and when he heard her car start, he got up from the table and went for the cupboard under the sink. There was nothing under there but cleaning supplies and an empty bucket. He looked in each of the cupboards in the kitchen and pantry, then made his way to the living room and up the stairs. After he had searched their bedroom, he had finally made his way into the upstairs washroom -- which had long since been labeled 'her' washroom -- and slid back the shower curtain.

There, in the centre of the tub, was the rectangular waste basket that should have been in their kitchen. Inside it were the stems of five strawberries, and one newspaper.

He pulled out the paper and brushed off the greens from it, leaving red smears behind on the headline which proclaimed a new highway was going to connect into west Hollywood, to be completed within the next five years. He sat on the edge of the tub and turned through section after section, briefly skimming each headline until he found the one that would have made Martha segregate the entire paper into the trash and then the trash into the washroom.

The crime section had it, and once he found it, he wondered how he hadn't checked there first.

"Murdock trial starts this week."

He read the first paragraph or two of the article, let out a deep sigh, then put the paper back into the basket, and the basket back into the tub.

He made himself more Cream of Wheat.

CHAPTER TWO

"Have you got this one?" Janet Nesbit asked, holding up a washed-out color photo of a tall man with well-coiffed hair and a puffy jacket collar that obscured part of his rough-shaven jawline.

Duncan Taggart looked up from the list of names he was hunched over. He clasped a red highlighter in his hand as though it would escape if he didn't grip it in just the right way. He was clean-shaven with a medium build that looked shorter because of the clothes he wore: dusters that came down past his waist and pants that bunched at the ankles. His brown hair was always neatly pushed back and there was always a cigarette behind his right ear, although Janet had never seen him smoke it. He studied the photo she held up for a moment, clacked his tongue against the roof of his mouth, then nodded.

"That is Harold Amir," he said, turning back to his list. He found the name near the top with the rest of the A's and put two dots next to it with his highlighter to point it out to her. It had already been crossed out. "He worked for Shane International for thirty years until 2015 and retired with full benefits. He's been back inside the building a total of five times since, each time for a charity ball or an event or some other such thing that they invite the old guard to."

Janet squinted at him as he turned over a page in the file next to him, which was a wall of text that detailed Human Resources complaints lodged against varying working members of the Shane company. Every time he came across a name, he would take out his black pen and put a dot next to it on the company register, which was a miles-long document of current and former employees and staff. They were currently working on only the A, B, and C portions of the alphabetical list. Those who were proven not to have been involved with the homicides at Shane were crossed off the list with red highlighter.

What gave her pause was that Duncan had rattled off the information on Amir without looking at any employee roll or HR form. He'd known it, the same way young children could rhyme off the stats of their favorite baseball players simply by looking at the photo on the front of the card they were on. She turned at photo over, looked at Amir's partially covered face, and frowned. It looked like a photo one would see on the cover of a supermarket tabloid, taken with a grainy telephoto lens. "He's crossed out?" she asked.

"He was at a Children's Charity event during most of the murders. In Uganda. It's on YouTube," Duncan replied under his breath, even as he added a black dot next to two names on the B-page. "As alibis go..."

She shrugged and nodded, moving the photo of Amir back into its rightful place in the 'out' pile.

Detective Janet Nesbit had been with LAPD12 her entire adult life. She'd started out as a traffic cop here, graduated to a 'Uni', then eventually made her way to the Vice squad. She'd been offered a promotion in Vice12 three separate times, and each time she had turned it down. She'd known that if she'd allowed herself to rise any higher in Vice12 than she had, she would have stayed there forever. She was that sort, always had been, and she recognized it. And what she'd wanted -- needed -- for as long as she could remember, was to be in Homicide. More specifically, to be at Homicide12. She'd been there for two years before she made Detective. The promotion had come with little extra pay and an unfeasible amount of extra stress that had begun to play havoc with her biology almost immediately, but she wouldn't have given it back for anything.

Duncan Taggart was not a member of LAPD12, a fact he had been made keenly aware of through most of his tenure occupying space there. Duncan was an agent with the Federal Bureau of Investigation (FBI to most) that had been assigned to Los Angeles to find the perpetrator behind a series of homicides targeting people who worked at Shane International -- a company with interests and holdings all over the world. As such, crimes which had been perpetrated solely in Los Angeles became of interest on a federal level, necessitating a link between the two: a link which happened to begin and end with his temporary placement at Homicide12.

On his first day, he had been given an empty desk near the front entrance and many, *many* disdainful glances from the local officers.

He leaned back on his chair, a comfy black mesh recliner that had been there since he took the desk, and pointed to a name on the sheet he held up. The name 'Dion Brusk' appeared in smeared typeface under his rough fingertip. "Will you come look at this?" he asked, sliding his chair back a little so that Janet could look at the file he had open without crowding her personal space.

She was about to move into the void he'd made for her, then she backed up, her hands pushing up into the air dramatically. "Oh no, I'm not falling for that."

He raised an eyebrow at her. "No, the guy... Brusk. He's been out of town for each of the murders. Business trips, yes, but... anyway, there's an HR file on him as long as my dick."

"Hand 'em over. I'm not going near that." Janet paused, his toilet humor finally registering. "Or *that*," she concluded.

He shrugged, moved back into his place behind the desk, and picked up the papers, handing the awkwardly stapled pile to her. "Not sure why you wouldn't --" He stopped, narrowing his eyes. "Please tell me this isn't about the curse."

He noticed two officers behind Janet cross themselves. They did it as a reaction, as though they did it automatically whenever those words were said aloud.

"Ahm... no. Nope," Janet said. She took the file from him before he could rescind it and began to look for the lines he was referencing.

Duncan sighed, strumming his finger across his upper lip. He contemplated taking the cigarette out from behind his ear, but didn't. "This is ridiculous," he said finally. "You're officers of the law. Pillars of the community.

Yet here you are, afraid to sit at a bloody chair because of some silly, superstitious curse."

The officer behind Janet crossed himself again.

"Don't you have somewhere to be?!" Duncan barked suddenly.

The officer jumped, startled, then nodded and turned and walked away from the copier he'd been at. It was still producing images he'd left on the tray.

Duncan turned back to Janet. "See that? Ludicrous. That's what you look like. That what you want?"

She smiled, then shrugged animatedly. "Look," she said. "Thomas Horton had that desk for twenty years. *Twenty years*, and there were only three cases he couldn't solve. Three. He kept the photos of the victims on his desk like trophies or reminders or something. I have a high solve rate, but you wouldn't be able to fit all my unsolveds on one desk. You'd need a place the size of the frigging LACMA."

Duncan snorted.

"You're the first motherfucker to take that desk since he left, and you've had one case, and it's *still* not solved. Not solved and no leads. That's some bad voodoo." She made two guns with her fingers and pointed at the desk. "And I ain't going near it."

He rolled his eyes, then went back to his notes on the desk. They stayed like that for less than a minute, each of them looking over their own sheets, before he pushed off from the desk with sudden force and rolled back. "Maybe you're right," he said, stepping up from the comfortable chair. "Maybe it's the desk that's the problem."

He grabbed a manila file folder and his phone, placing

one under his arm and the other in his pocket. He cocked his head at Janet, who was looking at him as though he'd started to Flamenco dance, head tilted and one eyebrow raised.

"I saw a grilled cheese sandwich place on the way here, looked okay. Lines were long but it's past the rush now. Is it any good?"

Her raised eyebrow raised ever the more.

"I'll pay," he said. He clucked his tongue against the roof of his mouth, then opened his desk drawer and took out a pink pill bottle, placing it into his pocket with his phone before she could see what it was.

She continued to look at his suspiciously.

"For fuck's sake," he huffed, motioning toward the desk. "You said it was the damn desk; let's get away from the damn desk. We can work just as poorly sitting in a booth and eating cheesy bread. There's a curse? I say fuck the curse."

Someone began to cross themselves.

Duncan jabbed a finger toward them before they could even touch their second shoulder. "I swear by all that's fucking holy, I will make a religious rights complaint against your ass, I shit you not."

The man balked, then lowered his hand and went back to his work. As soon as Duncan turned away, he finished the motion of crossing himself.

"Fine," said Janet, getting up from her chair and grabbing her coat.

The Drip was an odd restaurant, whose menu only consisted of many variations on two items: grilled cheese sandwiches and roasted red-pepper soup. The cheeses were different -- there was a build-your-own grill station, there were different variations and accoutrements -- but at the end of the day there were really only three choices: grilled cheese, red pepper soup, or grilled cheese dipped in red pepper soup. Even the walls were painted cheese yellow.

Duncan crunched into a grilled cheese sandwich as he read over the file in front of him, a lengthy HR report on a man named Ray Chaswick.

Janet sat down next to him with her own sandwich and a small ramekin of red pepper soup, not enough to be considered a meal itself, just enough for dipping.

"Have I ever said anything... inappropriate to you?" Duncan asked suddenly, looking up from his papers.

She stared at him for a long moment, chewing her sandwich in one cheek and looking like a chipmunk. "Fuck off," she said finally, after swallowing.

He chuckled and shook his head. "Sorry, it's just... reading these files, man, it seems like every guy has at least one sex harassment complaint in his jacket."

She nodded. "Way of the world." She looked down at her grilled cheese and looked to suddenly regret it, a look of concern coming over her face.

Duncan reached into his coat pocket and produced a pink bottle of pills, placing it on the table between them. They were antacids. They stayed there for a long moment as Janet lowered her eyes at them. "Have them, they'll help with the digestion," he said, making a shooing motion as if pushing them towards her.

She squinted, then picked up the bottle and shook

out two of the chalky tablets before taking them. She crunched them between her teeth before swallowing them with a gulp of water, then met Duncan's eye. "How'd you know?"

He shrugged. "It's not uncommon. Just about every agent with less than five years under his belt needs some digestion help or he'll shit blood for a week. Stress, stress is a killer."

She nodded, then took another bite of her sandwich.

"You seeing anyone about it?"

She looked back up, startled that the conversation was continuing.

"Sorry," he said, raising both hands in the air. "None of my business."

She nodded again, then swallowed.

Duncan paused, clicking his tongue against the roof of his mouth again. "So, what's got everyone on edge this week?" he asked, changing the topic as best he could.

Janet moved her tongue from one side of her mouth to the other, thoughtfully. "There's a trial starting up this week, trying a guy name of Victor Murdock."

He paused and waited for her to continue. "Is that name supposed to mean something to me?"

Her mouth moved from side to side. "Not really. Just some douchebag who got his rocks off hitting people over the head when they weren't looking. Allegedly." She paused. "It was the last case Thomas Horton worked before he was... before he retired. It was hard on him, I think. I was there for it, but I wasn't really *there*, you know?"

Duncan nodded. "Peripherally."

"Yes," she chimed, snapping her fingers and pointing

at him. "Yes exactly, I was there peripherally. Yes. Anyway, he retired just after the arrest, so he hasn't been around to see it through. I mean, I think we'll get it over the finish line... it's just Horton was so proud of that solved rate, I think if this one ends up in the loss column, it'll be too much like... tarnishing his record, or something."

He nodded again. He touched the cigarette behind his ear, brought his hand back down, then turned back to his file. He snapped it shut and waved it in front of him. "I'm not going to get him like this, am I?"

Janet pursed her lips, then shook her head.

He moved the cigarette from his ear to his lips, let it sit there for a moment, then put it back again. He cursed softly to himself, then put the file away in his briefcase.

"I am," she said finally, just as he was going back to his sandwich.

He raised an eyebrow to her.

"Seeing someone about it, I mean."

He held her eye for a long moment, then nodded. "That's good. Everyone should."

CHAPTER THREE

She hadn't known what to expect the first time she met him. She hadn't even known what to think of the building. She'd pictured LAFP as a long, spidery, one-storey building in the middle of the desert. Instead when she'd been dropped off by her cab, she'd found herself standing before a tall, white behemoth of a building in the centre of downtown, its shadow falling over the low-rent suburbs that the majority of its population was picked from.

Megan Greene had been in California for less than a month, and in that time had spent most of her energy acclimating herself to the fine details and difference between Maine criminal law and California criminal law. She was surprised to see how little there was... Most of the differences were in minimum and maximum sentencing. California had been quicker to adapt from the 'three strikes' view of drug sentencing. Beyond that the differences were miniscule, and typically centered around property law and family court.

She stopped at a security checkpoint halfway across the main floor, which itself was divided into large waiting areas, security stations, offices, and five small emergency courtrooms. The prison didn't start occupying prisoners until the third floor, she'd known that going in.

The checkpoint was a faux wall that was nonetheless treated like a real concrete barrier, rather than the building-wide rail it was. There were eight gaps in the rail where there was both a locked turnstile and a large body scanner. They used to be metal detectors, and there was still discolored tile surrounding each entrance from when they'd been replaced.

The line for the scanner on the far right had a much shorter line than the other seven, each of which had at least twenty impatient, shuffle-footed people in them. The far-right stall was for employees and legal aids only and was clearly marked as such. It did not stop the odd disheveled human or distracted middle-class traffic-court attendee from venturing aimlessly into the line as though they'd discovered some magical secret line that the others had missed.

Megan stepped into the line and waited while the person in front of her finished. She reflexively took out her phone and checked her notifications -- something she would have laughed at only ten years before and now found herself doing at any moment of quiet or patience. There were three messages from her home firm, two from Nathan, and one from the office account. She opened the first message from Nathan and began to read.

"Ma'am?"

The soft, falsetto voice made her look up. The guard was staring at her with a gray plastic bin extended to his fullest reach. It hung in the air between them like a disembodied lung, large and precariously weighted. The guard had a name tag that read Stephen, with no indicator of whether that was his first or last name. He was the same glazed tan color that everyone who spent any time in the Los Angeles sun adopted. Her unconscious brain spent the first several milliseconds of their interaction trying to place him, ethnically, into one box or the other, and the rest of the interaction chided herself with embarrassment for the first one.

"Sorry," she said, placing her phone into the bin. He retracted it and put it on the track of rollers behind him that led into an x-ray machine presided over by a tall woman who stared at the screen in front of her as though it were a federal crime to look away.

Stephen looked her up and down, taking in the total of her. Her suit was expensive, the sort that straddled the should-be-nonexistent line between traditionally power-ful and comfortably feminine. It was a hard line to parse and she didn't pretend to know how to do it, she paid a stylist for that, and the stylist had worked with her firm to produce a wardrobe that was 'on brand,' both for the firm and for her position in it. "You've done this before," he said. It was not said as a question.

"I haven't, actually," Megan corrected.

He frowned, then motioned to a worn line of tape on the floor a foot in front of the body scanner. "Stand with your toes touching the yellow line please. Remove your shoes. If you have any more electronic devices, please re-move them and place them in the bin. Remove any metal jewelry, pins, brooches, hair clips, necklaces, earrings or piercings of a ferrous-metal variety."

She pulled out her earrings and placed them in the bin. She'd worn clip-ons over her piercings even though she felt childish doing so, only because she'd suspected this would come up.

"Any non-plastic pens or cases, into the bin. Any implants or IUDs, this is the time to tell us and provide relevant documentation."

She shook her head.

"Please spread your feet until one is on either end of the yellow line. Please do not make sudden moves during the physical inspection. Please be aware I will have to briefly lay hands on you but that it is being done in accordance with federal law and is under the supervision of my peers." He nodded to the woman staring at the x-ray screen, who did not look up when she nodded in response. "Do you understand these instructions as I've explained them to you?"

Megan nodded, even as she spread her stockinged feet to either side of the line.

Stephen stepped up behind her, and in the moment he was out of her peripheral vision, she felt her heart rate quicken. No matter how many times this modern ritual was performed -- usually at airports -- it still felt *wrong*.

His gloved hands that smelled of rubber and starch were in her curly red hair suddenly. They did not tease the ends of the strands like a lover would, they bore in, pushing past the tangles and structure of product and plastic pins to find their way directly to her scalp. They rummaged their way over the whole of her head, not missing a single square inch, the sharpness of his nails felt even through the veil of rubber he wore over them.

She winced but tried not to, conscious of the others in the room. She had no idea which of, if any, the people in the room could end up opposite her in court and did not want to show her discomfort.

When he was done thoroughly dismantling her well-coiffed, burnt-red curls into a tangled mess that looked close to the way it had when she'd woken up, he moved down to inspect her torso. He patted at her with a gentle touch -- nothing like some of the work she'd gotten done by the TSA, but there was no touch gentle enough to make it not feel invasive. He cupped not her breast but the area beneath them, rising up to make certain there were no weapons hidden among her undergarments. He moved her skirt and ran his hand up her thigh to check for a concealed weapon and found none. On her second leg, he went up further than she was comfortable, and even though she was sure it was not intentional, she had to stop herself from making a snide remark at his expense.

When he was done, he came back around to her front and had produced a penlight. She wasn't sure where it had come from, and its appearance after he'd run his hand up her inner thigh was slightly jarring; as though he'd found it there and brought it around to question her on its use.

"Open your mouth," he said, clicking the light on with a snap of his thumb.

She noted that 'please' had been lost somewhere between her bra strap and her thigh, and recalled that it was not the first time.

She opened her mouth and he shone the light over all corners of her pink gums and white teeth, even putting that same gloved hand that had been in her hair into her inner cheek and pulling it slightly ajar to see as far down her throat as he could. She began to urge as the smell and taste of latex filled her senses, and he pulled away.

"Clean," he said, waving to an unknown observer

with a practiced motion. He did not apologize, merely motioned her forward onto the yellow X in the centre of the body scanner.

"No really, it's okay," she said, adjusting her skirt until it was back to its original position.

"Hole your arms up at ninety-degree angles," Stephen instructed, holding up his own to illustrate.

She did so, and a section of the scanner encircled her and made a loud mechanical buzzing sound as it did. She waited in that position for what seemed like forever, then eventually turned to the nameless woman at the x-ray. "Am I good to go?"

"Oh, yes," the woman said, as if she'd come to that consensus several minutes before and had simply forgotten to let Megan know.

Megan huffed, stepped out of the body-scanner with ease, and walked over to where her grey tray of belongings sat. Her newly minted visitors badge lay on top of them without so much as a 'there you are,' and she took it. She clipped her earrings back into place and picked up her phone, checking it reflexively. There were three more messages, all from Nathan. This time she hit ignore and headed towards the set of elevators on the far side expanse of the room.

There was a second line at the elevators, this one longer. People got on one at a time and swiped their badges before the door closed instead of piling in to capacity as they typically would. There was a second guard in the elevator that seemed to stay in it for every trip. He looked much like Stephen, but slightly taller and broader.

When the doors opened a third time and it was her turn, Megan stepped into the elevator alongside Stephen

2.0. The interior of the elevator was clean and white with a reflective sheen on the walls above the waistline. There were no buttons, only a card-reader slot and a keyhole. The keyhole was in an odd oblong shape that looked to match a key dangling from Stephen 2.0's waist.

She reached out her badge and swiped it through the card-reader, then stood back alongside him. Unconsciously, she caught herself mimicking his stance and posture as the elevator doors closed and it started to rise through the floors of LAFP.

"You've done this before," Stephen 2.0 said, in the same non-question way that his previous version had. His voice was deeper though; this one had clearly gotten an intimidation patch.

"No," she said, even as her stomach lurched with the inertia of the elevator's motion.

He frowned, as though he were annoyed. "Your badge will bring you to the floor you're cleared for. When the doors open, you'll see that floor's security desk. Please check in at the security desk. Your appointment should already be prepared for your arrival. Your floor's security will lead you to your conference room. If your appointment is considered of imminent danger --"

"He's not," Megan answered.

"--then a security officer will accompany you at all times during your appointment," he continued, as if she hadn't spoken. "If your appointment is not seen as critically dangerous, a member of the security staff will be stationed on alert outside the appointment area at all times."

She nodded. He finished just as soon as the elevator slowed to a halt, and the doors opened on what she only now was learning was the sixth floor. The doors opened and it was as Stephen 2.0 had described: a long desk with rounded corners and turnstiles on either end that led to two different doors. There were three people seated behind the desk currently, and no one else waiting. She walked up to the most receptive looking of the three, handed her badge and gave her name even though her badge had her name on it, and was escorted to the meeting room on the right.

When she pictured prison conference rooms, she pictured the ones back home, which looked remarkably like the ones on TV: grey, concrete and dull, either at a bland folding table or conducted via telephone from either side of plate glass. This room was none of those things; like the desk outside it was sleek and white with rounded corners that she guessed were a safety measure and yet looked good all the same. She felt like she was interviewing for a position as an iStore clerk, rather than interviewing a defendant.

The defendant sat in his oranges at the table farthest from the door, and when it slammed shut behind her, there were just the two of them in the room.

"Victor Murdock?" she asked as she neared the table and pulled out the collapsible chair opposite him.

He nodded, his sharp chin dipping slightly into the beam of sunlight he sat next to.

"My name is Megan Greene, I'm your attorney." She took off her coat and laid it on the vacant chair next to the one across from Murdock, then sat at the chair across from Murdock. The chairs were hard and all metal, the type you got when the comfort of the people sitting in them was the farthest thing from your mind.

She took a file out of her briefcase and opened it on the table in front of her but did not consult it or even spare it a glance. Her phone was next to the file, its edge perpendicular to the edge of the manila edge. She pressed it on, swiped to ignore three new messages from Nathan, then shut the screen off and turned back to her client.

He watched as she did all of this with a quiet smile, his longish nose coming in and out of the beam of light he sat in every time he took a deep breath. Without warning, he closed his eyes and dipped his face into it, looked up, then leaned back into the shadows again.

"You'll have to pardon me," he said. "My holding cell faces due south. I haven't felt a good sunbeam in weeks."

She nodded, then made a note in the margin of her file. It wasn't haphazard: there were lined sections specifically for leaving notes in the margins of the files she printed. She knew her habits and prepared for them. "I'll see what we can do about that," she said under her breath, making no promise.

His head turned to one side, and that small smile of his broadened just a little. "Thank you. There's something so nice about natural light... Light that comes from a place farther away than our grasp of things. We can't step behind natural light, can't see it from the other side. It's... real."

She clicked her pen shut and laid it on the file, perfectly in-line with its edge. She laced her fingers together and held them near the edge of the table close to her central plexus, made eye contact with him in that way only hookers and lawyers were trained to do, and smiled. "You were initially charged with six counts of aggravated assault and one count of murder, in the first degree." She said this coldly and clinically, even though she knew that he knew it. Still, she could not take the chance that anyone who'd come before her had looked him in the eye and given him the facts of the situation he was in before, so it was up to her to do so. "After reviewing your file, I've spoken to the office of the District Attorney and the Murder One has been downgraded to Voluntary Manslaughter."

"That sounds better."

She hedged, moving her mouth from side to side. "It's a maximum sentence of eleven years down from a maximum sentence of life without possibility, so... better, yes. But I want to give you no illusions, that's still not great."

"Without possibility?"

She paused, not sure what he meant for a moment, then smiled. "Of parole. Sorry. Like without possibility of parole."

"I see," he sighed. He laced his fingers into one another then turned away from Megan, staring at a stained spot on the floor for several seconds while he let those thoughts sink in.

She had seen this before and knew to let it run its course.

When he turned back, he made direct eye contact with her and his voice, though wet, was firm. "I have never taken a man's life."

She stared at him a long moment, then nodded. "It should be easy to prove that then."

CHAPTER FOUR

Thomas Horton drove a mole-brown Volkswagen sedan with rust creeping up the passenger-side door that he had yet to notice as he never used that side. The front seats of the car were clean, immaculately so, with the only thing out of place the red file folder that slipped around his passenger-side seat every time he took a hard turn. The backseat was filled with used coffee cups and a few fast-food boxes. He cleaned them out once a week, but they still managed to pile up. Martha had counted the number of coffee cups once when he'd been too sick to go out and had told him he averaged ten cups a day, not counting anything he drank at home.

He sipped his fifth cup of the day now as he pretended to do a crossword puzzle, glancing intermittently at the strip club across the street.

He'd been parked in a small spot just shy of a loading zone for nearly two hours. The street was full of businesses and people going to and from their daily destinations, and twice other cars had honked their horns at him to try and get him to give up his spot, thinking he was just lounging. One had stayed and pressed the horn so many times that it had created a line behind him, and Horton had had to resort to rolling down his window and giving him the finger.

Once he would have rolled down the window and flashed them his badge, but those days were gone.

Two doors up from where he was parked was a fast food establishment with cheap coffee. He'd already purchased two cups from it with the change from his dash but had drank one on the sidewalk and thrown the cup in a trash bin. The less that were in the back if Martha performed another raid, the better.

Two hours ago, he'd watched a man named Humboldt Trueman walk into Box of Delights, a strip club that did even less than most strip clubs to disguise the fact that it offered more than just a show.

Humboldt was in his sixties, making him an old man even in Horton's eyes. He moved with a deft step though, Horton had noted after weeks of surveillance; the type of step one acquired when one was accustomed to creeping without wanting to be heard. An Abductor's Dance, he had used to call it -- but Humboldt wasn't an abductor, at least not as far as he knew.

Humboldt had been in lockup three times in his adult life, the first when he was so young that Horton knew that there were priors that were sealed in youth records. That first stretch in lockup was because he'd driven drunk and accidentally ploughed his car through the middle of a man. He'd hit and run and driven home and sobered up, then had turned himself in. That had gotten him a year in lockup and a year house arrest after. The second time he

had been drag racing and the opposing car had flipped
when they'd both gone around a sharp turn at the same
time. The car hit a bungalow and killed three people, including the driver. They'd gotten him for street racing;
he'd turned himself in. The third stretch had been for arson, and he'd been just past thirty at the time. He'd started
a fire on a building as part of an insurance fraud, but the
dry winds of California had dragged the fire to a nearby
housing complex. Five people had died. His lawyer had
pled him down to three counts of involuntary manslaughter and he'd served ten years.

Most people would have said that Humboldt Trueman
was an idiot... Horton had long since decided the man was
an assassin. Not the type you hired when you wanted to
make a point -- the opposite in fact; the type you hired
when you wanted someone dead and it just *had* to look
like an accident. Because that hit and run victim had been
a low-level cousin in a crime family, and that bungalow
had belonged to a judge who'd been famously hard on the
mob and lenient with warrants... and the fire had torched
a building where three of the twenty units were used for
witness protection.

Last month, Horton had been digging through his files
on Noah Lane, and had found a photo of a partial print,
so partial it was all but useless, but it was of a right index
finger, and it matched the right index finger of Humboldt
Trueman.

Horton stopped taking a long swig of his coffee when
he saw Humboldt come out of Box of Delights. He tried
not to be obvious about it, but anyone who had been looking would have seen the way he stopped the motion mid-

stream and backwashed awkwardly into the lidded paper cup, some of the light brown coffee spilling out over the lid.

Humboldt didn't look like a man who was finding his way out of a strip club in the early afternoon. Clubs in town -- especially in this part of town -- readily exercised their two-drink minimum, and unlike average bars they did not skimp on the alcohol of those two drinks. They *wanted* their patrons drunk enough to make bad choices, like buying more drinks, requesting a lap dance, or checking into one of the private rooms. Or for that matter, eating from the lunch buffet. Humboldt didn't look as though he'd had two strong drinks in the span of a single hour -- in fact he looked as though he were stone sober, walking with a purpose and conviction that only clear-headed men on a direct mission could walk. He stepped into his car -- a worn Chevy that seemed designed to fade into the background of any scene -- and turned the engine over before his door was even shut.

Horton shoved his coffee into the cup-holder next to him and started his car as well. As soon as he saw an opening in traffic that he thought Humboldt would take, he entered the street himself. When Humboldt veered into the street, Horton was directly behind him.

CHAPTER FIVE

Tim White lived in government-sponsored housing set in the outskirts of middle-class Los Angeles. There wasn't much left of a middle-class in Los Angeles anymore, but what little there was congregated here. It was a quiet street with homes that had been designed to look designed, each one complimenting the next by an over-zealous urban engineer.

The home was only one of three on the block that was one level, the style typically called a bungalow. Tim had been injured in the line of duty as a Federal Agent, and as a result was unable to make most movements below his neck, save for some scant movement that had been saved in his left hand. As a result of his immobility, the majority of his time was spent in the main room of his home, on a bed with motorized wheels that could bring him into any room. It was easier, though, to just stay in the main area. It was a large open-concept room, with a big-screen TV above a fireplace that was never used.

He had insisted on remaining at work, if only in a re-search capacity. He'd been told repeatedly that he could and would be allowed early retirement, with commendations, but would have none of it. Some reasons for that were the cases on his plate that hadn't been solved yet -- other reasons were more complicated.

"Rae Stephens," Duncan said, tossing a glossy photo of the man -- taken during life -- onto Tim's bed.

Tim could do nothing about it. He could not even feel the weight of the picture on his lap, though when he saw it fall sometimes his brain filled in the sensation from the visual cue alone.

"Peter Andrews," Duncan continued, tossing a photo onto the pile with each name. "Daniel Harvey. Tilda Stine. Whelan Davis. Chelsea Robbins. Grace Bennett. Samuel Lawrence. Walter Haybrook. Carl Silverski. David Jill. Shane Employees and murder victims all of them; you know what else they all have in common?"

Tim shot him a wry look but did not respond.

"Exactly!" Duncan tapped the file with his middle finger. "Not a *god damned* thing!"

"Have you dated since you moved out here?" Tim asked, suddenly and quickly.

Duncan straightened himself, the question taking him off his guard.

"I remember you dating. You had that girl, what was her name?"

"Skyler," Duncan drawled.

"Yes, Skyler. She was something else, fun. Have you been dating again since you moved out to Sun Valley? I didn't get around much before this, but I noticed there was some fine flesh on display -- if you're into that kind of thing."

Duncan stared at him, then turned away and licked his lips, glanced back, then looked away again. He was trying not to laugh and to ascertain where this line of conversation was heading all at the same time. "What's your point?" he asked, finally.

"My point is that you need a break."

"I can't take a break."

"I didn't ask if you could take one or not, I said you *needed* one. And I'm still on the Bureau, I could recommend it be made mandatory."

Duncan lowered his eyes at him. "I swear by all that's fucking holy, I will put The He-Man 'What's Going On' song on that TV on repeat and leave. And call your care worker and tell her you're out for the week." He pointed to the large TV across from Tim's bed, as if to emphasize the veracity of the threat.

Tim smirked. "When was the last time you were laid?"

Duncan balked.

"I'm not usually this blunt... but it's you."

He shuffled. "I saw a girl while I was on suspension. Nothing serious, but she was nice."

"None since LA?"

Duncan made an annoyed, dismissive motion toward the pile of photos on Tim's lap. "You see this shit? This is the one thing on my plate. One. You know over at that damn station they've started saying I've cursed the desk. This Latino brother crosses himself every time he walks past me. *Every time*, Tim." He brought his fingers to the side of his scalp and pantomimed shooting himself. "I'm beyond bananagrams. I need your help, this is... this is bananagrams. There's eleven victims with nothing in common except this one huge, massive, all-consuming thing they have in common, and since number eleven the whole thing has gone dark. No threats, no assaults, no nothing, not so much as a stray sound down a hallway... and yet here we are, still looking for this motherfucker. Fucking with me, he is." He let out a long, frustrated huff. "This feels... this feels genetically engineered to mess with me. Exactly me. For everything to happen so fast and so crazy that I can't keep up, and then to recede back to this... boredom. This wait. That's... it's like he knows the pace I work at and is doing everything he can not to work at that pace."

While he'd been talking, Tim had called up the case files on the eleven dead onto his screen. "Anything come back from the HR files?"

Duncan rolled his eyes.

Tim frowned, not needing further response.

Duncan played his hands over his open mouth. "I've been thinking about getting some details public, see if we can shake something loose."

Tim's jaw loosened. "That's a dangerous game with someone who's killed eleven people."

Duncan sighed. "Yeah."

"You know who you need to talk to."

Duncan paused, took a deep breath, then nodded.

Xander Drew stood above the sunken, misshapen remains of the Joucastle Childhood Care Facility. Sweat arced its way down from his wetted brown hair in long, steady streams, falling their way onto his bare chest. He stood back from the piece of rubble he'd just moved -- a chunk of stairwell that had crumbled and been pinned by two jagged shards of asbestos-laden wall, and looked at his work as the Los Angeles sun beat down on his naked back.

The Joucastle had been a tall building on the southern edge that bordered urban and suburban Los Angeles, the strange non-linear line that divided the skyscrapers from the backyards and patios. It had been built up, not out. The main building had been large and long and rectangular. At each of the four corners new floors sprang up, the way spires sprung up from the corners of old castles. They came up in rectangles, some bizarre fusion of medieval and modern architecture.

Xander had sat bleeding in the stone stairway that had led up to the main entrance and watched it crumble in on itself, a cave-in underneath the building causing the sub-basement to crumble, and the basement level above that to fold into where it had been, and so on and so on, space occupying where nature abhorred the vacuum of it until everything but the spires were too unsound to walk on and even they were condemned.

His arms were covered in the blood of the many scrapes and gashes he'd acquired while moving the rubble from one area of the lot to another, trying to separate and organize it. There were no scrapes or scars though, just the red ribbon leavings of where they had been.

"Have you found anything?"

Xander turned and looked over his shoulder back in the direction of the street, his hair falling into his eyes.

Duncan was standing at the edge of the destruction, where the sidewalk had been swept back. Only the toe of his shoes were over the line into what had been the Joucastle property, but even that was enough to send shivers down his spine.

"Go away," Xander said, turning back and reaching for a large segment of concrete that had become lodged in the remains of the Joucastle kitchen, having fallen from one of the dormitory spires. He picked up a large sledge-hammer and raised it up high, then brought it down on the slab. The slab did not budge, but the reverberations of the impact made their way up the shaft of the hammer and into Xander's arms, then finally into his teeth. He bore it, then hit the slab again, harder.

Duncan clucked his tongue against the roof of his mouth, shoved his hands deep into his pockets, and sighed. When that long sigh was done, he took off his coat, folded it, and laid it atop the warm hood of his car. He took his cigarette out from behind his ear and looked at it, rolling it while holding each end between the thumb and forefinger of each hand. He turned and looked at Xander, who was again making crashing strikes on the concrete slab with rebar sticking from it, and tapped the cigarette against the cup of one hand. He made a long sucking motion, then put the smoke in his jacket pocket.

He rolled up his sleeve to the elbows, walked the edge of the sidewalk, then stepped over the displaced stone barrier into the remains of the Joucastle lot.

Xander hit the concrete slab again, and a large chunk came loose, splitting along the fracture line of the rebar inside it. Xander dropped the hammer without a pause and reached forward, grabbed the hunk of weight, and pulled it back out of the way. When he heard Duncan's feet scrape against the pebbles that scattered along the remains of the old flooring, he turned around.

"I said leave," he said, his voice haggard from the dust, and lack of sleep.

"Yeah well, it's a free country," Duncan said.

Xander cocked his head to one side. "Not really." He took the stone piece he'd knocked loose by the rebar as though it were handles and continued to pull it. It moved only inches at a time, but he did not let up.

Duncan turned to look from one side of the rubble. He raised a finger, pointed to the southeast spire, and used it to orient himself. "We're in the kitchen?"

Xander nodded. "Just past it. I think this hunk of fuck," he kicked the concrete slab, "is blocking the entrance down to the tunnels."

Duncan turned and looked over the rubble. There was ample evidence of other such places where Xander had decided the remains of the entrance to the secret lower levels of Joucastle was, tiny segments of order that had been made from the chaos of the place.

Xander strained, the veins in his neck bulging as he gave the chunk he'd broken another heave.

Duncan picked up the sledgehammer, raised it high, and brought it down onto the main section of blockage.

Xander stopped and gave him a critical raised eyebrow.

"I'll hit, you pull," Duncan said simply, swinging the hammer again. It dislodged a piece of concrete about the size of his head. He was sweating already, large dark spots forming under the armpits of his shirt.

Xander nodded.

They moved six large sections of the blockage like that in silence, save for the labored grunts that both men made when the stone did not budge as expected under their pressure.

"That tunnel was narrow," Duncan said finally, motioning with the hammer's handle to where he guesstimated its remains to be. "Nothing saying when you find the entrance it won't be caved in."

Xander sniffed, his nostrils filled with dust. "Good thing I've got nothing but time then."

Duncan nodded, then sat, drenched with sweat.

Xander stepped toward him, reached into an alcove, and produced a bottle of water that had been kept cool in the shade. Duncan took it, and when he did, Xander held out his hand. Taking only a moment to understand, he handed over the sledgehammer and Xander took it, going back to work.

Duncan watched him for several minutes, taking deep, exhausted breaths between long chugs of water. When that bottle was done, he reached into the same crevice Xander had and produced another and drank it, too. "You ever rest?" he asked, finally, as he splashed some of the water onto his brow.

"Not really. Black out once or twice," Xander replied without turning toward him. "There's some beds in tower three that are stable, if things get real bad. But not really."

Duncan allowed his gaze to wander past the place Xander was striking, to the null area where both men thought the caved-in remains of the secret stairwell to be. His breath slowly became shallow and steadier as he focused on that absent space, everything else becoming a blurry mix of color from a moment in the wake of the oppressive gray. "I'm having trouble with the Shane case," he said finally, then took another swig of his water.

Xander cocked his head, then took another swing at the concrete. "There been more victims?"

"Not since the board got hit, no. Fucker's gone like a fart in the fucking wind, nothing behind but bodies and fallen stock and me, trying to make sense of it all."

Xander winced. He wiped the salty sweat from his eyes. "Have you considered terrorism?" he asked. He turned toward Duncan to say it, but grabbed a piece of concrete that had fallen loose while he did.

Duncan's mouth curled. "Don't say that. You have any idea the dumpster fire that would be?"

Xander shrugged. "The whole reason you're involved is Shane has projects and interests all over the country. All over the world, really. If the company's in trouble, maybe they can't provide whatever they're providing to the government by way of weapons and --" he stopped, then stood and turned to Duncan. "What are they selling the government?"

Duncan shot him a droll look. "That's pretty far above my pay grade." He pushed the heels of his hands into his ocular orbits until he saw spots. "Terrorism. You did not just say terrorism."

"Just an option." He cocked his head again, a motion which Duncan was starting to see as him loading a new idea-bullet into the chamber of his mind. "Could be domestic, too. Someone wanting to grind that same sale of arms to a halt that's homegrown." He paused. "Not that I take issue with that, in principle."

"I hate that less. I still hate it, but I hate it less."

"Maybe it's time to stop looking for connections among the victims. Maybe the connection is Shane... just a general connection that is Shane. Someone with a hate for Shane."

Duncan straightened. He took a sip of his water.

Xander finished dragging that seventh slab into its spot, organized with the others along the new stone wall he was inadvertently constructing between himself and the city street. "Like, if we were trying to catch a serial rapist that targeted redheads that all jogged along the same trail, you wouldn't go looking for what the victims had in common *besides* those two things. Anything else would almost be incidental."

He nodded. "Trying to fix this is driving me nuts. Homicide 12 is jittery as fuck because some great detective's last case is about to go to trial."

"Victor Murdock?" Xander asked, standing and looking at him.

"...Yeah. How --?"

"I was there for that mess. Some of it, anyway."

Duncan raised his eyebrows.

"Not that mine is a name you want to say around that place if you want to stay on their good side."

He nodded appreciatively. "I've been shooting around this idea of sending out a false lead, see if we can get the killer to show himself. Something plausible, but wrong... like saying we've traced the blade that cut the victims' throats ear-to-ear or something, and that we have a lead on the owner."

Xander squinted, thinking. "Were the victims' throats cut?"

"They were not," Duncan replied, pointing at him.

"Dangerous game."

"It's where I'm at."

"Still, I wouldn't."

Duncan nodded again. He paused a long moment and finished the second bottle of water. "I could use your input on it, if you'd come back and look over what I've been doing."

Xander regarded him a long moment, then shook his head, and picked up his sledgehammer again.

Duncan watched him. He motioned toward the slowly emerging entrance to the passage they were uncovering. "Last time I saw that I was dragging you through it, and you were damn near dead."

"I wasn't."

"You were, and you know it." Duncan glared it him with deadly seriousness that was rare for him, his veneer of sarcasm falling away for just a moment. "Now you heal faster than anything I've ever seen, and that's weird... but that woman that I found down that hole with a knife in your belly, she was weirder."

"Celena," Xander corrected, his voice almost a growl.

"Yes. She took hits harder than anything I've ever seen, and I do not know how she did that: but nobody could survive a cave in like that. Nobody. She is *dead*."

Xander shook his head. "She isn't. Until I find the body, she's still out there, looking to prey on more children." Both men stopped and remembered the files on the children whose deaths they had attributed to the woman, and how many there had been. "So until I get a better lead, I'm going down the tunnel."

Duncan stood and nodded. He turned and walked back to his car, sliding his sleeves back down as he did. When he reached his coat, he unfolded it and put it back on, then reached into his pocket and pulled out the cigarette.

He walked back into the remains of Joucastle, the Children's Care Facility that had taken the lives of hundreds of children, and handed the cigarette to Xander.

Xander took it, and as Duncan got in his car and drove away, lit it.

CHAPTER SIX

Megan sat at the end of the hotel bar, at a seat with no adjacent seat that could be occupied. She swallowed the last of her Bourbon -- neat -- and signaled for the bartender to bring her another. It was her seventh.

"You sure?" the tender, a tanned man in his late twenties, asked.

"Literally the only good thing about this hotel is that I can drink all I want and then walk back to my room," she said, her voice perfectly spoken despite her inebriation.

The bartender nodded and poured her another drink.

Horton shifted uncomfortably.

Humboldt Trueman had gone to the Laundromat and then eaten at Burger King. Then he had driven in circles around one of the better middle-class suburbs for some time and Horton began to think he'd realized he was being tailed, until he eventually found an out-of-the-way bungalow and delivered a package wrapped in brown paper and string to a woman who looked young, with stress marks under her eyes that made her look old.

He'd gone to an upscale restaurant just shy of the Hollywood Boulevard named *Morgana's* and had sat at a table for two beneath a large iron window. He had not ordered anything and had barely drank his water, but he sat there for forty minutes before getting up to leave. His next stop had been a deli shack, where he'd ordered two hot dogs with everything and a large Pepsi.

He had made three more stops that had taken him well into late evening before Horton lost him in midtown traffic, and now Horton was sitting in the dim light of the *Espresso Express* coffee shop looking through the pictures he'd taken covertly during the day. As he scrolled back through the most recent, he found the shots of Humboldt at the table at *Morgana's*. He'd had those long, lanky arms of his situated with his elbows between his legs, his hands pressed back under the table. Most of the time they laid slack, but every so often they rose to a forty-five-degree angle, remained for an awkward amount of time, then dropped again.

Horton fished a red sharpie out of his breast pocket and rummaged about his passenger side seat for paper, pushing aside the newsprint about Victor Murdock's upcoming trial and pulled a mostly blank sheet from its red folder. He scribbled: 'Morgana's: Drop Point?' in the wide orphan space at the end of the page, then planked it back down with the rest.

He let out a long sigh, squirmed in his seat, then shifted uncomfortably again. He turned and gave a side-long glare at the coffee cups in the foot-well of the passenger seat, as though it were somehow their fault and not his own that his bladder was currently pressing on the borders of its space within him. He sighed, rested his head against the steering wheel for a moment, then got out of the car.

Espresso Express had long since closed for the evening, the only light he'd been in the light that kept the sign illuminated through the night. He looked at his watch and realized it was later than he'd thought. Frowning, he took out his phone and texted Martha: 'Dinner?'

He waited. The three-dotted 'typing' animation came up at the bottom of his screen. 'Ate yours,' came the response. 'It's in the washroom if you want it.' He snorted, then put the phone back into his pocket and looked around the street for a washroom.

The street was tightly packed, all streets in the part of town were. Businesses maximized floor space because that maximized product space, building their storefronts right to the margins of their property lines until all that was left were a long wall of brick and steel and mortar. There was a small section of office spaces, a furniture store that looked to have less furniture in it than his own home, and a pizzeria named *Charlie's* that had patrons inside and a thin man in a white shirt tossing dough to their amusement.

Horton smiled and crossed the street, willing his bladder to hold onto its cargo long enough to get into the pizzeria washroom.

He stopped.

In front of him, directly across from *Espresso Express*, was the large bay window of a convenience store. Within it were racks upon racks of salted treats and confectionary and seemingly random grocery items: baked beans on the shelf alongside Lays potato chips and chocolate bars and bags of pre-portioned cotton candy that hung from the endcaps. On the window, in green letters with an orange outline, it read Powell's Convenience.

The last time he'd seen it, Fabian Mitchells had been slumped through it, a long stalagmite of glass pressing through his neck and sending blood gushing down over them that eventually dried in place and left those jagged peaks of glass looking like mountains with red frosted peaks.

Horton stepped over to it, the image of the last crime he'd even officially worked for the LAPD flashing back and forth with the reality of the scene now: the storefront window back in place and better than it had been before. Before it had been clear plate glass; now the owners had sprung for vinyl letters to further advertise themselves. The insurance money must have more than covered the actual pane, Horton assumed.

He reached out a hand and pressed it against the glass, that quick coolness seeping into his palm even on a hot Los Angeles evening.

His phone went off, and as he reached for it there was a second sound, behind him. Too close behind him for the empty street this time of night. An exhalation of a long breath. He turned quickly but only made it halfway, before a forceful shove sent him cascading up and through the newly minted window of Powell's Convenience.

"Dammit!" he bellowed as glass found its way to his flesh at multiple points at once. A millisecond later, he hit the black and white tile floor of the store and skidded into the wire rack of chips. Salsa fell from its perches and shattered all around him, sending starburst shapes of red and green chunks in all directions.

Horton reached for his gun, but before he could get it out, his attacker was on him.

CHAPTER SEVEN

The elevator doors opened with an audible ping, revealing the vast-yet-cramped department that was Homicide12.

The Homicide division of any city was busy, but today when Duncan stepped through the archway into the department there was an eerie calm over it. The room that was typically a living, breathing entity under the always-hot sun was currently holding its breath, and the pressure of it was palatable from the second he stepped past the window with the blinds which were always shut and into the rest of the office, with the glass walls on either side.

People were standing. In the time he'd been warehoused at Homicide12, Duncan didn't think he'd ever seen people stand. People moved, walked, went from place to place. People went to and from the printer, to and from the interrogation feed, to and from the vending machines. This wasn't a job that allowed for the downtime to stand around, and yet here were fifteen of the city's finest, each occupying their own personal space and not moving an inch from it.

Sergeant Lake leaned against the doorframe to her office at the far end of the hall. She was giving it her whole weight, as though she wanted it to break, to bring down the entirety of the department and the building it was housed in in one volley of constant pressure.

Janet stood in the centre of the room, in the brief null space between the Tetris block configuration of her desk and his own. The knuckle of her right forefinger was in her mouth, between her teeth. The bone of her neck was arched out, pumped tight from stress, and she was staring off into the vacant space of his desk.

He stepped up to her, careful to walk around the statuesque officers that stood between she and he. "Jan," he said in a hushed tone, influenced by the atmosphere in the room. "What's happening?"

She turned to him with eyes that were bloodshot. He realized suddenly that there were tears behind the eyes of every man and woman in the room, although none had managed to shed any yet. They were all in that painful, awkward space between needing the release and being unable to overcome years of culture that told them to hold tears back.

She reached out a hand and placed it on his shoulder. When she tried to answer, she couldn't.

CHAPTER EIGHT

"Can I interest you in some custom jewelry?" a man in his late thirties asked, holding up a long necklace with a charm featuring a woman's face in white profile. The man was standing next to a table of similarly made pieces molded from resin, and there was a young girl at the table behind it. She smiled shyly.

Shiro Gilbert looked at the piece. It was beautifully made, one of the best in a Market that was overcrowded with custom and costume jewelry. It had been molded on white and the brown background painted on; he could see the tiny brushstrokes.

The man placed the charm into Shiro's hand. "My granddaughter made it," he said proudly, motioning behind him to her proudly, without turning to look at her.

Shiro turned his almond-shaped, eczema tinged eyes toward the girl, who blushed slightly and turned away. He looked at the charm, small and delicate as it rested on the reddened dried skin of his finger.

"Get it," said a woman behind him. She was a tallish natural blonde with smiling cheeks and small blue eyes.

She looked to be in her mid-thirties but without the stress that typically comes from that age, so he immediately assumed unmarried with no children. She was wearing a flowery dress, and when she spoke it was like hearing what silk felt like. "Look at her, she's sweet. The table's full; she hasn't made many sales. Get it."

Shiro smiled and looked up at the man. "How much?"

The man told him five and Shiro paid it. When he continued past the table, he nodded and said, "Thank hew," to the girl, the one word he had been unable to shed his Asian accent of. As he walked away, he stared at the broach with the white woman on it and held it up, as if comparing it to the blonde that followed him. "It looks like you. It's like they took a mold of Krystal and printed them by the dozen."

The blonde woman, Krystal, rolled her eyes. "My cheekbones were never that high."

Shiro smiled, even as he pocketed the necklace and let his eyes fall aimlessly out over the rest of the crowd that had gathered in The Market.

The Market was a massive collection of strip malls and restaurants that might as well have been its own tiny, self-contained city. Concrete streets ran between businesses separated into perfectly equal square lots of glass and brick, each with their own separate address and power. There was an adults-only street where clocks were literally always set to happy hour. There were three food courts, which in the early mornings were cleared of chairs and used as a workout area by out-of-work mothers. It had its own daycare, fire hall, and security station that property owners came to refer to as the 'local constabulary.' The downstairs doubled as a bingo hall and community centre. All said, there were over two hundred businesses located in the walls of The Market, selling everything from fresh-cut chicken to bargain-basement tattoos.

He stopped at a pawn shop specializing in used electronics. There were three televisions of different sizes and shapes on in one corner of the small front section of the shop, behind a wall of nearly new game consoles that looked as though they had roughly fallen off the back of a truck. Each of the three TVs was turned to the same station, a news broadcast that couldn't be heard from the hall but had a still image of a man in glasses and a brown duster over the anchor's right shoulder.

Shiro and Krystal stopped at the exact same moment and turned toward the screen.

The man over the anchor's shoulder was Thomas Horton.

As Shiro approached the screen the volume of it came into earshot, and the image switched to an image of a man with a set jaw standing in front of a large stone edifice. He was in his early forties, with thick brown hair that showed no signs of graying and smile lines around eyes that were the exact same shade of blue as Krystal's. The man appeared remarkably thin, though it was hard to tell beneath the long black robe draped over him, accented only with a purple sash slung easily around his shoulder. The crawl on the lower edge of the screen identified him as a Reverend. Reverend John Trask.

"The things that this has done to my church, my community, it cannot be overstated," Trask said, looking past the cameras as a cluster of microphones pushed their way up close to him. "My community has been under a sustained attack for months with hate crimes that have escalated into full murders and the best the LAPD could do was to arrest one of our own -- one of the *victims* of this assault on our way of life, as much as any other -- and is now putting him on trial like any other drug pusher and pervert that makes our streets unsafe for children."

Shiro narrowed his eyes, even as Trask's seemed to sway slightly from the journalist he'd been making contact with to look directly at the camera. Through the lens of technology, it was almost as if they were locking eyes. Krystal folded her arm in around the hook of Shiro's as he watched and tried to tug him away, but he did not budge or break his icy stare at the screen.

"Victor Murdock is innocent. He has always been innocent, and yet he remains held while he awaits trial at a bail that is and remains unaffordable. We in his parish have collected money for his release but as the trial approaches, we have consulted Mr. Murdock and put it towards his defense instead. We have a fine lawyer, and we are confident she will see that justice is done... but it cannot undo the injustice of this act. There is a sustained effort against our community, to make it into something... sick. Something foreign."

Shiro bristled at that.

"We must descent from the fear. This heinous act against a good, moral man proves to me, without a shadow of a doubt, that the efforts against our community are continuing. These acts are the work of one man, and that man is not Victor Murdock. The LAPD must find this man and prosecute this man and keep our community safe, but first they must let the scales fall from their eyes and release the innocent man, Victor Murdock, currently in their custody."

"Are you buying or should I get you a couch?" said the large man behind the counter.

Shiro turned his burning gaze from the television to the man, burrowing into him with his glare.

The clerk stopped and shrank.

"Come on," Krystal said, pulling on his arm to no affect.

Pushing his teeth together, he turned and made his way out of the pawn shop, then out of The Market altogether.

CHAPTER NINE

Xander heard Duncan's car pull up but did not turn around, instead choosing to swing his sledgehammer at the beam of wood that bisected the exposed tunnel at the base of Joucastle. He paused and perked his ears when he heard the car door close, listening for (but not hearing) Duncan take off his coat in advance of the LA heat again. He hit the beam of wood again, cracking it.

Duncan turned when he got to the place where the boulder of concrete had been just the day before, and now stood like a haphazard monument. He looked from it to Xander, then back again and let his gaze rest there, continued until he was firmly in the mouth of what had been Joucastle's kitchen. "Stop this," he said. It was an order, not a request.

Xander hit the beam again, and the ripple of the strike made hairline fractures through to its peak.

"Thomas Horton was killed last night."

Xander struck out again, with such force that the obstruction beam and the one next to it crumbled, bringing down new debris into the frame but rendering those at least to dust and crumbled sections of driftwood. He dropped the sledgehammer, took several deep breaths tinged with sawdust and dust, then turned back to Duncan.

Both men turned and walked to Duncan's car without a word.

CHAPTER TEN

Xander took off his shoes, bracing himself against the wall of Tim White's home with one palm as he did so.

He unlaced them in deft pulls at the laces, grabbing each with military precision. When he'd loosened each enough, they fell to the floor, the toe hanging at an awkward angle compared to the heel, resulting in a break between the two that would have rendered them unwearable in any city except Los Angeles. There was little worry of moisture squirting up through the gap here, only sand and the occasional stone.

Tim watched this on his monitor, as Duncan stepped in behind Xander without removing or brushing off his shoes.

"Sorry I've been away," Xander said, unbuttoning the top clasp of his shirt and fixing his collar so that it hung loose.

"I'm sorry to bring you back with such bad news," Tim said with heartfelt empathy. "I know you were close."

"He learned my *name* from *you*," Xander bristled. "We weren't *that* close."

"Bullshit is what it is," Duncan added, grumbling. He looked through the different windows on Tim's screen. "If you counted every time a murder happened in LA as a copycat of whoever's about to go on trial, we'd be drowning in acquittals. This guy--" He pulled Tim's screen toward him and tapped on a still image of Reverend Trask with one knuckle. "This guy is bullshit. Have you got anything?"

Xander moved to the other side of Tim's bed. Without comment, he took the corner of the screen between his thumb and forefinger and moved it back to its original position. "Has the physiotherapist been by today?"

"She wasn't feeling well," Tim said, his pupils moving to meet Xander's. "I let her have the day."

"Did she send the alternate?"

"It was short notice. She was almost here when she called; she was running late."

"That's why they have alternates." He walked to the foot of Tim's bed and pulled the sign-in sheet that hung there, like a hospital chart. "There's three signatures missing this week. Was the alternate not in or is he just not signing?"

Tim frowned, and avoided Xander's gaze.

Xander put the file back down with a harsh clang, the metal back of the clipboard hitting the metal rail of the bed. "I'm gonna have a talk with them when they come in."

"That's not necessary."

"If that was true, there'd be three more sets of initials on that sheet," Xander pressed, even as he made his way back over to 'his' side of the bed.

"Can we get on with this now?" Duncan asked. "Is this, like, important bitching? Should I get a chair?" He tapped the screen twice with one knuckle. "What'cha got?"

Xander frowned at him, then turned to Tim. "Anything new on Joucastle since I've been out?"

"Still no word on Jeremy Piper," Tim said, his tone shifting to a deeper, more authoritative one as he swiped left on his optical mouse twice. The booking photo of Jeremy enlarged from its containing folder, coming into full, almost life-size view. He had a wide gash on his forehead from the struggle of getting him in, and he glared at the camera with contempt. "He got out of lockup and nobody's seen tooth or nail of him since."

"He's hiding," Xander said. His voice had changed too, becoming a low growl as he locked eyes with the image of Jeremy Piper. "As well he should be."

"Any kids missing that fit his M.O.?" Duncan asked. He stroked his lower face as though he had a goatee but didn't.

"No," Tim said. "There's still missing kids, but none from homes. I think he's gone to ground."

"Or he's changing his pattern," Xander added.

Duncan nodded at him.

"But this is why you're really here," Tim said, and with three swipes over his mouse pulled up the shattered image of the Powell's Convenience storefront window. There was a man in a loose-fitting coat slumped over it, the shards of glass that remained fixed to the base of the frame slicing up through his neck and throat.

Duncan pulled back from the screen. Xander leaned

forward, part of the color draining from his face.

"Warn me next time," Duncan said, cursing under his breath. "That's a cop, man."

"That's the same as last time," Xander said, his voice hushed. "Can you pull up the photos from the Fabian Mitchells' murder?"

"That wasn't federal. I can though, in a bit."

"Print them for me when you do," he said. He motioned around the image without leaving any grease-stained fingerprints on the screen. "Print both on the same page if you can because this is... this is the same. The placement, the body, the... everything. This isn't a murder scene, it's a tableau."

"What's a tableau?" Duncan asked, fortifying himself and then coming back into view of the screen.

"Ah, it comes from art," Xander explained, raising back to his full height. He pantomimed making something with clay. "Your teacher ever get you to make a scene from a book with toys and things?"

"Like a diorama?"

"Yes!" Xander said, pointing to him. "A diorama is a type of tableau, yes." He turned that same finger to the image on the screen. "How accurate is this diorama?"

Tim furrowed his brow.

"You know what I'm asking."

"I really don't."

"Was the symbol on the ground?"

Tim's brow tightened even more, and with several swipes of his fingers he brought up the rest of the images that had been taken at the scene. They showed the last moments of Thomas Horton's life from multiple angles, but none showed the interior of Powell's Convenience. "No pictures."

"That's not a 'no'," Xander said, then pointed to Duncan. "Take me to the scene?"

Duncan nodded, then turned back toward the door.

"Xander," Tim said.

Both men stopped and turned.

"You should talk to Martha Horton."

They paused: Duncan only briefly before he continued walking ahead, leaving Xander to linger in the weightless space between Tim and the door. He didn't speak or make eye contact with Tim.

"I would. But it's not the sort of call you should make over the phone."

Xander's upper lip twitched. He turned away again.

"Xander," Tim called a second time.

He turned again.

"Before you go. Under the bed."

Frowning with one eyebrow raised, Xander lowered himself into a squat and looked under Tim's bed. There was a long, rectangular box there with an ajar lid. He pulled it out and placed it on the bed without opening it. "What's up?"

Tim looked from him to the box.

Xander opened the lid, removed a small tuff of wax paper, and withdrew a sleek black pair of new sneakers. They were expensive, the type that professional runners wore. They'd been pre-laced and had the sheen of polish to them, the stitches that held the leather together so tiny they were almost unperceivable.

Xander looked at them for a long moment, moving the

shoe he'd produced from the box around so that he could see it all: the stitch, the material, the tread. He turned to Tim. "Why?"

"Same reason you should see Martha," Tim said, with a sort of kind seriousness that only he was capable of. "Because someone else needs it."

CHAPTER ELEVEN

"Thank you very much, Joel," Kendra LaMire said as she turned her attention to Camera Two. "And thank you for joining us. Today we're talking to Reverend John Trask of Los Angeles' own Church of the Holy Heavenly Father and author of the new book *Policide*. Thank you for joining us, Father."

Trask winced slightly but retained the smile he'd practiced in the mirror while his makeup had been being applied. He had told her three times during the setup that he was not referred to as Father in his parish, and yet each time had not influenced her next flub. "Thank you for having me," he said, in that too-polite way every person on television said it.

Morning LaMire was a morning news program that aired on stations local to Los Angeles six days a week. Its host and namesake, Kendra LaMire, was a blonde woman in her forties that perpetually wore blue pantsuits with big brass buttons and a lavish, manufactured smile. Her teeth were perfectly white, straight, and had cost upwards of twenty thousand dollars to be made that way. The set had the orange and yellow hues of a sunrise, because even though this would air the following morning, it was being taped in the mid-afternoon.

"So, we invited you on because you wrote a book about the negative effect of police on our society, you've been maintaining that the former member of your parish -- whose trial starts tomorrow – is innocent, and yesterday the arresting officer of said trial ends up dead at the same location as the first murder... does that sum up your week?" She leaned forward when she spoke, and Trask could see the line of her white blouse poke up from behind the wall of perfect blue. Her suit was not a shade of blue, it was the perfect, unencumbered, total *blue*.

Trask shifted in his chair so that he could lean forward as well, trying his best to take cues from her on how to move and act for the camera. "I'm here for the same reason I wrote the book, because Victor Murdock is a *member* of my parish and he is innocent of the crimes of which he has been accused." He placed emphasis on the word 'member,' in his mind to combat her characterization that Murdock was a 'former member' of the Church.

"Yes, let's talk about your book. In it, you say --"

"You didn't read the book," Trask interrupted, waving his hand at her dismissively.

Kendra's eyes flicked toward Camera Two, and the producers beyond it, but maintained her expensive smile.

"Nobody reads books anymore. People don't write books to be read, they write them so that they can get on shitty TV shows and talk about their book and hopefully get the ear of thousands of people."

"We're on in the morning, you can't say that," Kendra said through tight teeth.

"Then I assume you'll edit it," Trask said. He unbuttoned his blazer, then re-buttoned it one clasp down to give himself some extra breathing room and readjusted himself in his chair. "In my book, I talk about the police's sustained -- if uncoordinated -- attacks on urban centres. Society has moved towards a secular belief model, and that's fine, I'm not here to tell anyone what to believe -- but we've moved away from priests as the patrons of the soul and moved toward police as them, whether we want to admit that or not. You can't be for Rule of Law above all else and not also be for Police as the Priests of that Lawful, Legal Church of Laws... but I think what we've been seeing more and more is something akin to the pedophile Priest scandal in the 90s... we're seeing these new men of conviction for what they really are, people who come after our brothers and sisters with no cause or evidence and take them in the night so that they can pad their solve rate."

Kendra stared at Trask, wide-eyed. After a long pause, she spoke: "That kind of message is going to be hard to swallow for some of our viewers, given that you're on to respond, in part, to the death of a policeman."

"Thomas Horton was a good cop, from all I've seen. I met him once." Trask nodded. "But his solve-rate was off the charts. I have to wonder: if we looked through those cases, how many were there like Mr. Murdock, arrested because... why? Because of a rock?" He made a sound with his mouth, puffing air through his lips. "That wouldn't hold up in an episode of CSI, let alone a court of law. That wouldn't hold up in Night Court."

"I'm going to stop you there, Father. We're not here to --"

"Influence, I know. And it's not Father, it's Reverend. As in 'Revered,' although I don't use it that way. And it is ridiculous to say we're not here to influence the public on the matters of law... that's all this is for. That's all political TV is for. You guise it under education, but it's closer to reeducation, in the Orwellian sense of the word." She tried to interrupt, but he continued: "This is the world we live in. We've replaced the Church as a centre for knowledge and community with a system that acts against us, that can turn on us and say it has proof. But it's a proof we can't understand, we just have to trust their results. It's sick, and it's just replacing one unknowable with another. The only difference is that we," he patted himself on the chest, "acknowledge that our answer is unknowable."

Megan sat and shifted uncomfortably in the uncomfortable chair across from Victor Murdock, who was once again dipping his head into the beam of sunlight that came in from the window next to him. He bobbed down into it, then returned up into the shadow cast by the window frame, looking like a bird searching for worms.

She shifted again, pulling her suit to one side while she shifted to the other. Stephen 1.0 had jostled it to one side while frisking her this morning and she was having a hard time forcing the fabric back to a position that felt comfortable and natural. She placed a file from her briefcase on the table then slid a photo out of the file and turned it around so that it was on the table between them, facing him. It was an evidence photo of a piece of concrete that had been broken into a corner. The outer edges were smooth and polished, while the verso side was jagged and pointed in sections. On the photo, the slab was on a gray table almost the same color as it, and next to it on two sides were rulers placed for scale.

"This is the main piece of evidence against you," Megan said. She tapped the white border around the picture from where she'd had it printed. It made the picture look like a bygone style of Polaroid.

Victor craned his head forward without adjusting his shoulders much, taking in the whole of the picture. After a moment he picked it up and looked at it, the glean from the sun reflecting off its glossy finish. There were other pairs of people in the room today, and even though they were at the far end of the far table, Victor still spoke with a hushed voice. "This is concrete."

"This is the concrete that was taken into evidence from your home on the day you were arrested," Megan corrected. "This was yours, wasn't it?"

He shrugged. "If they say so. Honestly, one piece of concrete is like any other... but mine had that kind of smooth corner, I think that was why I got it... so yes, that was probably mine. There's no reason to think it isn't."

"Well," Megan said, then let her voice trail off. "I wouldn't go that far. If you honestly can't tell when it's in the room, don't cop to it. If you do recognize it in the room, do, but only if you're *sure*." She plucked the picture from him and laid it back on top of her folder, then put both her elbows on the table and brought her hands forward to illustrate what she was saying.

"There are three main components to a criminal trial," she said, pantomiming making three piles between the two of them. "There's motive, opportunity, and weapon. And all of it is on them, don't let them make you think otherwise. As much as we put faith in our system, a shocking amount of convictions go through because people aren't educated that the burden of proof is on the accuser. That's why you're entitled to a lawyer." She pointed both fingers back at herself. "Opportunity is the hardest to prove, that's always... nebulous."

"I'm not sure I understand it," Murdock said. His brow was furrowed and a wrinkle that shot straight up from the tip of his eyebrow was now finally understood.

She smiled. "Basically, were you there when the murder happened. That's what that amounts to, were you in the vicinity. Can they place you in the vicinity? And if you have evidence to the contrary -- movie stubs, witnesses, alibis -- then opportunity gets thrown out the window."

"I was at home, I think. Just watching TV."

"And that is the crux of why opportunity is bullshit," she said, pointing directly at him as though he'd made some epiphany-worthy argument. "Because no American is *required* to have people surrounding them twenty-four seven. You aren't required to keep a diary of your events or keep a schedule or a planner." She pointed to her own planner in a manner that suggested she despised it. "This is the problem with opportunity. They can't prove you were there, and you can't prove you weren't, but since the burden is on them, the whole thing is a wash." She swept that imaginary pile to the floor with one brush of her hand. "Motive is another place where they're struggling," she said, motioning to the second invisible pile.

As Victor's eyes were on it, she flipped through her file and brought out several typewritten documents.

"These got handed to us during Discovery. Which is less fun than it sounds." She laid them out before him. They had been collated into three separate units. "These outline the ways in which they've alerted us that they may come at us for motive." She paused. "All of them are bullshit. I've read them, you don't have to. These are... theories, based on their assessment of you, of the victims, of the crimes. Your best defense is to not comment on them, which is why you're exercising your right to have me speak for you, so that they can't trap you in anything."

"I am?"

"You are," she nodded. "As for weapon... they say they have the weapon. I've got some people picking apart the science behind it. It's bad forensic science, honestly. I think we have this. But I do have to ask about this guy," Megan pulled out a screen shot of Reverend John Trask from the television spot he'd done the previous day. "This guy is campaigning for you pretty hard, and we need to talk about that."

"I haven't seen Reverend Trask since I came inside," Victor said, almost sadly.

"Ooooh I know. I've checked," Megan said. "So, this guy's campaigning for you and he's basically running on, there's been a new murder, this is the real murderer, this person is innocent. Which has worked before, fair. I've worked cases where that's won. Hell, I made my career on a case where that won. But I think with you it's especially poignant, because they lack motive, they lack opportunity, and when I'm done, they'll lack a weapon."

Victor nodded, leaning into the light again. "Can you get me a room that faces east?" he asked, quietly, in a way that was unconnected to everything that had come before.

She straightened up slightly. "...Yes. Yes, I should be able to arrange that."

His eyes cast down to her pale hand, then back again. "Are you married, Miss Greene?"

Again, she straightened. "I'm not here to talk about that. I'm here for your case."

"I'm not either," he said, leaning back on his own chair, becoming more relaxed even as she became increasingly tense. "I could never find that... person. It's become harder to date as a person of faith, if you're looking to date within your faith... if you have a close community, it can be like dating within the family, even though it's not."

She paused, then nodded.

He took a deep breath. "When I get out of here, I need to work on that. There's so much... awful in the world. I'd like some normalcy. Some marriage."

Megan smiled at the phrasing. "Don't count your chickens before they're hatched, but yes. Yes, I'd say our chances took pretty good." She smiled and started pushing her photos and files back into her folder. "And I'll talk to them about your cell. I think we've been very accommodating to the State of California; it's about time we started flexing some muscle to show we're not fucking around."

Victor bristled at her language, but smiled.

CHAPTER TWELVE

Powell's Convenience was once again crowded with police and emergency service vehicles for the second time this year, creating a slog of traffic as commuters came around the blind turn on their way to work and were caught off-guard by the fire truck blocking their passage, then awkwardly found the space needed to turn around to find an alternative route. This happened in both directions, causing congestion of honking, U-turning traffic on either end of the road. The sound was enormous and clamouring, becoming almost a living thing onto itself.

Xander stood on the bumper of the fire truck and held onto the rail that went up its side and over its top. The wind was in his hair as he looked over the gathered professionals and gawkers that gathered whenever there was a body in the street -- like crows gathering around a fallen member of their murder and cawing its passage to heaven into the morning sky.

Duncan was standing next to Travis and Fredericks, the three of them looking down at the space where the body had been only hours before. The glass still had smears of

Thomas Horton on it, petri dishes of a man that was for a brief time and never would be again. As Xander watched dispassionately, Duncan rested an empathetic hand on Travis' shoulder. Travis drew back, slightly, unsure what to make of the choice. Duncan seemed not to notice the discomfort his action had caused. He walked through the front door of Powell's and took a bag of Lays chips off the rack, placed a dollar fifty in change on the register, then opened it and exited the business again. Fredericks and Travis followed him with steely gazes as he went.

Xander frowned, the red from the blood in the sun catching his eye like red-pepper jelly. He watched as Travis pointed, outlining the flaws in the tape outline of where Horton's body had been. 'Placing' bodies that rested on three-dimensional space was far trickier than bodies that lay splayed flat like starfish. Any attempt ended up looking like an amorphous blob, arms disappearing into the outline of the torso and merging with heads until no right-minded person could look at the frame and call it a human. The only thing distinguishing the oblong that was the head from the rest of the body was the splash of red that came from it, echoing out from the neck like accusing fingers pointing back at their source: "There's the culprit, sir. That's where we came from."

"You want to be seen?" Duncan asked, striding up alongside the fire truck. He had opened the potato chips and popped two into his mouth.

There was a red smear on the outside of the bag -- almost imperceptible -- that Xander noticed but did not comment on. "Today I don't care," he said, holding his head high to the breeze as it twisted and changed direction, bringing a cavalcade of fresh scents to his nostrils. Copper was chief among them. "Did you get a good look inside?"

Duncan held up the polyethylene bag and shook it, as if to say, 'You watched me make an ass of myself by getting these, right?'

"Any symbols inside I can't see from the street?"

Duncan took a bite from his chips. "No swastikas. No twenty-threes. No eighty-eights. No arrowhead crosses. Nothing that would mark this as a hate crime."

"It's a good cop killed," Xander said, biting the words. "That's an attack on the smallest minority of them all, far as I'm concerned."

Duncan narrowed his eyes at him but did not respond. He turned and sat on the same protuberance of corrugated metal Xander was standing on. He ate several chips, waiting for his frustration at Xander's comment to subside while simultaneously weighing it against his own experience and coming up short. "How much media coverage was there around the symbol last time?"

Xander stared at the red tainted glass for a long moment, then crouched down into a squat that brought him nearly to Duncan's level. "Not a lot, from what I remember. They didn't want a circus about it, and it was hard to see unless you stood back from the glass and noticed the pattern in it... it was a big part of Horton's *original* thinking on the case, but not a lot in the coverage. And there wasn't much coverage, anyway."

"Original thinking?"

"Hn?"

"You said the symbol was a big part of Horton's original thinking. That sort of implies his thinking changed."

Xander's hands drew together, forming two O's with thumbs and forefingers that became interlaced like links on a chain. "I changed them, I think. He had a guy arrested at first -- this poor dumb motherfucker who I don't think knew where he was half the time -- mostly because of opportunity and the fact that he had an old swastika tat."

"You're defending Nazis now?"

Xander shook his head. "I don't, and he wasn't one. His parents were and he... I don't know the term. Evolved? Left the faith? I feel weird calling anything associated with that ideology a religion."

"As am I," Duncan agreed.

"Yeah. Anyway, Horton had the wrong guy and I... I dunno. I told him, and eventually he got turned on to Murdock and made the arrest."

Duncan ate several chips, staring out at the crime scene. The crowd of pedestrians was slowly moving in, encroaching on the area sectioned off by police tape with every shuffle and jostle. Soon they would have come too far and Fredericks would have to shoo them back, and the whole process would start again. "Where's the original suspect now?"

Xander adjusted his jaw, taking a long tense moment before answering in which he did not look at Duncan. "Witness protection. He got targeted by a vigilante who didn't want to see past his ink."

"...You?"

Xander's head snapped to him. "If I was at all vigilant, this wouldn't have happened." He gestured towards

Powell's Convenience.

Duncan clicked his tongue against the roof of his mouth. He stared at the scene as though it were made of moving, motorized, articulate Lego-characters, travelling about their tasks on tracks with hidden levers. He took it all in, every misshapen piece of glass and red smear and hastily drawn diagram of blood spatter. "How close is it to the original?" he asked finally, when he couldn't find a single, solitary detail to link to.

"Exactly it," Xander said, after a pause. "Aside from the symbol, exactly it. Down to the square foot the body is at. I'd have to get out the pictures and hold them up to be sure… but it's exactly like I remember seeing it back then. Exactly."

"It's a copycat," Duncan said. He spoke immediately after Xander had finished, as though he'd been waiting to chime in with his opinion on it. "Only copycats get things exactly right. They're devoted to the original, they try and xerox it if they can. Serials, they're always similar to their past selves but never the *same*. Like with artists: no two versions of *The Scream* by Munch are exactly alike, but plenty of copycat artists get the brush strokes dead on. It's a copycat, and he didn't know about the symbol because it wasn't in the paper, that's why it's not copied."

Xander furrowed his brow. "You comparing serials to artists?"

"Nope," he said, equally quickly, as though he had expected the criticism. "Just calling it like I see it."

Xander let out a deep sigh. "I don't agree," he said finally.

Duncan raised an eyebrow and turned to him, incredulous. "Oh really? Do tell, Sherlock."

Xander pointed at one of the shards of glass coming down from the upper echelon of the window. "When I met Horton, I was shooing him off another case… a worse case. One that would have gotten him killed, I think." He paused, the weight of the irony of that hitting him. He looked down for a moment, composed himself, then returned. "I told him to keep working this case, because it was normal police stuff. It was the type of thing he was trained to handle: a horse, not a zebra."

"Zebra?"

"Medical school thing I picked up," he explained. "Trying to teach you to challenge your assumptions. If you hear an animal approaching and you hear hooves, you assume a horse. But sometimes it's a zebra. It's trying to remind you that evidence can have more than one conclusion."

Duncan nodded. "Good analogy. I'll steal that. So, you got him to pair to the Fabian Mitchells case *because* it was normal. What's the issue?"

Xander pointed to the broken window frame again. "*This* isn't normal. No matter how you slice it, this isn't normal. Assaults that accidentally lead to murders do not inspire copycats, so that makes no sense. The copycat theory only makes sense if this was a zebra, and if this was a zebra… then I was wrong from the start and maybe it's not Murdock. Maybe we've assumed more than we think and this is… the same thing. A serial assaulter that graduated to murder without trying to and went underground until the trial brought him back. He thinks he's out of the rough with the trial starting and is looking to make a splash, throw a monkey-wrench into the system."

"Don't think that," Duncan said firmly. He aimed a stubby finger at Xander. "Do not go down that road. You do not want to fuck with an active case by calling in that kind of… doubt. That way lies badness, you have no idea."

Xander nodded. "I agree. Still."

"Still *nothing*," Duncan emphasized. "The court thinks they have the guy, let them sort that out. That's their domain. This," he gestured to the scene the same way Xander had, "this is different, treat it like it's different. It's a copycat."

"It's *too* exact."

"That's why it's a copycat."

Xander huffed, then got down off the fire truck. "We all burn down here," he mumbled under his breath.

"Pardon?"

"Nothing."

The Church of the Holy Heavenly Father was, somehow, quiet. Despite the bustle he'd been creating, somehow the media was still obeying the rules of sanctuary and staying out of the church. Despite having been on the evening news and three local daytime talk shows in the last day, Reverend Trask was still mostly alone in his chapel.

There was one man seated near the front of the church, in the furthest pew away from the flickering flames of hope that cast all rows in an ominous Halloween glow. The man himself looked to grow out of the dark shadows of the pews and join with the subtle glow of the flames that reached him.

Trask watched him at first, holding himself against the faux-French doors at the rear of the chapel. The only light in the room came from the candles, of which only the first row was actually flame. The rest were lights, each controlled by a switchboard and turned on as people donated. There were lights behind each of the stained-glass windows as well that were currently off, the Saints displayed on them dark. There was no natural light behind them, only more downtown structures. The flood lights had been installed behind them to provide the illusion of luster.

Trask took a deep, steadying breath. He still had makeup on from his performance with Kendra LaMire, and the flesh on his cheeks was the reddish yellow of a spoiled orange. His sweat clung to the harsh powder and became sticky, horrid clumps that he could feel on his face yet had not had a chance to properly expunge.

He pushed off from the doors and started his way up the long hallway between the two columns of pews. It shifted slightly to the left, eventually curling and coming to a cul-de-sac around the Light of Hope. When he was halfway to the end of the hall, he spoke. "I apologize, I didn't see you come in. It's been quite a day… the Lord never gives us more than we can handle, but today He sure tried."

The man sitting in the pews did not react, turn, or respond. He was not looking at the lights as most people who sat at the front did, he looked off to his right at the shadowy nothingness between he and the wall.

Trask hesitated, continuing his gate up the hallway, but slowly. As he rounded the slight left turn that took him temporarily away from the worshipper, the man's front also slowly came into view. His face was shadowed still by long black shadows under each eye. Each cheek had dry, flaky flesh on it that gave way in spots to reveal the wetness of pink new skin underneath. The man's face looked raw and painful and Trask winced when he saw it, imagining even chewing to be agony for the man.

Trask stood at the edge of the row of pews with his hands on the endcaps of each, waiting.

The man's hands were clasped in front of him as though he were praying, but it didn't look like prayer. They shook, and if Trask had had to guess in any other setting, he would have said that they were shaking with anger. The man lowered his arms, then turned finally and met the Reverend's gaze.

His eyes were pointed like almonds and his hair was as patchy as the flesh on his cheeks. It was balding in small, damaged clumps that did not look to be naturally occurring. They looked like damage from a fire or from radiation. It was hard to tell from underneath the shadow of his brow, but it seemed as though this man were staring at him.

"Is there anything I can help you with?" Trask asked. His voice took on a quieter, more gingerly tone than when he spoke on-camera, and after the day spent in-studio he was suddenly aware of it. In person he realized he was almost doing an unconscious impression of his own pastor growing up, Reverend Keitel.

The man continued to stare at him from those black

holes under his brow. "Yes," he said finally.

Trask tugged at his shirt collar, suddenly hot. "Whatever you need. I was saying, I apologize for not being present when you came in. The Lord never gives us --"

"I saw you on the television," the man interrupted.

Trask stopped, readjusting. "I see. And what is it I can do for you?" The man stood to his full height, looming a full six inches above Trask. There was length to him, drawn out by a thin frame that made it appear as though his image had been skewed in Photoshop. He looked unnatural, a caricature of what lanky, gaunt men looked like.

The man took a step toward him roughly, as though his legs were asleep. He moved with the jagged unpredictability of badly rendered film footage.

Trask turned and eyed that display of candles along the far wall in his peripheral vision, then back to the mysterious tall man. He smiled. "You don't come to chapel much, do you?"

The man stopped in midstride. "Pardon?"

Trask motioned back to the candles. "People who don't attend often typically avoid the candles... they're not sure what to make of them. Obvious, physical signs of faith... they unnerve those who are transitioning from secular answers. It's like anything... first you feel it privately, then you sometimes graduate to feeling it publicly. But when you're still in that private zone the public outpourings can be... overwhelming."

The man glanced in the direction of the orange glow. "That's not why I sat in the far pew." When he spoke, the word 'pew' had an elongated E sound to it.

"But you don't deny you don't often attend," Trask smiled, pointing at him with two fingers.

The man was silent for a long moment, maintaining eye contact. He licked his lips -- which Trask now noticed were also quite dry -- and it didn't help. "My wife was. Catholic, as a point of fact."

"I'm sorry."

The man crumpled his nose. "What?"

"You said she was Catholic. If she had converted or lapsed you wouldn't have called her Catholic at all, you wouldn't have brought it up. Was implies that it's she that is no longer. I'm sorry."

The man stopped, taken aback. He looked away toward the flickering candlelight from the other side of the room... then continued forward, passing Trask so closely they bumped elbows and then continuing out into the hall between pews toward the exit.

"I'm sorry, was it something I said?"

"No," the man said with a dry bark, but did not turn around. He continued to talk, but to himself, in a voice too low for Trask to understand, until he left the chapel completely.

Trask sighed, loosened his collar, and retreated into the back of the chapel to wash his face. It had been a very long day thus far and wasn't over yet.

CHAPTER THIRTEEN

Megan's hotel was a suite with French doors dividing a living room/social area from one of the largest, fluffiest beds she had ever slept on. The bedroom had a TV that appeared from behind a remote-controlled door when it was turned on. The bathroom was large, a standup shower and a Jacuzzi fitting in with more than enough room to move freely between the two, and had doors leading to both the bedroom and the living area.

Megan had pushed the glass coffee table back to give herself more room in front of the couch. There were dozens of pages of black text on white paper arranged into piles, and on each pile was a single word in bold, dark font that took up the entire page: 'OPPORTUNITY'; 'DISCOVERY'; 'EVIDENCE'; and 'RAYMOND COUP'.

She changed their order, taking entire stacks and rearranging them and then sitting back to look at the order again, often while taking a hearty mouthful of the neat scotch she'd poured herself two fingers of. She took a long slug of it even now, bringing the sum total down to one finger.

"Ooooh, fuck," she said to herself as the orange tang of the alcohol stung the back of her tongue. She took another small sip, just to dull it. She took a pile called 'MOTIVE' and moved it to the front of the stack, stretching far to do so and spilling some of her drink onto the carpet. "There are trials in South Africa where men and women are still tried as witches to this day, because someone they held a sincere grudge against was hit by lightning. Do you know what even those trials have that the case against Mr. Murdock does not? Motive. Even in South African witch trials, they know that in order to convict someone you need motive." She moved her hands as she spoke, the alcohol sloshing in the glass but not spilling. It was the way she moved when she was in front of a judge or a jury: stay moving, stay animated... stay engaging. Keep all eyes on you, at all times.

She took another drink from her tumbler.

Between where she sat against the couch and its edge was a stack of seven green file folders. Each was for a different alleged victim of Victor Murdock, but only the top file -- Fabian Mitchells -- had been a murder. The other six had been assaults, all of whom had lived but had been hit from behind in the dead of night and had no clue who their attackers were. All had belonged, at one point or another, to the Church of the Holy Heavenly Father.

She glowered at the pile as though it were mocking her. She'd been over them so many times that she knew them by heart by now, and she'd spent most of that time looking for the thing the police couldn't find -- motive. There was connective tissue between the victims -- same church, same community -- but nothing that called out the motive into the night. Which was fine, it wasn't her job to find motive... unless she could find one that exonerated her client, at which point it was absolutely her prerogative.

She turned on her cell phone, opened the contacts, and typed in the letter T. When the list of names came up, she closed the phone app again, checked her inbox, then put the phone away and ran her fingers roughly through her hair.

She looked at the pile of papers marked RAYMOND COUP and stared at it for a long moment before turning away, grabbing the pile that said EVIDENCE and moving it to the front of the lineup.

"Evidence is key to any investigation into the truth, and that's what we're here for," she started, even as she polished off her scotch and reached for the bottle again. "Evidence is what divides a case without merit from a case with merit. In a world where evidence doesn't matter, our justice system falls to whims... and that's what this case is, a whim. It was described as a 'sudden epiphany', but strong police work is not made on epiphanies; it is made on a foundation of measured, pragmatic measures of cause and effect. "

She reached over the file with her client's name on it and forced it open with her one free hand, rummaging through the images therein and spreading them wide until they were scattered like flies in a spider web. "I can't link any of these images. There is no cause and effect, only... snapshots. With this level of dismissal of evidence, we could arrest anyone. We could arrest you, Judge..." she paused, searching her files for the name, "Mandis.

Or you," she feigned pointing to a stenographer, "or anyone."

She took another long dollop of alcohol into her mouth. Her gaze cast over the photos and summaries she'd scattered from the Murdock case... it hadn't been the case file itself; it had been the images from it. A 'visual history' she'd called it, trying to find images that best represented the stages of the case. Each one was printed with enough glossy photo-paper on the bottom to write a remark on, like Polaroids pinned on the inside of a locker.

There was one photo in the centre of her timeline, taken as a screenshot from a security camera at LAPD12. It showed two men hunched over the same computer in the Homicide 12 main office. One was sitting in the chair and looking at the screen, his face well-lit yet partially obscured by the other man, Thomas Horton, who was standing next to him and observing what he was doing on the screen. The sharpie-scribbled note along the bottom of the photo was: 'Horton works an arson case.'

On the photo Horton was circled and named, the unknown computer user... was not. He was young, younger than Horton by at least twenty years. The footage was grainy and gray and hard to make out, but there were wisps of dark hair that made it into the man's face, and his hunched posture belied a set of strong arms that pressed forward at off angles in the screen shot.

Megan squinted at it for a long moment, drinking her drink. It was only those block letters that said RAYMOND COUP that drew her attention away, and when they did, she picked up the pile and started to move it to the front of the row, then stopped herself. She sighed and placed it back at the end, running her fingers through her hair and then pantomiming an explosion for nobody but herself.

She turned on her cell phone, opened the contacts, and typed in the letter T. When the list of names came up, she pressed Tony Jones and the app changed over to the black screen of a dialing phone. She cursed, put her fingers through her hair and gripping her scalp angrily as she waited for the ringing to switch to voicemail.

There was a click, followed by a "Hello?"

The color drained from her face and she sat up a little, her tongue turning into a swollen trout inside her own mouth. She tried to speak but no words would come, and she laid her drink down between her crossed legs as though that would help.

"Hello?" the voice on the other end of the line said again, and there were sounds of ruffling fabric. It had grown agitated.

Megan cursed silently, looking up at the ceiling. "Hi, Tony," she said finally, her voice straining for artificial chipper-ness and coming up short of it. She sounded like an early text-to-speech recording, her voice landing somewhere in the furthest dip of the Uncanny Valley and staying there. "I'm sorry, I thought you'd still be at the office, was leaving you a message." She took the phone away from her ear and looked at it, confirming it read five pm.

"Time difference, it's eight here," he said. His voice was somehow matter of fact and annoyed at the same time.

"Ahh. Ah."

He sighed. "Jesus, Greene, what time is it there? Are you drunk already?"

She paused, swallowed, then pushed her glass tumbler away from her legs as if the proximity of the unconsumed alcohol held sway over her speech. "No," she lied, unconvincingly. "No, it's not that. I just... I wanted your advice. On a case. Ah... got a bit of an atom bomb and part of me wants to drop it in the opening statement but I'm not sure I --"

"Call Nathan," Tony said, cutting her off briskly. "What kind of bomb? Is it -- no, call Nathan." He paused. "Was there something else, or --"

"No, no, sorry," she smiled so that he could hear her smile, but as soon as she was done speaking it reversed. She reached for her glass and took the last of its contents quickly, pressing the whole to her neck so that he couldn't hear. "I mean, how are you? I was wondering... how you were?"

There was silence from the other side of the long.

"Tony?"

Tony sighed, making no effort to turn away from the phone's mouthpiece as he did so. "Get some rest, Greene. Seriously." He broke the connection.

She turned her phone screen to watch as the app registered the end of the call and closed, lingered on it for a moment, then tossed the phone across the room. It landed on the plush carpet of the hotel room with barely an impact.

She made herself another drink, then grabbed the green folders of the victims and pulled them over to read again.

CHAPTER FOURTEEN

"Churches creep me out," Duncan said, as he closed the door to the Church of the Holy Heavenly Father behind him. He was holding a green file in his left hand, both of which were dangling at his waistline. Xander was standing just a foot in front of him with his back to him, backlit by the far-ahead wall of memorial candles. "They all smell the same, you ever notice that? Churches and high schools, they all smell the same." He stepped up next to Xander until they were shoulder to shoulder and watched where he watched, looking up toward the empty rows of pews and vacant alter. "I used to joke that back when the churches ran the schools, they saved money by buying bleach in bulk, enough for two thousand years. Then when they split the church and state, they split the haul of cleaner between them, too."

"That's dumb," Xander said under his breath.

"Yeah but, two-thousand years' worth? Think of the savings."

Xander turned slowly, until his wry look met Duncan's eye.

Duncan cocked his head toward the alter. "You got religion?"

"I'm Catholic."

"That a 'no' then?"

Again, Xander shot him a look.

Duncan frowned. "Loosen up, you look like death. It's bad when meeting non unsubs."

Xander paused, nodded, then adjusted himself to try and loosen the tense posture of his shoulders to little affect.

"You still go to church?"

"Haven't been in a long time, no... had a bit of a falling out with my Priest."

Duncan paused, longer than typical. "...Oh. Uh... sorry."

"Nothing like that."

"Okay. Good then... good? Good."

Xander took a step forward, crossing the Rubicon from the shadowy arch that housed the entrance into the line of light that surrounded the church.

Duncan held up the file and shook it meaningfully without opening it, as though weighing its importance by its empirical weight. "How you wanna play this?"

Xander took another step forward, craning his head to see if there was seating above the door, as there was in some venues. There was not that he could see. He turned his head slowly into all directions his neck could manage, taking it the whole of the church after a fashion that looked like a yoga warmup.

The Church of the Holy Heavenly Father was possibly one of the oddest churches Xander had seen in his life. It was at least the oddest that was still in regular use. The Church had started as a townhouse that fit with the townhouses on either side of it. There were only townhouses in this part of the city, each painted a vibrantly cheap colour. This one had been repainted an earthy brown, but there were still hints of a more spectacular colour underneath that coat.

The building had originally been three floors, but now it was one high ceiling, with the remnants of the third floor still circling the ceiling in a tedious ring of stairs and storage space.

There were seven stained-glass windows, three on each side and one at the head that had not been visible from the outside. Light shone through them regardless, and Xander could see the light fixture behind the false back of them.

"Horton came here looking for answers," Xander said, distantly. He was quiet then for a moment, then turned and gave his full attention to Duncan for the first time since they'd stepped foot through the faux-French doors. He was alert again, whereas before the ambiance of the building had been seeming to weigh on him. "He didn't have a lead when he came here, he was just getting a sense of the victim. The mother -- Fabian's mother -- she'd mentioned that her son went here, so here Horton went, just... trying to get a feel for the man. Who his friends were, if they knew anyone that would hurt him, that kind of thing."

"Standard legwork," Duncan nodded. "I'd've just creeped his Facebook, but that's me."

"That is you, yes," Xander said, snapping his fingers

and pointing at him. "But Horton came down here, he needs that personal touch. That's one of -- that was one of the things that got me about the man. He was not an Armchair Anthropologist; he would get up and get in and see everything. He had to see every square inch of this place where Fabian Mitchells came every week: how does it look, how does it affect him, how does it measure who he is." Xander spread his arms wide, encompassing the entirety of the church.

Duncan stepped forward, looking around at all the places Xander had looked, turning his whole torso to do so.

"And because he came down here, he met Trask and Trask gave him the names of the other alter-men that hung around with Mitchells and bam, you look into those two and you've got your suspects. When someone was killed, he'd just look at who was in their orbit, who was close to them, and keep expanding out." He brought his fingers together and then spread them out to the fullest length of his arms, as if to illustrate. "Pick apart every one until you find which one did it." He shook his head, smiled, then let the smile fade. "He was a good cop."

Duncan turned to him, incredulous. "You saying I'm not?"

"You're a good *investigator*. It's in the title, the 'I' in 'FBI.' But Horton was a good *Detective*. That was his whole title, and it was all he did. And I'm not... I think I could have learned more from him. Start next to the victim, that's the sun of your case's solar system. Expand out, look at the people and planets closest to him, then the next closest, then the next... examine them until it makes sense, because it will make sense. I don't think he ever got to Pluto, if you follow me. Or if he did, he stayed on that shit for the rest of his life."

Duncan grumbled, "Pluto's not even a planet anymore."

Xander sighed, then shrugged. "Maybe that's the point. Maybe once you get out that far you're not even sure what you're looking at anymore, how to class it."

Duncan snorted, opened the folder briefly, then started walked the slowly left-leaning hall up to the altar.

Xander followed him. "I know almost no people who would have wanted to hurt Horton, and the few I do are already behind bars. And are remaining there." He paused. "Nobody in his close orbit -- the Mercury Zone, let's call it -- would have done this. So, let's move out, and let's pick at the people we see. And there are two orbits: there's the case's orbit and there's Horton's personal orbit, and one of the first places they intersect is John Trask."

Both men reached the end of the pews and were led by the slope of the hall to the left of them, where the first row of Light of Hope candles had been snuffed out, leaving only the artificial flicker of the fake candles. Xander leaned in and saw that the bulbs of each were actually in the shape of tiny flames, so that the light would appear as natural as possible.

"Reverend Trask while we're in here at least, I prefer," came a soft -- yet firm -- voice from behind them.

Xander and Duncan both turned. Trask was behind them, behind the far row of pews at the wall between the first two stained-glass windows. He was backlit now, the glow that came off the blue and yellow pieces of glass reflected soft-hued light onto either of his shoulders.

"Apologies," Xander said, forcing a smile. Then, under his breath and to Duncan: "Good or Bad?"

"I'll be Bad," Duncan answered, in the same hushed tone.

"I'll be absent until I'm needed," Xander said, stepping away off to the right of the flames even as Trask approached. They passed each other, and Xander smiled and nodded at him. "Again, sorry, Father."

Trask smirked and stopped, pointing at him: "Catholic?"

Xander nodded.

"All the Catholics call me Father. I never was nobody's Daddy. It's Reverend. Reverend."

Xander nodded. "Apologies again then." He continued to the row of pews and took a deep breath, in through his nose and out through his mouth, breathing in that two-thousand-year-old bleach smell that Duncan had joked about. He winced, his nose twitched, and he moved into the second set of pews.

Trask continued toward the light until both he and Duncan were just shadows in front of it. "I'd ask you what you were doing here, but enough men with folders of paper have come through in the past few months that I've learned to recognize the LAPD."

Duncan pointed the folder at him. "FBI, actually."

Trask stopped, then made an exaggerated nod. "G-Men, one and all. I didn't recognize the difference, if there was one."

"Not like the difference between Father and Reverend," Duncan drawled, rolling his eyes. "That's way different. Wouldn't want to fuck that up, otherwise your imaginary friend would get mixed up with someone else's imaginary friend. Can't have that."

Trask extended until he was ramrod straight, his shoulder coming apart like a peacock that had been startled.

Xander made his way to the halfway through the row of pews. He was taking his time, running his hands along each Bible and Hymn Book he found along the way, picking some up and thumbing through them. His ears were perked, trying to hear everything he was pretending to be missing with Duncan and Trask's conversation.

"You're here about the murder, then?" Trask asked, his voice audibly filled with agitation now.

"Well, this was the first stop after Mitchells was killed, seemed a logical first stop now. If the killer's copying that case, stands to reason we should, too," Duncan spoke lackadaisically, his voice taking on an uneven sing-song cadence as he ran his fingers along the cool edges of fake melted wax never to him.

"Only if you want to arrest the wrong person again, as well," Trask said. It was odd to hear a Reverend using sarcasm so openly, like listening to your second-grade teacher curse. It felt wrong in the ear.

"And *that*," Duncan said loudly, pointing the corner of his folder at him, "brings us to why we're here. Full circle; love it. Love when I can get there naturally." He waved the folder in the air between them, as though it were a carrot he was offering the Reverend.

"If you think that was natural conversation, I know why your ring finger is empty."

Duncan smiled at him and shook the folder again, as if

congratulating him. "So, you were the first person Thomas Horton came to when he wanted to get to know Fabian Mitchells: fair enough. The kid was a religious guy, you go to his religious leader. Not my cup of tea, but then again, I hate tea." He paused, smirked at Trask, then continued. "But now we're here. Now it's months later, and this shit is finally going to trial. Public defenders didn't do shit with shit, so you hire a fancy criminal lawyer from out of state. Defended serial killers and shit."

Xander looked up briefly, then turned away again. He pulled one leg up over the pew, then the other, until he was now in the first row of pews, not the second. He sniffed back again, clearing his nostrils so loud it echoed off the walls.

"I didn't hire the lawyer," Trask corrected. "The Parish did. We raised money through collection, as a community. That's what a Church is, Mister --"

"Taggart."

"Mister Taggart, it's a community."

"Lovely. But you called the firm, right? The Church itself didn't uncouple from its foundations and stomp on over to Maine and go in for an appointment? You didn't put the whole flock on group-call, did you? You called. It was their money, but you called."

Trask glowered at him.

"Great, just so we're on the same page. So, you hire this fancy lawyer and she's going through the case, and then you start telling people that someone else did it and that there's still another killer out there somewhere, and then, all of a sudden, there's this dead body that looks a lot like the first dead body." He paused, then smiled. "You get that that looks bad, right?"

"For your case."

"Fuck me," Xander cursed, under his breath. He was standing at the far edge of the pews, very close to the wall.

Duncan ignored Xander, his eyes only darting toward him for a second. "No, no, for you. See with murders we always ask ourselves, 'Who benefits?' Like, you find out some broad died and that the husband took out life insurance on her a month before, that's a clear benefit. He benefits from her being dead, so we look at him... your case, your 'you got the wrong guy' argument... that benefits a lot from Tom Horton showing up dead. You, by extension, benefit from that. You see why that's a problem?"

Trask stiffened again. "I was meeting with a community group when the tragic event happened," he said, his voice stiff but also holding contempt.

There was a flash of light from the pews as Xander held up his phone and took a picture of something. He looked at his screen, swiped it several times, typed something, then put it away and cursed again.

"You were?"

"I was."

"I can check on that then? I'm sorry, said that like it was a question. Meant to say: I'll check on that, then. You know, in case you're making up stories." He let that hang in the air, as he looked around the chapel. "You know, stories. Make sure those friends you were meeting with aren't imaginary, too."

Xander stepped into the negative space between the two men. "We're out of here," he said, thumbing Duncan's shoulder.

Duncan shot him a surprised look he tried to hide.

"Apologies, Reverend," Xander said to Trask, then took Duncan by the coat and started away.

"What the fuck?" Duncan hissed when they were halfway down the hall. "I was under his skin. I was like an enema I was so far under his skin. What are you --"

"Listen, shut up." Xander held up his phone screen and thumbed it on. It opened to a washed-out picture he'd taken in the wood of the pews... showing a burned section in the rough shape of a handprint, smeared and distorted but still clearly what it was.

Duncan raised an eyebrow. "What the fuck is this?"

Xander sighed. "Trouble."

Tim's door came open with enough force to startle him. There was an awkward moment -- there had been many of those in the past few months -- in which Tim's body forgot that he was paralyzed and tried to react to the sudden, sharp stimulus by jumping. The result was an uncomfortable disconnect between mind and body, the former expecting to have to adjust for the latter's sudden flexing and then having to readjust for the lack thereof. It took mental effort that was, although unconscious, taxing. He could feel the beginnings of a migraine from it even now.

Xander stepped into the room without taking off his sneakers. He let the door close behind him, a pressure-hinge forcing it shut after it almost connected with the opposing wall. "Did you get it?" he barked, before he'd even crossed the room.

Tim let out a sigh that was an attempt to let go of some of the adrenaline that was rushing through him with no use. He swiped his fingers and an enlarged version of the picture Xander had taken appeared on the screen: the burned handprint he'd found on the pew at the Church of the Holy Heavenly Father. "I got it," he said. "I don't know what I'm supposed to do with it."

"Look up Shiro Gilbert in the Federal Registry. That's Shiro with an O, not an H."

Tim squinted, then swiped to open a window. A gray screen with white boxes loaded, the only flourish on the site the small, slightly-off gray imprint of the Bureau's symbol emblazoned in the top right corner of the site.

Xander stepped into the view of the screen. "No, Shiro's the first name. Gilbert last."

Tim made the correction and hit enter. A head shot covering the entire left side of the screen materialized. The man had wispy dark hair with bald patches checkering it every few inches. His mouth was small and the skin on his face was tight, with eczema nipping at the corners of every orifice. The pupils and sclera of his almond eyes were an ashen gray that stared relentlessly into the camera, so glossed and bloodshot they seemed like fake lenses. "To whom do I have the pleasure?" Tim asked.

"He's powered, like me," Xander said, his words clipped and firm.

Some of the color drained from Tim's face. "He's another Engen experiment?"

Xander bristled, taken aback by that. "No, I... No. I don't think so, anyway. He just... has them."

Tim looked from Xander to the photo of the Asian

man with the burned flesh, and suddenly the sclera of his eyes no longer looked like the sort of fake lenses someone bought at a party supply store to look intimidating... suddenly, they actually intimidated. "What does he do?"

"He generates heat. I'm not sure how much control he has over the creation of it actually, but he can sure direct it at the least. I've been on the receiving end of it a few times and it is less than fun. Felt like my insides were cooking from the inside out... I don't think my powers were made to handle that kind of assault. It wasn't something that Engen worked into their design."

Tim scrolled down the file. It listed Shiro's last known address as being in Wichita, over a year ago.

"When Engen made the Black Womb, they made it so it came out when I lost blood or when I was unconscious... it was a defense mechanism. If I lost blood or I was knocked out, this thing would come out and deal with whatever threat I couldn't handle and get the fuck out of dodge." He tapped Shiro's chin with his knuckle. "He overrides that. He cooks you from the inside out and even my Healing Factor doesn't know how to deal with that."

Tim raised an eyebrow, then continued scrolling. "He killed his --"

"Don't even. I know. I met him while Horton and I were working the Fabian Mitchells case."

Tim turned to him, shocked. "That's not in here."

"Nor would it be. Horton had been investigating sex workers that had been burned alive, and I'd managed to get on his radar as a suspect."

"I remember," Tim said. "That was one of the files that got me to come here in the first place."

"Right. So, Horton's working the Fabian Mitchells

case at the time, and it all gets tangled up together -- all of it. Me, this fucker, everything. Because it turns out this guy doesn't have a hate for sex workers, he has a hate for *criminals*. Any criminal. Motherfucker would probably kill a shoplifter. He killed his neighbor because he was hitting his son... *and* he killed the son."

"Why?"

"I have no earthly idea. *None.* But this guy... this guy is beyond fucked up, and when you add him to a situation, that situation gets worse. It just happens, you can't control it. He got it in his head to kill the first suspect Horton arrested for Fabian Mitchells."

"In error," Tim said, frowning.

"Yes, exactly. So then that became my day, protecting this idiot with a nasty tattoo from this..." he tapped the screen again, "whatever the fuck this is. So now Victor Murdock is on trial and people are trying to make the case that he might get off because..." He swallowed. "Because Horton was murdered. This Priest is on the local news yelling about how he wants just that, and then I go to that chapel and I see this." He pressed Tim's screen and brought the photo of the burned handprint back to being in the most forward window. He looked at it for a moment and let the image hang in the air, then turned to Tim. "You feel me?"

The color had drained from Tim's cheeks. He wasn't moving, and it took Xander a moment to realize that he had meant to nod and had forgotten that the muscles of his neck would not translate that into motion.

Xander pointed to the screen. "I need you to get the word out to your local people that he's here."

"That won't be easy to explain."

"Doesn't matter. Don't care. He will be at that prison and that trial tomorrow... if he thinks for even a second that someone he thinks is guilty is going to get off, he'll fry them like chicken, and anyone who tries to stop him will get the same." He stepped away from the screen and looked across the room, where the printer sat. "Is that mine?" he asked, pointing to a stack of papers.

"Ayuh," Tim replied. He was already calling up his All-Points Bulletin template. He watched Xander. "Did you go talk to Martha Horton yet?"

Xander was flipping through the stack of pages he'd printed on Murdock's alleged victims and did not look up from them. "What? No. I don't think she'll have any information." He paused, considering. "And I don't think she's a target."

Tim's face pleaded with him. "That's not why you should go see her."

Xander's head snapped up. There was something acerbic on the tip of his tongue, but it left when he saw Tim's face. He swallowed it back, paused, then nodded and went back to his reading. "Yeah. Okay."

After another moment of typing, Tim paused, his attention turning back to him. "How were you so sure Gilbert would be in the Federal Registry?"

"I looked him up, months back."

Tim stared at him.

Xander finally looked back at him and shrugged. "If you'd wanted your password to be hard to break, you failed spectacularly at that."

Tim sighed, then went back to the work of drafting his email.

CHAPTER FIFTEEN

Martha Horton sobbed, her face scrunched and reddened. She had been crying for hours that felt like years and was currently at the tiny kitchen table that -- for the first time -- seemed too large and vacant and agoraphobic for her to stand. On the table in front of her was a meal of pork and baked potato that she'd made the previous day. Although friends had brought their own meals and casseroles and desserts, she'd wanted to eat the pork while it kept. She'd made it unsalted and now salted it with a steady stream of tears.

She'd eaten her portion of the meal yesterday and had saved this plate for Thomas when he'd gotten home. She hadn't realized it until after she had unwrapped it from his shelf in the fridge and warmed it in a microwave that he hated (and that he swore hated him back) and had sat down, fork in hand, before actually taking a bite.

Her first -- and as yet, only -- bite of pork had been in her mouth, when she realized she was eating the last meal she would ever cook for her husband.

She had broken into a fresh crop of tears, not knowing what reserve of water her eyes were harvesting them from, and had not stopped since.

Xander watched Martha from the shadows outside her home, hidden by the last light of the setting sun. The porch that led into her kitchen was in better condition than the last time he had seen it, a welcome symptom of Thomas' retirement he was sure. Beams that had shown rot had been replaced, and there was a fresh coat of weather proofing glass over the entire thing.

He stepped forward and moved to the formerly dilapidated porch steps, his feet resting comfortably on the third. There was still enough width to the steps that a second man could have stood there next to him, and in his mind's eye he remembered when Horton had: on the night he had come and told him about Shiro Gilbert, months ago.

He started to step forward into the light of the kitchen, toward Martha, mouth open to say something. No words came.

He stopped after a moment and bent down to reach between the steps. The sticky sound of tape stretching cut through the night air, and he withdrew a plastic cigarette pouch, still grasping shards of mangled packing tape. He peeled off the top, took out a cigarette, then closed the pack and put the rest in his pocket.

After another moment's hesitation, he turned and left Martha Horton to her tears.

CHAPTER SIXTEEN

Megan stood in the centre of the elevator with her hands clasped tightly on her brown file folder. She held it against her crotch, like a teenage boy trying to hide an erection with a book binder. She was wearing her blue blazer that one client had once told her made her look like Hillary Clinton, and she had spent many attempts to wear it since trying to parse out whether he had meant that as a good thing or a bad thing.

The folder was an accordion type that was held shut with a piece of leather string that wrapped around a designed strap to close it. It smelled new, the welcome scent of polyethylene and leather and paper coming to her nostrils in pleasant waves.

Stephen One and Stephen Two were both in the elevator, one large man on either side of her. The elevator was free of dust and dirt and had a white glossy finish, looking more like the inside of a case that would house a new smart phone than a human.

"Slow day?" she asked, smirking out one side of her mouth.

"No," both One and Two said, just shy of together and in the same tone of voice. If they had both been standing on one side of her she would have thought it had been one person speaking they sounded so similar. It was only that the answer had come in in surround sound that had made it unreal.

"Good, you'll be kept on," she grumbled, then looked at her watch. It was close to twelve, she realized, the minute and second hands ticking their way closer and closer to all three standing at perfect attention. She fiddled with the straps of her file folder, as if worried that the papers within would grow legs and scamper away if it wasn't held shut.

The elevator doors opened before she even felt their downward motion slow to a halt. There was no ping or ding or chime: the doors just opened with lightning speed to reveal a packed courtroom where everyone was sitting. Everyone turned to face her as one and followed her as she walked up the hall between the aisles with Stephen One and Two behind her, the only sound the clack of her heels against the tiled floor.

There was a large display in the centre of the courtroom, in front of the judge. It was a life-size recreation of the window at Powell's Convenience, fully intact, with the vinyl lettering on it popping as though it were new and unbleached by the sun. She smiled as she stepped until she was in front of it, Stephens One and Two breaking off to either side. She turned, facing the gallery of attendees for the first time.

They were all people she knew, she realized suddenly. The faces in the crowd were not the journalists and family members and looky-loos that came out of the woodwork for every other major crime, they were *her* people. Tony was there in his best pressed suit, and sitting next to him was Nathan. Neither were smiling; both looked as though they'd been carved from marble: inanimate, unmoving.

"Fuckers," she said under her breath.

Everyone in the court galley shuffled as though they had heard her, even those standing against the back wall, unable to have found a seat in time.

Her parents were in the third row back, shaking their heads. Next to them was Natasha Mayer, a tall woman with close cropped black hair and a nasty gash along her cheek that Megan realized, without thinking how strange it was, had been the blow that killed her.

The entirety of her high-school basketball team was seated in the middle of the crowd.

Seated in the furthest row back were two teens that she recognized: one a tall blond boy with freckles, the other a short teen girl with shoulder-length black hair.

"I've figured something out," Megan said to them, and this time it was as though only they heard, even though they were farthest away. "I need to speak with him."

"He's gone," the girl, Cathy, replied. Suddenly she was sitting alone on the bench. A man who'd been standing behind her stepped forward, dressed in black. She only recognized him when he placed a heavy hand on Cathy's shoulder: it was Xander Drew. "He won't come back."

The hair on the back of Megan's neck stood on end and she turned to look over her shoulder. The stenciled vinyl green letters of Powell's Convenience had been re-shuffled, pushed together to make a shape like a child making art out of alphabet magnets. They formed a cross with equal distance from each spoke from the centre, and each tip producing a short protrusion to its right. It was a green and orange swastika, made out of jumbled letters in Bauhaus font.

A shocked hush fell over the crowd and she reached, instinctively, for her file folder. She unraveled the leather cord with a quick flourish motion and shoved her arm deep into the guts of the case, returning it a moment later clasping the neck of a bottle of twenty-year-old scotch. She tried to unscrew its top without looking, instead keeping her gaze locked on the hateful symbol, as if waiting for it to move again, daring it to shift into something else.

A young girl screamed in the galley, and Megan started to turn to see what it was. She hadn't even completed the motion when a sudden impact launched her into the window, her right temple connecting with the tip of the swastika and shattering both.

Megan jolted awake, displacing the stack of paper she'd been reading as she did so, the file on Raymond Coup. They were stained brown from alcohol, the glass she'd been drinking empty on the floor beside her. "Fuck!" she hissed, suddenly awake. She braced herself to get up, her hand finding its way to a sliver of glass. It pushed through the skin just enough to draw blood before she recoiled. "Fuck!" she yelled again.

Someone banged on the wall of her hotel room and yelled something that could not be heard through the wall above a mumble.

"Fuck off!" she yelled back, then made her way to the washroom to soak her bloodied hand.

-Ssssss!-

The sound of rainwater sizzling as it touched down against the hot metal of the heating pipe made Sly Irons jump, startled. He turned quickly away from his tool kit, facing the hot copper pipe, just as the droplet vanished with a tiny puff of steam.

Rain was a rarity in Los Angeles. When it came, it came in short, hot bursts that even the most seasoned meteorologist had difficulty predicting, covering the dusty, dry tarmac of the city with a blanket of water it was not equipped to contend with. Roads washed out, earth was displaced, and before anyone could even mount an effort to combat the flood it was gone, the heat of the sun valley evaporating it as though it were never there at all. Within ten minutes of its stopping, the only evidence that it had been there at all was the destruction it left in its wake.

In most geographies, a sudden downpour would make people take shelter. Los Angeles was different: the rain drew people out. Rain in LA was hot and humid, more like a pleasant shower than the frigid onslaught of colder climates. People left their homes to walk in Los Angeles rain, strolling hand-in-hand like lovers.

Sly chuckled to himself as the rain beat down and walked over to the pipe.

"What a night to pull shift," he grumbled to himself, walking over to the pipe as even more rain droplets hissed against its boiling hot surface. He tapped his wrench twice against the pipe's exterior, almost idly, not paying any attention to the sound that the pipe had emitted.

Sly was the building manager at the Yardside Apartments complex, a series of a hundred and twenty-one apartments divided between two buildings that had no yard, despite the name, but did have cheap rent. The building was primarily home to those with low-income: families with more kids than they had dollars to feed them and groups of men working illegally packed into two-room apartments filled with sleeping bags. Sly made his way through the halls answering pages two-hours past the time he said he would most days and could often be seen mumbling to himself. He spoke aloud when he saw potential problems with the building, as though some invisible assistant were following him around and taking down the notes he dictated.

The tenants had been grumbling for about four months that the heat refused to be turned down. The building was heated by hot water pipes, all of which were fed by the master pipe Sly now stood beside. Finally, after months of cajoling, the landlord had broken down and called for Sly.

With a look not unlike a detective examining a scene, Sly placed a gloved palm onto the metal pipe. He pulled it back immediately, cursing as burning pain shot up his arm: "Geez - us!" he shouted, taking off his thick insulated glove and examining his hand.

The flesh was an odd pinkish color he had never seen before, like an embryo. It had already begun to blister.

"Damn it," he muttered, shaking his head.

He stared down at the hissing metal pipe angrily. There were pressure valves and checks and balances in place that should have prevented the pipe from getting that hot. He had already checked all the gauges several times before coming out in this downpour of rain, and everything had turned out fine. His gaze followed the path of the pipe up to a closet-sized service room at the end of the alley.

There was a faint orange glow seeping out from the cracks along the door, and it flickered violently against the darkness of the night.

"Homeless kids," he mumbled, frowning. He swallowed, then stretched his neck and summoned all the authority he could. "Anyone taking shelter in there?" He paused. "You might think you're smart starting a fire in there, but you don't know the trouble you're causing."

Sly patted his wrench to make sure it was on his belt. It was, hanging at his side like a gun in a cowboy's holster. He then slowly strutted over to the door, paused, then pressed his hand against the metal frame.

He pulled back again, taking a step back in shock.

"Damn!" he shouted again, more violently this time. The door was searing hot, possibly even more so then the pipe had been.

"Fire must be right by the door," he realized, gritting his teeth. "All right, you fuckers, party's over! Come out, right now, or I'm coming in!" He raised his wrench slightly. "And you don't want that."

He put his faded green working glove on over his hand, then slowly reached out and grabbed the doorknob. It was hot but seemed to be growing cooler by the moment. He hesitated for a moment, then pulled the door open in one swift motion, raising his wrench high against whoever lay within.

Nothing.

Nothing but darkness, and the low humming sound of the pipe's heat generator boiling away at the large, underground hot water tank. There was no fire, nor was there any trace of where one had been, within the confines of the small shed.

A cold rush of gooseflesh passed over Sly, sending shivers up and down his spine. He shook it off, raised an eyebrow as he leaned into the shed and looked from one corner of the shadowed, humid room to the other, then closed the door behind him.

High above in the street that connected to the alley, a light flickered, making the shadows of the rain dance and leap against the stone walls, creating haunting images of demons to those who had the imagination to see them. Sly took a look around, then gazed up at the failing light source. "Screw this," he muttered.

He pulled the remainder of his tools into his belt and was about to leave the alley, when he heard a sound he'd heard many times before: heels against concrete. He stopped what he was doing and listened, his face suddenly going slack of all expression, as he watched the mouth of the alley illuminated with light from the street. As the *tap tap tap* of the heels drew closer even his breath drew quiet.

When the sound was so loud it was all he could hear, even above the roar of distant thunder, a woman appeared in profile at the left of the alley. She wore a thin, laced pattern black shirt that was almost see-through, enough so that you could clearly see her black bra. Her black leather pants were skin-tight and held up by a belt made up of large, shimmering silver rings. Her face was beautiful, and her lips were small and dark and puckered. Her hair fell short around her chin.

Sly's breath caught in his throat, and he pressed his back against the wall so that he would not be seen. He knew her, had seen her many times. She was one of the few white women who lived in his building, something he'd taken note of and had taken care not to say aloud. She was the women from apartment 21B, and he knew her well. He had watched her jog in the courtyard twice, and once he had been inside her one-room apartment to fix the faucet. He had left the job half done to have a reason to return but had never been called back. He suspected she'd hired an outside contractor.

He smiled to himself, cracked his knuckles, then gripped his wrench again.

He moved to turn swiftly around the corner and raise the wrench high -- and suddenly, there was a hand on him.

"What the hell?" he shouted. It was loud enough that the woman from 21B must have heard it, though she didn't pay the exclamation any attention as she continued into her building.

Sly turned, and to his horror, large, scarred hands seemed to appear out of the shadow that had been the wall. They grabbed at Sly's wrists, burning four thick lines into each of them.

"Aaah!" Sly screamed, as he was thrown into a heap on the wet ground. His arms fell into the puddles of water and hissed like the water pipe had, the wet retreating from the scorched heat of his forearms violently. "What is this? What's going on?"

A man moved forward, gaining light and depth and dimension with the addition of orange-hued light that seemed to come from nowhere and everywhere all at once.

Shiro stretched out his deformed and burned palms. They came from the shadows of the wall as though being fed through it, forearms protruding from the wall then joined by arms, and finally shoulders and face. A large, broad-shouldered figure emerged from where there had previously seemed to have been only nothingness. He gritted his teeth as he stared down at Sly. There was a searing hatred to that stare that Sly had seen before, though never in someone he had just met.

"Wh- wh- wh-" Sky stammered, pain leaching from his arms and exploding everywhere in his mind, making performing any task other than fight or flight anathema.

Shiro raised both his hands, which were black with burns. As the rainfall became more forceful, smoke and steam rose from him with the same hissing sound that had previously occurred upon contact with the metal pipe, until the entire alley was filled with steam.

Sly screamed loudly, scrambling to his feet and trying to run.

Shiro grabbed at Sly's exposed arm, his flesh burning at the man's hot, dry touch.

Sly screamed.

"You were about to harm that girl," Shiro stated matter-of-factly, giving Sly a small nod. "Now you will not."

"I didn't do nothing!" Sly protested, still cradling his wounds.

"You were about to. Should I have waited until you committed the act?" Shiro asked, his voice a harsh whisper. He reached out, taking Sly by the neck. His scaly fingers sizzled once again when they touched the soft skin. Sly brought both hands up and grabbed Shiro's arm to try and force it off of him.

Shiro raised one hand, opening the palm and spreading the fingers wide. The deep blacks of his eyes grew bright, small orange sparks dancing in them like the embers of a midnight wildfire.

He pressed his open palm against Sly's face. Sly's skin turned pink immediately, and Shiro held his stance despite Sly's screams and squirming. The flesh then began to peel back, revealing steaming muscle underneath. A sickening smell began to fill the air of the alley as Sly screamed even louder. Boils formed across his face as tears streamed down it.

Then, without warning, Sly stopped screaming.

A moment later, he stopped moving altogether.

Shiro let him fall to the floor, revealing the searing handprint on his face. Smoke came out of Sly's skin where Shiro's fingertips would have been, as bubbling blood dripped from his ears onto the gravel ground.

Shiro watched until the blood mingled with the rainwater all around him, then turned and walked from the alley, the soft hiss of boiling water following him wherever he went.

Xander closed the window of his apartment. He stood at it for a long moment, the fingers of each hand resting on the lip of the ledge. The window was dirty and its view led out to a solid brick wall across the way. He stood with his forehead resting against the glass, shifting focus from the grime on the glass to the contours of the brick.

He took a deep breath, then released it as five short huffs. He did this again, and on the fifth huff he turned quickly and stepped away from the window, into his apartment.

The air was thick with heat, stale and milky-tasting -- the result of atmosphere trapped for weeks on end and the hot California sun. It stank of baked ozone.

He stepped until he was in the centre of his kitchen, only a step away from the archway that would take him into the living room. His bedroom was off from that. Adjacent to the archway was the bathroom, and to his immediate left was the room off the kitchen that was tugging at the corner of his eyes.

There was a plastic bag under Xander's arm that was packed full of the papers Tim had printed. They bulged the edges of it, straining the edges of the fibers until they threatened to pop at the seams. He stood with the weight of it and the spare bedroom in his peripheral vision as the dusty air of his apartment filled his lungs with each breath, making his chest tighter, not looser.

He took a deep breath and huffed it out in portions again, then stepped over the divide between the rooms into the living room.

There was a large map of the city that covered most of the floor, bunching at some edges unevenly. There were Lego bricks strewn about on it, most knocked on their sides and broken apart from the tower they had been in.

There were teeth marks on some of the red pieces, the scrapes and gouges of scavengers.

He pulled up the map and bunched it into a large paper ball, sending the Lego bricks scattering every which way. He threw the ball into the kitchen without looking and started pulling stacks of paper out of his bag. He lingered over a space of open floor as if considering it on some unseen merit, then dropped the first stack of paper onto it. He stepped two feet away from it, then dropped the second stack.

When he was done, there were seven stacks of white paper with black text, arranged in semi circles that expanded out from the far wall. He bunched the plastic bag and tossed it the same way he had the map, ran his fingers over his mouth, then sat in the centre of the stacks.

The guest room was just barely visible around the corner of the archway. Its door was ajar, he realized for the first time. He swallowed, then pushed himself back with the arches of his feet until his back was against the wall, and the door out of sight.

He picked up the stack closest to him and started to read about an assault victim named Omar Frits.

CHAPTER SEVENTEEN

The courtroom was narrow, the seats on either side of the hall unable to sit more than four average-sized people. It was dark, the varnish on the walls and seats just a slightly too-dark shade of brown compared to the rest of the building. There were no windows or natural light or natural ventilation, just a bad air-exchanger and a rotating fan placed at each of the four corners of the rectangular room.

The room was small but crowded, everyone already in their seats when Xander entered. He stayed near the back, leaning against the wall between the door and the fan, letting it push the scents of the stale-aired room towards him every time it rotated in his direction.

He recognized many of the players that were seated in the galley, most of them from the files he'd read last night. All of the living assault victims were present, most surrounded by small clusters of two-to-five people that looked and acted like them, for support. Family and friends, people of the same economic status, coworkers. Each victim had a tiny solar system of people that surrounded them, circled them, insulated them.

There were others. Journalists he recognized by the equipment, though there were not many, and the equipment was slight. Memo pads, pencils, and iPhones that were open to record at a moment's notice.

The Reverend, Trask, was there. He sat alone, apart from the victims who had -- at least at some point -- been a part of his community and church.

There were guards, easily recognized by their uniforms. There was one outside the door and one standing against the wall to the opposite side of Xander. There was another stationed at the far side of the courtroom, standing in front of a second door that the accused entered and exited through. That one was portly, with the sort of sagging jowls and tits associated with a sedentary lifestyle.

The two counsels sat at two separate tables at the front of the room, their backs to everyone except the judge and the stenographer. The counsel on the right sat alone, a lanky man with slicked-back black hair and a poorly shaven jawline. The counsel on the left had a generous mop of red curls flopping onto the shoulder of her blue blazer. She sat next to Victor Murdock.

Murdock sat on the edge of his chair, his head just slightly turned so that he could see into the assembled crowd just by shifting his gaze, not turning his head.

There were others in the room -- two dozen or so -- that were not separated into camps based on their profession or affiliation with a victim... people who had no outward, obvious reason for being there. Xander tracked them, marking the place of each in the room in his mind's eye. He eliminated those that had characteristics mutually exclusive from those he was looking for -- male, broad, patchy hair -- and what remained were just over ten.

Which was far, far too many.

He frowned as the fan alongside him brought a fresh crop of scents to him: Alka-Seltzer, deodorant, and stale fabrics. Nothing out of the ordinary, nothing alarming. He tried, and failed, to appear relaxed as the judge banged his gavel and invited the lanky man speaking for the prosecution to begin.

Gordon Cross stood up, stepped away from the prosecutor's bench, and into the open space between it and Judge Mandis' position. From here he could feel the breeze of all four fans -- the two in the back having less effect on him -- and the way they each pushed the tail of his suit into different directions. He buttoned it once, just below his central plexus, straightened it, then placed both hands before him as he began to speak. Only Judge Mandis, who had seen this several times now, knew that it was a ritual Cross performed before every opening argument to steady himself.

"Fabian Mitchells was murdered. That, at least, is indisputable," Cross said, with all the gravitas and weight he could muster. "That's the only thing in this case that is. That is the *nature* of a murder investigation. We present you with the evidence as we understand it and the conclusion we've drawn from that understanding… and ideally, the people then choose whether that's enough or not." He pivoted his body to point at the Defense without turning away from Judge Mandis. "That's not what the Defense wants to happen here. The Defense is arguing that there isn't enough evidence -- that the best and brightest of the LAPD are wrong -- not enough evidence to even warrant the trial. The Defense is attempting to deny the State and her people the right to a fair trial: to see everything laid bare and make their judgment, together, as a community." He paused. "Fabian Mitchells was murdered. If we deny the court the opportunity to hear that, we kill him twice."

Cross stepped back around to his side of the prosecutor's table, casting a quick gaze across the gallery as he did so. That was the truest measure of how his message would land, he'd found... judges were less arbiters of truth than gauges of the crowd they sat before, in his experience.

The crowd looked angry.

The fans shifted some of the air currents in Xander's direction as he watched Cross return to his seat, bringing a fresh selection of scents to his nostrils. Cross's words had caused some members of the gallery anxiety, and others excitement, both of which resulted in the same: sweat and heat that turned a wide variety of scented deodorants to vapor. The air of the courtroom was suddenly thick with scents of lavender and pine and the chalky, dusty scent that was supposed to be unscented deodorants. And then, along with it, was the faint smell of carbon. That same weak smell that somehow excited the senses more than any other, the same stench that lingered in the air for hours after a match was struck.

Xander stood straighter and scanned the gallery again,

looking out at those eleven possible versions of the man he was here for. There were three with hoodies, one navy blue and two a gray that looked startlingly similar to charcoal black. They sat on opposite sides of the gallery and Xander struggled to keep them both in his field of vision at the same time.

The smell of it was overpowering, so much so that it started to come in waves. It would wane for a moment with the abatement of the fan, pause, then return. The somehow comforting smell of activated carbon and gunpowder, and the salty stench of burnt flesh and singed hair. It came in such steady patterns that his heart started to beat to it, the way it seemed to synch to the bass of a loud song. The steady thrum of it started to reverberate at the edges of his vision, pushing them in each time the scent tickled his nostrils until he had tunnel-vision set on the man in the ashen grey hoodie to the right of the gallery.

Xander stepped forward until his midsection touched the edge of the seats. He was as close as he could get to the man without stepping over attendees.

The smell of burnt matches became steady, as did the encroaching black around the corner of his eyes.

Megan stared at the five cue cards in front of her. Victor Murdock sat next to her, his breath growing harsher and more anxious the longer she took to answer. Each of the five cards had a single word on them, a visual representation of the argument they presented. They were: 'Opportunity', 'Discovery', 'Evidence', 'Motive', and 'RC'.

She held RC in her hand now, tapping it against her opposite palm.

"Ms. Greene?" Judge Mandis called, turning a bushy eyebrow up in her direction.

Making a decisive sucking sound between her teeth and top lip, she moved the card marked RC to the top of the file and stood up, both hands on the table. "The best and brightest of the LAPD. That's what you're focusing on here: the one piece of evidence and the summary judgment of the," she pretended to check her notes for effect, though she knew the name by heart, "LAPD 12 Homicide Department, that right?"

Cross did not move or nod. He kept his eyes on her and the root of his fountain pen nestled against the concave of his lip, waiting.

"So, let's talk about that evidence. That almighty stone upon which the court is building the structure of this trial," Megan said, turning back to the judge. She held her hands out in front of her, as though measuring the weight of the slab of concrete herself even now. "So, what they have is this stone, this big slab of concrete, that they took from Mr. Murdock's home. And they've looked at that slab and they've tested it and they've said that it's the right shape and right material to match the weapon used to hit Fabian Mitchells over the head and cause his death."

Despite himself, Cross nodded.

"Do you have motive?" She shrugged dramatically. "Don't need it! We have the murder weapon, in his home. Opportunity? Don't need it, he can't account for his every movement, and the murder weapon was in his home! See it's easy to say that good police work has been done, but I say -- I say -- lazy police work has been done."

At the back of the courtroom, Xander bristled at that statement.

"I say they found what they thought was the Holy Grail and then, then, they stopped looking. Just like they almost did with the UnSub prior to my client."

"Your Honor," Cross started.

"It's a preliminary hearing, counselor," Mandis drawled. He turned to Megan. "That said my time is finite. Arrive at your point soon, Miss Greene?"

"Yes," Megan said, clapping her hands. "Of course." She turned to her file again, again for effect, then turned to Cross. "So this evidence, that your whole case revolves around... you sure it's unique?"

Cross lowered his eyes, but otherwise did not respond.

"I've seen the discovery you sent over, the lab results and experts and that. But see, I've had it tested, and I say that it's just the same mix of limestone shale that you find anywhere in the city... anywhere in the country, actually." She paused. "But still, it was in his home. He's a rock collector, and that's *why* it was in his home, and I say there's nothing unique about it... but it's your evidence. It's what you based your whole case on. So let's take a look at it."

She pulled a sheet of paper from her file and slid it over on her desk. "So this was sent with the discovery. It's the Chain of Custody of the evidence." She paused, then turned to Cross and smiled. "You're familiar with Chain of Custody, yes?"

Cross nodded, despite himself.

"Great, so the first member of LAPD in the Chain

was the arresting officer, Thomas Horton. Yes? Okay, and he has an exceptional solve rate, and an even better appeal rate, which I'm sure you're going to point to at some point. But needless to say, he was fired -- rather, encouraged into early retirement -- less than twenty-four hours after the arrest was made." She raised her head to make eye contact with the judge. "I have expert testimony that will show that this termination came about due to shaken faith in Horton's ability."

Cross opened his mouth to speak.

"Then from him," Megan continued, loudly, before she could be interrupted, "the cement slab goes to the Trace Department at LAPD12. Now that's a fair-sized lab, but we know from the Chain of Custody who handled it, thankfully." She picked up the paper and held it up to Cross, even though he couldn't read it. "The initials you sent there, RC? You see that? There's only one person who has worked for the LAPD 12 lab in the last year with those initials... care to take a stab as to who that was?"

Cross shrugged, then looked to the judge as if to coax him to end this... but the judge's face was losing color, as though it were slowly dawning on him where this was going.

"I'll give you a hint: RC stands for Raymond Coup," Megan said finally, laying the paper down and looking in her file for another.

The color was now draining from Cross' cheeks, and there were several murmurs from the crowd.

"Raymond Coup, who a month after processing the evidence in this case went on to become the first serial killer in the state of California to have been an active member of law enforcement at the time of his apprehension."

The murmurs in the gallery became a roar, and Mandis started to bang his gavel for attention.

"So just so we're clear," Megan continued, "the evidence that you based this case around went from a discredited cop to a serial killer before forming the basis of your entire prosecution." She looked back at her cue cards. "No motive, no opportunity... no evidence. Nothing, Your Honor. We want the case against my client dropped because the State. Has. Nothing." She bit the last words, then sat.

She fixed her hair, took the first steady breath she had in minutes, then turned to her client.

Victor was smiling at her, with something akin to awe in his eyes.

"Your Honor," Cross started, rising to his feet, "the Prosecution requests time to... review the evidence in this case, and the amount to which Raymond Coup taints its use --"

"My client has the right to a speedy trial," Megan said, without turning away from Murdock. "He would like to exercise that right. Or he would like to be released."

Mandis moved his considerable lips back and forth. "We will reconvene tomorrow, 3pm," he said. He turned to Megan. "I trust that's speedy enough for your client?"

Megan nodded. "It will do." She turned and smiled at Cross, who was already going over his version of the Chain of Custody that Megan had had only a copy of.

The stench of ash and smoldering atmosphere was

everywhere now, to the point that Xander could notice several other patrons of the court reacting to it -- looking from one direction to the other in search of the source. He was straining, fighting the steady thrum that was coming from both his heart and the right side of his gut -- it was that twitch that darkened the corners of his vision, more and more making him unable to focus on anything except the man in the grey sweatshirt.

The Defense and Murdock stood. A moment later the Prosecutor did, and the judge moved toward the entrance to his private chambers.

The man in the hoodie stood and started toward the aisle. He was blocked by other attendees, but Xander could see the path he was heading on, and how it would cross with the Defense's just as they were making their way down the aisle.

"Hey," Xander said, firmly. A few people turned in his direction, neither of whom was the tall man in the ash gray hoodie. He was tall -- Xander could see that now -- just as he had been the last time they'd fought.

His hands in his pockets, the man made his way past the weeping couple he was standing next to, getting closer to the space between the aisles.

"Hey!" Xander repeated, lifting his leg and stepping into the row in front of him.

"Excuse me, sir?" One of the guards started, stepping toward Xander. He went ignored.

"Hey, hey!" Xander yelled, stepping over the next row of seats. Only two rows stood between he and that sooty sweat-stained hoodie. There was a woman in a blue flower-print dress between them, and a long row of attendants after her, shuffling their way toward the centre aisle.

"Sir!" the guard said, with more authority and less coaxing.

Xander stood, took in a deep breath that squared his chest, then yelled: "Shadow Flame!"

The man in the ash gray hoodie turned, revealing a deep African American complexion that was as far from what Xander had been expecting as possible.

"Fuck," Xander whispered, stopping his forward momentum short. He turned quickly and scanned the crowd, many of whom had turned toward him... one wearing a navy-blue hoodie on the opposite side of the gallery stared with a bright orange glower and gnashing, clenched teeth. "Fuck!" he yelled again, even as Shiro turned and started toward the nearest exit.

Xander stepped up onto a chair and jumped back to the previous row of seats, even as patrons of the court moved to avoid him, making the squeals and derisions that all crowds made when one of its member started acting out of turn. He pressed forward even as the guard -- who he could tell was closer than he should have let him get -- started to yell. He moved from seat to seat deftly, skipping over the line of the crowd as Shiro pushed his way past those in his way with the same force as he would have an inanimate obstacle.

The stench of burned flesh was everywhere now, inescapable.

His vision collapsing like an iris, Xander pushed off the last chair he touched with the ball of his foot, launching himself through the air and into Shiro. The crowd screamed and parted even as a guard's heavy hand found its way onto Xander's shoulder and hauled, hard.

"Off! Me!" Shiro bellowed, his voice roaring like an old wood-powered oven when his mouth opened.

Xander reached back a clenched fist and brought it down hard against Shiro's lip, hammering it and scorching the flesh of his knuckles at the same time. He pulled back the fist a second time, but his arm was bound, and when he turned two white-clad arms from the same man were holding him.

Shiro scrambled to his feet, turned, and the crowd was too busy watching Xander to notice that his eyes were glowing white hot. "You," he snarled, his voice thick with contempt.

Xander's eyes went wide. "Look--"

A wave of heat erupted from Shiro's general direction, boiling the air and frying the oxygen. It pushed Xander and the man who held him back, and for a moment, Xander's vision went completely black. There was a brief, weightless, floating sensation... followed by his skull connecting with the hard floor of the courtroom, then his shoulders, then the rest. The impact reverberated through him like shattered glass, and for the first time in what felt like forever, he felt bones break and re-knit themselves. The impact made the solid color he saw switch from black to pure, blinding white.

There were hands on him before his vision returned, and even before he knew what he was doing he was pushing them off.

When his vision returned, Megan Greene was looking down at him: the red curls he should have recognized while she was defending Murdock to the judge falling to either side of her face.

"Fuck," Xander cursed, forcing the guard's hand off of him.

Shiro was gone.

"Xander?" Megan asked. The tone of her voice was sure, just leaving enough room for doubt, their time apart having haggard his features and made him gaunt.

He pushed away from the guard and spun out of his grasp. He pointed at the guard when he started to speak, then to another man who was encroaching on his space. There was blood on his forehead, but the bleeding had already stopped. "Where'd he go?" Xander asked, avoiding Megan's gaze. But he didn't expect -- nor did he receive -- an answer. He knew Shiro was gone.

When he was close enough to the door, he lunged for it, pushing through into the hallway. He ran down the hall to exit the courthouse entirely, hearing the shouts and yells of people chasing behind him. There were journalists outside and they raised their cameras but didn't click them -- it wasn't him they were looking for -- and they ignored him until he ran to one side with the quick, restless abandon of someone being chased.

There was an alley next to the courthouse and he turned down it, ran its length, then stopped at the corner and turned back to see if he was being followed.

People ran by the mouth of the alley, the blue Los Angeles sky behind them framing the entire thing like a piece from The Marx Brothers, the bright light of the city making it sterile and clean even though it was anything but.

Very few looked down the alley, and most that did did not see him, and none that saw him ventured down toward him. He wiped the blood from his forehead as the ring around his vision finally recessed back to normal, smiled, then laughed.

He reached into his pocket, withdraw a cigarette from the pack he had listed from the Horton household, lit it, and took a deep drag.

"You think I don't know you that well?" came a voice from the other side of the wall he was resting against.

He paused, let the smoke curl from his lips, then turned and rounded the corner of the alley.

Megan Greene was standing at the mouth of the alley, leaning against the grime-slick wall with her arms folded.

He nodded, cursed, then took another puff of his cigarette.

CHAPTER EIGHTEEN

Between the entrance to McGreggor's and the building next to it was a small alley that, depending on the view from which one approached it, seemed to fade into the brick of either building and not be there at all. Down the steps of the alley, two floors below street level, was a bar that had been, appropriately, named The Brew. It was named this not only because of its fine choice in alcoholic beverages, but because trouble just seemed to brew there.

The Brew was well hidden and didn't show up on Google Maps or Yelp or Zagat. There was no signage on the street alerting unknowing passersby to its presence. Word of mouth was nonexistent, as it wasn't talked about much by the people that went there. Those who found it wanted it to stay hidden. In the '20s the location had been a speakeasy, if the owner was to be believed, and he enjoyed maintaining that position.

Xander held the beer stein he'd been drinking from in front of him, watching the drink within it move back and forth. Only a tenth of his drink remained, and yet somehow it still had a head on it, a trick of physics he did not quite understand. He watched it for a long moment, looking for the world like a drunk who had found secret meaning in the bottom of his glass, then tilted the glass back and let it slide down his throat as one continuous drain.

Megan watched him, her own glass nearly complete on the bar between them. Hers was darker, but both had come in the same sponsored stein and been delivered as one after they'd sat down. She smiled at him out of the corner of her mouth as she watched him, despite herself, and laughed.

"It's weird to see you do that," she said, her voice humming as she took a drink from her glass.

He finished his drink, let out a subdued 'ah' of satisfaction, then turned his head until he saw her over hunched shoulders. "It's weird to see you at all."

"Touché," she laughed and nodded, raising her glass to him before finishing it. "So, you left Coral Beach after--"

"Yeah," Xander bit, cutting her off. "Yeah, I did."

She smiled, even as a portly man with a bushy white mustache came up to them. He was wearing suspenders and a checkered shirt and a smile that pushed his cheeks high.

"Good day, sir," Megan said.

"Sir was my dad, I'm Henry." He extended and hand and she took it. He spoke in a folksy way that was anathema to Megan's preconceptions about Los Angeles, and she liked him immediately. He motioned to their glasses. "More of the same? Xander?"

Xander nodded.

She raised an eyebrow, realizing that they'd met before and laughing, then shook both her hands to stop the bartender. "Fuck that," she smiled. "Don't bring him what he had, can you get us both something... local. Get me a Dark Ale local brew. Something."

Xander started to shake his head.

Henry ignored him, smiling at Megan. "We got Tarte Noir. It's sour, but it's good."

"That, then." She grinned and patted both palms on the table as Henry walked away.

Xander stared at her, his eyebrows knit and dubious. A moment later the ales were delivered, their bodies thick and so black that none of the light from the bar penetrated them. Xander lifted it, spun it, then took a small sip -- followed by a longer one.

Megan watched him as if waiting for him to test a new poison. Once he took the second sip, she picked up her own class and brought it to her lips. She drank it back quickly, her throat bulging and subsiding with several swallows, and when she was done, she licked the foam mustache she'd made with a fluttering pink tongue.

"I know you're the Black Womb," she said finally. She stared at him while she said it, and after, watching for the subtle changes in his rough-hewn features that she'd seen twist and shift many, many times before. His right eye closed a little -- more than a wince but not quite a wink -- just as it had when he had been younger. She watched for the tells the way she'd learned to watch for tells from anyone and found very few.

He turned to see her out of the corner of his eyes,

paused, then turned away again and took a drink.

"I don't pretend to know exactly what that it, but I get the gist, and I know you're it." She paused and waited for him to ask her how she knew, but he didn't. "It was the testimony transcripts for Jaden Mal. The way he described the monster he'd seen... it was too close to the way Adam Genblade described the thing he said you transformed into. Black and inky with those big red eyes... 'Black Womb,' that was what Genblade called it."

Xander took another drink from his glass, held it in his mouth a long moment, then swallowed.

She paused, watched his face and the scant movements of it, then continued. "I didn't realize you'd left. I figured it out after you disappeared... it just kind of stayed with me and I had to look into it, and I found all these parts of *you*. Going after the gangs, taking on Phillips... all the way back to that first September, when everything started going to hell." She paused, trying to gauge if she should push the points of the deaths that happened that September further, and deciding not to. "That's what I thought of them as, parts of *you*. That's the weird thing about being a lawyer... you start to define yourself by the battles you pick. And I guess you start to define other people by that too."

She paused, but he didn't move.

"I called Cathy a little while after I figured it out."

Xander's eyebrows raised slightly and he moved, shifting in his seat until he was no longer letting her linger in the corner of his eye. He sat sideways on the barstool, almost facing her. He took another swallow of his ale but did not answer her.

"I didn't know you were gone, not then. She let me know... she didn't tell me anything. I'd already had it all figured out... but she was worried, I think. It didn't help the way I phrased it; I think she thought I knew where you were. She misses --"

"It's better you know," he said finally, cutting her off. He took another drink, all but downing the half-full stein, then leaned away from it to face her. "It'll make this next bit easier. That man, in the courtroom--"

"The one you attacked."

He nodded. "His name is Shiro Gilbert. Ess, Atch, Eye, Are, Oh and then Gilbert, like Gilbert and Sullivan."

She nodded, his emphasis making her make a mental note that transcended the light fog that the Tarte Noir was causing.

"He's powered. I don't know how he got his powers, but he has them."

"Like you?"

"Not like me. He makes this," he shook his hands in front of himself, vibrating them in the space between them. "*Heat.* He makes it like it's from nowhere, that's why he has those burns. The heat that comes out of him, it burns even him. Call the Feds and ask about him when you leave here... call Tim White, you still know Tim --"

She nodded quickly.

"... Call him. Ask him about Shiro Gilbert. I met him just after I started really laying down roots in this city... when I knew I was here for the long haul. I was making war against this mob boss name of Stephen Fields --"

Henry came over to check if the duo needed more to drink, heard that name, then pivoted and continued past as nonchalantly as he could. Megan noticed, however, and watched him continue on to the end of the bar.

"There was a mishap. I burned down one of his whore houses, when it was empty, to try and get under his skin... I was trying to hurt his business, make him mad, get him to fuck up. Anyway, Shiro had been killing prostitutes, and the local PD thought the two were connected and pinned me."

Megan raised an eyebrow. "I did a lot of work trying to find you, and that didn't come up."

He held out his hand, palm up, and splayed his fingers. The tips were scarred with white lines intermixed with smooth flesh akin to that on a scalp.

She narrowed her eyes, reached out, and took his large hand in both of her own. She ran her thumbs over the flesh of one of his finger pads, feeling the way they slipped, the ridges of her fingers finding no purchase on his own.

"It's the claws," he said. Even as he did, he let the one on his index finger poke out, just enough to draw blood, then recede. The blood stopped. "The skin heals when they pop but it doesn't heal quite right... it messed up my fingerprints. Made the arresting officer think I was some hardened criminal, so that was fun." He took a sip of his drink, turned to the bar, and watched his vision tunnel again. He cursed, rubbed his thumb and forefinger to either side of the bridge of his nose, then watched it return to normal.

"That was Thomas Horton?" Megan asked, finishing her drink as she watched him massage his face.

He nodded. "He was working the Fabian Mitchells case, that was when it all got tangled up together. I got the hint that the person who was killing the prostitutes was out of Horton's league, so I went after him, and I ended up helping out with the Mitchells case, too. Which got Shiro involved in the Mitchells case, and that is exactly when the fun stopped. Full stop, do not pass go." He took the last of his drink, held the empty glass high, and Henry nodded. He took a deep breath. "He fancies himself a vigilante, I think. I tried to trace the pattern of his kills, but it's hard. It's like --"

"Like trying to track you," she said curtly. Henry brought Xander a new drink and took his empty glass. "I'll have another as well. And a Burt Reynolds shot each, please." She took a fifty dollar bill out of her clutch and slid it over the bar to him. "Let me know when we've outspent that. With tip."

Henry nodded, taking the money gratefully and sticking it into the front of his apron.

Xander took a large mouthful, getting most of the beer's head. "The victims we found, they were all of them criminals... except his first two. But even the criminals, you've gotta get in his head to see it the way he sees it, and that is a scary fucking place to be."

"How so?"

He paused, his mouth warbling. "He kills criminals indiscriminately. He has no sense of... proportion? Yeah, proportion. He'll kill a sex worker the same as he'll kill a police impersonator the same as he'll kill a murderer. For him it's like, the ultimate equality. All crimes are created equal."

Megan bobbed her eyebrows and let out a breath of air. "That's... I mean, the sex workers I've seen I'd call them the victims more than the criminals."

He nodded. "My point, exactly. But it's worse. The day we met it was because he'd killed his neighbor, this douche bag who'd been coming home drunk and beating on his wife and son. You've seen the type, each one a normal domestic argument escalated by the inclusion of one crazy fuck."

She nodded.

"So Shiro, he hears this through these super thin walls every day, and this one day he's finally had enough. He goes next door and just... fries the guy. I mean there's nothing left but soot and bones at the end. I'm told it looked like Uncle Owen and Aunt Beru."

It took her a moment to place the reference, and when she did, she did not comment on it. "Sounds like the guy had something coming. Maybe not that... but something. I've seen a fair share of nasty bruise photos from my time in family court... I'd never condone it, but I get it."

Xander nodded, knowing the next part but letting Megan absorb that point-of-view while he sipped his drink. "Mmm-hmm. So, then he kills the wife and the son too."

She stood up straight. "I... pardon?"

He nodded solemnly. "That's what we're dealing with. That's the kind of brain he has... where his logic goes. He killed the abuser, sure... but the mother watched him abuse the son for years and didn't say anything, never called the cops... she had a duty to protect and inform and didn't, so she gets to burn, too."

"And the kid?"

Xander grinned and tried to hide it. "Took me a while to figure out that one. It's hard to get in his head... I'm still not sure I have it. It's a statistics thing. Something like seventy-five percent of abused teens grow up to be abusive themselves." He paused. "It was *preventative*."

Megan squinted, then held out three fingers and counted on them. "The criminal, the person who didn't report it, and the victim who might grow up to be a criminal... all tarred with the same brush?"

"Mm. This is what you're dealing with. This is the level of... fuck, that he is. Imagine someone with that mentality, someone who doesn't respect *life*, with powers. And now realize that he was there for the Fabian Mitchells case. I had to stop him from killing Leo Brooks in his cell, and now he thinks Victor Murdock is going to walk, too."

Megan nodded, got out her phone, and started to text someone. "That's... fuck. Yes, thank you."

Henry brought Megan her drink, along with a shot for each of them.

They moved to a booth when a booth became available. There were fresh glasses of Tarte Noir in front of each of them, and Megan had had to pass another bill to Henry, who had pushed it into his apron alongside the other.

"He was a good man," Xander said, speaking of Horton, which the conversation had circled back to. "I realized it the first time I met him. In an interrogation room, of all things. I'd only just been in LA and it got me by surprise, how effective this cop was. I mean... you remember the crap I got up to back home and managed to never get the blue after me."

She nodded, smiling.

"None of that here; Horton saw through that shit right away. He was a good cop in a good department."

Megan snorted. "Raymond Coup."

He gave her a side-on glare. "Not the same. Good argument, though, by the way. I forgot how much I liked watching you work."

She smiled at him, watching him from over the top of her beer stein. "Yeah?"

"Yeah, during the Genblade thing and the Mal thing... listening to you pack a better punch with words than I can with my fists, it's cool. You lead people along and there's this -- this tingle moment -- when you've reached your point, when you're really on your game. It's awe inspiring, honestly."

She smiled, and when she felt her cheeks grow hot, she took a drink again.

He paused, his face slowly drawing out, a thought dawning upon him. "He's dead. I guess you don't know that, but he is."

"Horton?"

"*Genblade*," Xander stressed.

She flopped both hands on the table dramatically, her mouth agape. "You're *kidding* me."

He smiled. "You can't tell anyone, but yeah. He's buried less than ten blocks from here, unmarked plot. Cremated, actually, but whatever."

She ran her fingers through her hair. "Fuck me. Adam Genblade is dead. There's just... there's so much of all this I didn't know."

His hand was resting flat against the table between them, veins bulging and knuckles protruding and white and raw. His flesh was taut over most of the hand and rough at the joints -- they were the hands of someone double his age, and without thinking of what she was doing, Megan reached out and plucked it between her thumb and forefinger. She guided his hand gently, turning it over until it was palm up again, then splaying out the fingers and examining the scar tissue on each. While each finger's scars were made of straight slices, neither could be said to be exactly like the other, and almost formed an odd new form of fingerprint in and of itself. She ran her fingers along those smooth, straight lines, some of which went all the way down to the second knuckle.

"So there are claws," she said, her eyes on the scars and not on him. "And Genblade, he was who he said he was."

"He was."

She swallowed, adjusted herself in her seat, and maneuvered her soft hand under his to cradle it, even as her opposite hand continued to examine it. "What else don't I know?"

He stiffened.

"I mean... about you. There's claws, and Genblade was honest about there being experiments... what else is there?"

He swallowed hard, paused, took a drink with his free hand, then swallowed again.

"It's okay."

"It's... hard. It's always with me but at the same time always separate. Jekyll and Hyde is the closest example. I have this... extra organ, The Womb."

"So not the same as --"

"No. And don't ask me where the name came from, I don't know. But it carries all this extra material, this black flesh that covers me -- that oily blackness from the court transcripts. But it needs a way out, it feeds into my blood and it forces its way out."

"Does it hurt?"

"Every time." He paused, then took another drink. "More than you can imagine. More than I can imagine... the brain, it has a way of blocking it out. Anyway. Back in the day it used to come out when I was too emotional, or when I went to sleep, or when I lost too much blood. And depending on how it came out would dictate who was in control -- me or it."

She sat up a little straighter.

"It was like sleepwalking -- it would act on my thoughts, the way thoughts work in dreams. It was a fucked-up time. After a while of locking myself up at night and such, things started to get better. Still happens when things get out of control... and you can always count on it to make shit worse in those situations... but I've got a handle on it at night now."

She smiled. "No more nighttime excursions?" she joked, but her voice had little humor, belying the attempt to let the air out of the situation.

"Not since I got to LA, I don't think. Not since... not since." He let that stand, treating that as though it were the end of the sentence.

She waited, then nodded. She had continued to run her fingers over and between his during the explanation. The ridges of her fingers had found purchase only twice, each time near where the prints met the first knuckle of the ring finger. The prints were so thoroughly obliterated that she couldn't have been able to say if he had arches or loops, spirals or whorls. His hands, much like the man himself, was nothing like the person she'd known back in Maine. Both were enigmas now, and yet both maintained the vague shape of the man he'd been. She could see that man if she squinted at this one, carried around like a shadow.

"Do you need another drink?" he asked, spying Henry approaching.

"I think I'm good," she said, nodding. She curled his fingers up into a loose fist and then gently pushed his hand back toward him, as if returning it to him.

CHAPTER NINTEEN

Shiro sat in a padded chair at the end of a long, empty room, reading a battered, aged paperback novel. There was a man on the cover who was lounging against a veranda, having a cigarette as he looked out over an expensive and expansive property. There was a lake and luscious green trees alongside a Victorian-style house with a pale blue roof. In truth, the artist had paid more attention to the architecture and scenery then the man who was nominally the focus of the piece... he looked drawn out and sad, his free arm cocked at his hip at an odd angle, giving him the general appearance of a sad mime impersonating a teapot.

It was *The Great Gatsby* by F. Scott Fitzgerald.

"I hate that book," Krystal said. She was across the room from him... across the entire apartment, really. It was a studio.

Shiro's eye flipped up, peering at her from over the edges of the page.

"Actually it's *Daisy*. I hate Daisy. I hate that line... that all a girl can hope to be is a beautiful fool... I mean really, who the fuck talks like that?" She was leaning against the bare wall of his apartment, one foot rested against it, in a position she often relaxed in and that reminded him of Greasers, or at least the way they were presented in film. He didn't think he'd ever seen an image of an actual Greaser.

The chair he was in was soft. He'd found it in the garbage room of the building, and aside from some slight wear it had been in good condition. The polyester fibers had begun to fuse on each arm, melted together and becoming smooth, ridged things that reflected even the scant bits of light available in the room.

The room was hot, the sort of humid, smoldering heat that was sticky and uncomfortable. The room stank so much of singed ozone that it had begun to take on an entirely new aroma, an aftertaste that was somehow akin to bile, although Krystal made no mention of it.

Shiro raised his book and narrowed his eyes in the dim light of the room, continuing to read.

In my younger and more vulnerable years my father gave me some advice that I've been turning over in my mind ever since. "Whenever you feel like criticizing any one," he told me, "just remember that all the people in this world haven't had the advantages that you've had."

Far in the distance, too far for it to have been coming from his paltry studio, Shiro could hear the sound of a baby crying. It was that sort of blistering, all-is-lost wail that a child had when hurt suddenly and unexpectedly, the way all pain was to an infant. Infants knew pain the way man knew the Universe: not at all.

As he continued to read, the screaming got louder.

Without seeing the child, he could picture it: his entire face red with effort, a thin mop of black hair atop him, his mouth open to its widest and seeming all the wider for a lack of teeth. Shiro knew the child was a he even though he couldn't see it... there was something about the intonation that made the knowledge just come to him, unbidden.

The scream was everywhere, suddenly, coming from all directions, until he couldn't even read the words on the page anymore: they sat like hieroglyphs, his brain too distracted and agitated to read them.

"Krystal, could you see what's --" he lay the book down in his lap and then jolted back into his chair. Krystal was standing with arms and legs spread in the middle of the room, engulfed in roaring, consuming fire. She was so overtaken by the orange and bright, bright yellow that it should have pushed her features back and made them unrecognizable, but he saw them nonetheless: she was scowling at him, her mouth agape and alight, steaming at him with a full-throated demon's bellow that even still could not be heard above the flame.

The infant that was screaming was next to her, engulfed in flame himself. It rose up and tickled the ceiling with the tips of its sparks, as though the screams of the child were in and of themselves accelerant. The child was crumbling, turning to ash even in front of him, slowly crumbling into gray dust that found its way out and onto a breeze. The child's eyes remained whole until the last possible moment, slanted and almond-shaped but blue all the same, until the sclera in them popped and they oozed out over the burnt remains of the cheek, like butter slithering its way over hot broccoli.

"You!" Krystal bellowed, thrusting a finger full armed toward Shiro. The word was almost lost in the roar of the fire, the whoosh of its churning timed with the 'ew' sound as if on cue. "You'll burn too!"

The child was gone now, a pile of ash where he'd been and several small teeth that were still perfect: they had never been chewed, hidden inside the babe's gums until they'd been torched and melted away. Now they were twenty tiny charms on a bed of gray dust, sticking out like misshapen white pearls.

Krystal stepped forward as though she were about to grab Shiro by the throat and shake him. He remained paralyzed in the chair, unable to look away from the burning inferno that was her eyes. "You... will... too!"

Shiro woke with a scream as he hit the floor in front of his chair, banging his knee and sending it bending back. He cursed and hissed as he smelled the familiar scent of burning paper, and when he looked, the battered paperback copy of The Great Gatsby was in flames. He grabbed it off of the floor and beat it against the wood until it was out -- but only the last of the pages remained.

So we beat on, boats against the current, borne back ceaselessly into the past.

He allowed the lingering embers to take the last pages of the book slowly, until there was nothing left but a pile of ashes resembling the one in his fast-fading dream; then he found his way to a struggled sleep there in the middle of the floor.

CHAPTER TWENTY

There were streets, in fact entire suburbs, on the west end of Los Angeles that people just knew to steer clear of. They didn't need to be told; there was something in the very architecture of them that called to something base in the people who approached: stay away, bad things happen here. Roofs rose at steep angles and walls remained in partial decay until what could have been normal was an obscene parody of it, sparking some long-dormant DNA to respond: *danger*.

Duncan had always felt for the people who had to live in those communities... because biology was a hard thing to fight, and that anxiety that outsiders felt coming in was felt by those who lived there too, he was sure. Even though it was their home, the tension inspired by those steep spires and crumbling edges would remain and be omnipresent. It was no wonder to him that so many who grew up there would end up hard. Tension was only his day job, and he was hard. He had heard someone say once that that hardest thing to do was convince a paranoid person that everyone wasn't out to get them when at least one person really was... and he imagined that what he saw now acted as that same sort of confirmation bias -- things are bad here, and they won't get better.

There was a body in front of him, a woman of about thirty-five. She was lying face-down in such a way that would have been painful had she been alive, her nose likely crunched against the pavement, but even from this angle Duncan could see split tissue and the redness within it on either side of her neck. There was very little blood on the street, the dents and impressions of the pavement undisturbed and enhanced into clear view by the streetlights above.

"I wish we could move her," Janet said, her voice tinged with empathy that she rarely let show when she was on the job.

Duncan was squat near the body, careful to leave at least a two-foot width around it from even the tip of his shoes. Janet was behind him, standing over him and alternating having her arms crossed and having them on her hips, as though she wasn't quite sure what to do with them. "Not until Travis gets here." He checked his phone to see if there was an update from the poor-sighted coroner. "Which should be soon."

"I know," she nodded, even though he couldn't see. "I do. It's just --"

"Yeah," Duncan frowned.

The woman was brunette and had the sort of pale skin that one had to work to maintain with sunblock and lotion in Los Angeles, that much he could see from here. The marks on her neck looked to have been the fatal blow and Duncan imagined they went all the way around, but until the coroner came, they were unable to move her to be sure. Still, there should have been blood on the street and there was none. There was a suspicious clump of it on the back of her head though, soaking into her hair and turning it an unnatural shade of red. There was a gash there that he could barely see and what may have been the beginnings of a bruise, but the body didn't continue raising bruises long after it was dead and so it was stuck in place like half-risen bread. She was wearing a light blue blouse and black pants that expanded out halfway down the calves, with what he could tell even from here was a large belt. She was barefoot at the moment. The shoulders of the blue shirt were speckled with blood, some of the only blood he could see on her from this angle. He imagined there had to be more in the front, from the nature of the wound.

"What you think, a professional?" Duncan asked.

Janet cocked an eyebrow at him. "What, you mean a prostitute?"

"No... no. Like a professional. Business-type. Office worker." He paused. "From the clothes. I'm asking, not telling. I have no clue about women's clothes."

Janet nodded largely, understanding. She turned to the victim, looked her from head to heel and then back again, then nodded. "Yeah, yeah that sounds about right."

Duncan turned around, looking along the street. They were on Bezos Place, a long col de sac that went in a straight line for a full block before ending in a wide oval, like a Florence Boiling Flask. They were roughly in the centre of the expanse, between the mouth and the belly of the cul-de-sac. The houses loomed all around but there were gaps enough between them that he could see to the next street and the houses on them -- nicer houses, not perfect, but nicer. It never ceased to amaze him how close the dregs and slums were to the habitable areas here. "I don't see a store," he said finally. He fished his phone out of his pocket again.

"What's that have to do with anything?"

"I'm here," Travis said, exiting his car. His tone was a perfect mix of exasperation and apology. "I'm sorry, there was construction on the Boulevard." He stepped up next to Janet and Duncan, motioned to them both, then moved to address the corpse. He placed a gloved hand carefully on the side of her head, then reached for his thermometer.

Duncan opened his phone to a Maps app and typed in the word 'convenience.' The hourglass icon spun as it communicated with its servers, the tiny burner of a cell-phone struggling with all its might to complete the request. Finally, four icons materialized on the street-map of his surroundings, a tiny blue dot in the centre indicating his relative position. It was off by a street and oscillated back and forth, trying to correct its error and expending battery doing so.

The closest location to him was Powell's Convenience. He held up the phone and showed it to Janet.

"Fuck," she cursed, turning to look at the body with new antipathy. "Nope, not going there. Nope."

"There's a blow to the head," he said, even as he stepped away from her and rose onto his tip-toes, as if that would help him see further than the next yard between the houses of Bezos Place. He stepped sideways along the street, trying to find a particular gap between the houses, stopping when he located it.

She followed him, still muttering objections.

"See that?" he said, pointing with his whole arm between two houses, one beige and the other unpainted. Residents of those homes that had been looking out their windows stopped and stepped away uncomfortably. Janet turned and looked where he was going. "That trail between the houses connects Reach Road, which empties out onto the street that has --"

"The Church," Janet sighed heavily. "The Holy Heavenly Church."

Duncan nodded, looked at the map on his phone, looked around at the street surrounding him, then back to the body and Janet. "There was a blow to the head."

"Hey!" Travis called back over his shoulder, before Janet could have a chance to respond. "She's seventy-nine. What's up?"

"Looks mid-thirties to me," Duncan said in a snarly tone.

"*Degrees*," Travis clarified, echoing Duncan's contempt. "She's seventy-nine *degrees*. She's been dead... at least twelve hours." He looked around the street. "What gives?"

Duncan stepped back toward the body and looked it over, this time looking around her instead of on her person. The ground was clear of dirt and her arms were splayed out to either side. Frowning, he walked around and stood straight in front of the victim, the toes of his shoes pointing down the length of her body.

Janet walked around with him. "What are you doing?"

"Calculating the path of least resistance," he said, lining his arm up with the corpse and following its line straight until it found its way to a two-storey building with three street-facing doors. Again, people looking through the windows at them from that building mysteriously chose to stop when Duncan gestured in their direction.

"Pardon?"

"I'm a lazy fuck. Most people are. When I assume other idiots are lazy fucks, I'm usually right." He started walking toward the multiple-dwelling home, carefully stepping past the body even as Travis began to turn her over. Janet followed him, and they both walked across the street until they were in the front lawn of the house -- the lights were now mysteriously out completely.

Duncan turned around, his eyes down to the ground and the fake grass that had been laid there.

"What are you looking for?" Janet asked, scrunching her nose at him.

"There," he said finally, pointing to a large patch of wet, weighed-down astro-turf. "Right there. That's where the body was." He motioned with his hands from the spot to the corpse, and despite her initial hesitation, Janet had to admit that she could see the rough shape of the corpse in the pattern of downed grass... and that the blades leading from that oblong to the edge of the lawn were all slanted in the direction of the body, as if something heavy had been recently pulled across them in that direction.

She cursed, then thumbed the clasp off her holster. "We both going in a door, or going in one?"

Duncan waved her off. "Don't bother." He motioned

to the area where he suspected the body had been, then all around it. "No blood here either. This isn't our kill site, this is the first dump site..." He raised his voice considerably, "*Guess* someone *in that building wanted to report a dead body but didn't want the pigs snooping around, so they dragged her out into the street.*" He paused. There was a shuffling behind one of the window blinds, but little other movement. He lowered his voice back to its typical low cadence. "Unless we find something else, leave them be. They're rats but they're good rats... they wanted the body found but they didn't want to be involved."

She glowered at him but re-buckled the clasp that held her gun in its holster.

Both of them walked back over to the body, which -- having been photographed and examined -- had been turned over onto its back. Even from across the street Duncan could see that his assumption had been correct: the gashes that he'd seen along the neck below each ear were actually one continuous cut that went all the way along her neck, opening it wide.

"Yeah, there's no way she was killed there," he affirmed, thrusting a thumb over his shoulder toward the multi-dwelling without turning to look at it. "There would have been blood *everywhere*. There wasn't any. That was a drop site." He motioned from there to the street. "This is just the second site."

As they got closer, her features came into view. Her lips were pale, small things in the centre of her face, but her eyelids were darkened an ashy purple color, fluttered upwards to sharp points. She had worn makeup to her job -- at an office, Duncan presumed -- but not lipstick. His face scrunched as he puzzled that, but when he looked at Janet, she didn't seem to take exception to it and so he tried not to either.

When they got closer, he saw the thin outline of her face, coming down to a triangular point, and that her eyes -- now glassy and fogged -- had been a pale shade of violet in life. There were piercings in her ears he hadn't been able to see from the back, not danglers but sharp pinpricks with single gems or charms in them that stayed in place for as long as they were worn.

When he got within two feet of her, Duncan stopped in his tracks. "Fuck me," he cursed.

Janet turned to him to ask what was wrong, but he was already on his way back to his car.

"What's his deal?" Travis asked her, under his breath.

She shrugged. "Pervasive developmental disorder, if I had to guess," she said in a tone that made Travis unsure if she were joking or not.

Duncan stood in the open door of his car and leafed through a banker's box full of files there, pushing past one page after another until finally coming to the file he wanted. He pulled it out -- a five-page HR file stapled together at the top left corner. He held it up as he turned back toward Janet, as though it were a grail he'd discovered and was displaying.

"Laura Bennett, age thirty-six. Single, cancer-survivor from early childhood," he recited, as he stepped back over to Travis, Janet, and the newly-dubbed corpse.

"How can you possibly know that?" Travis asked, an eyebrow raised.

Duncan handed the file to Janet. "I have her personnel file."

Janet took it, and saw that the picture in the top left-hand corner of the page was in fact the woman who was laid on the street before them -- the picture and the corpse even had corresponding makeup, no lipstick and a color-ful eyeliner, although the shade of eyeliner was different in the photo.

On the opposite side of the top of the page was the pressed logo for the Shane International HR Department.

"Fuck me," Janet said, huffing.

"Get in line," Duncan growled, even as he took the file back and started to read it.

CHAPTER TWENTY-ONE

Megan laughed as the door to her hotel finally jostled open. She tumbled forward, her shoulder losing the frame it had been pressed against. She caught herself, dropped the room keycard and watched it bounce across the floor, then snorted and righted herself again.

Xander put out a hand to stop the counter-weighted door from coming back and hitting her in the head.

She laughed again, made her way to the swivel-chair next to her writing desk, and started to pry off her shoes. When the first one came off, she stopped, reveling in the moment of freedom after hours of constriction. "You have no idea how good that feels," she said, moving the joint of her ankle from side to side, then wriggling her toes freely for the first time that day.

"I really don't," Xander agreed, bending down and unlacing his still-new sneakers. The soles still maintained a cushiony, cloud-like bounce to them, and the pushback of the aged fabric of the hotel-room carpet actually felt harsher on the arches of his feet.

She laughed again, then pushed back on her toes until the chair's wheels brought her back to the hotel mini fridge. When she was fully on the other side of it, she edged the door open with her toe, then let herself fall forward to look into it. She cackled, reached in, and pulled out a tiny bottle of gin and a can of off-brand cola. "Stocked!"

There was a glass tumbler upside down on a paper coaster on the writing desk. She picked it up, blew in it absently, then punched both drinks open and started to combine them.

Xander stepped forward cautiously, stepping in front of the hall that branched into the bathroom and into the suite proper. The doors to the sleeping area were open and the bed dominated it, large enough to fit three. He kept it in the side of his eye as he stepped in, slowly making his way to the couch that was its mirror image.

Megan watched this out of the side of her eye as she poured the second glass of alcohol. "Go ahead," she said finally, as if perplexed that she had to provide him with permission.

He sat on the couch and turned to her and smiled, though his head kept turning toward the fluffy, plushy monolith that took up the majority of the adjacent room. After a moment he let his shoulders work into the leather of the couch, the cushions beneath adjusting to his frame, and he let out a deep, impactful sigh.

She raised an eyebrow and then stepped over to him with his drink. When he took it, she didn't release it for a moment, and they stood like two parts of a connecting circuit. "Got a thing for couches?" she asked, finally letting it go.

He smirked, then took a drink. "I've got a thing for

cushions. Been sleeping on my floor since..." he paused. "I've been sleeping on my floor."

She nodded. "Spent a few nights there lately myself." She sat on the floor and started to take the pins out of her hair, laying them one by one on the coffee table in front of him. Each one made a small metal *tak* sound on the glass finish, lined up equally spaced apart like tally lines.

Her hair came down and he realized that he was watching her as her curls spilled unfettered down over her shoulders and clavicle. He turned away, first toward that huge bed with the cream-white sheets, then finally letting his eyes drift up to the pattern of the moldings above the doorway that divided the living-suite from the bedroom. He took a long drink from his glass, cutting its contents by at least two fingers.

When there were eight metal tally-marks on the glass, Megan pushed her nails through her hair all the way to her scalp, teasing it out and making a sound similar to the one she'd made when her shoes had come off -- the release of pressure that, until that moment, hadn't been apparent to anyone but the recipient of it. She smiled pleasantly, then leaned back against the couch, using the seat next to Xander as an arm rest and bringing her drink to her lips. She also took two fingers, watching his glass as she did so, as if unconsciously trying to keep up. "What keeps you on the floor?" she asked, letting her head loll onto her shoulder. "It's not the drink, I take it."

He regarded the glass, took a mouthful, then shook his head. "It's not, no."

She stared at him with those massive green eyes of hers, waiting for him to answer, as he tried his best to keep his gaze fixated on the doorframe.

When he turned to her he found her a mix of bright colors: all fiery red hair and green eyes and pale white flesh. Her hair spilled around her face despite her attempts to keep it clear, framing either side of the green.

"I don't like my apartment in general," he said, gesturing to the room as a whole. "I used to have people living with me. I was there alone first for months and I didn't notice it was empty, but then they were there and now they aren't and it's just..." he trailed off.

"A vacuum," she finished.

He nodded. "There's no air where they were, and they were everywhere there. It was a house and they made it a home and now it's just... a place again. There's no soul to it." He took another long drink. "I don't like it there without them."

"Was one of them a girl?" she asked, an eyebrow raised surreptitiously and a wry grin on pink lips.

"They were both women," he said, correcting both points. "But it wasn't like that."

She continued her knowing look at him, laughed a little in the back of her throat, then turned away and took another drink. "It was for me. There's no shame in it... I've had roommates and I've had romances, and in my experience, roommates don't imbue themselves onto a place like that. Romances, they do. They linger like ghosts and haunt a place after they leave it, ghosts of the past." She turned back to him. "Nothing like that?"

He pursed his lips. "Maybe the start of something like that. But if it was anything, it was only a start -- nothing I wouldn't feel silly talking about."

She winced with discomfort and finally shed her blazer, revealing the light blue button-down underneath. She stretched her arms up like someone pantomiming bird's wings, and it wasn't until he saw her move that he realized how little she'd moved in those directions before -- the level to which she constricted herself, and how those levels were peeling away.

"So, it's too silly to talk about... but serious enough that it keeps you out of your own home?" she said.

She was laughing a little at his expense, he realized, but didn't mind. He nodded, moving his head to one side to acknowledge the dichotomy of it.

Megan took another drink, the last of her glass. "Well, you don't have to stay there tonight."

Xander smirked, feeling the couch grow even more comfortable underneath him, as though it were responded to the stimuli of her voice. "Thanks... really. This is probably the most comfortable thing I've been on in weeks, but I can't --"

She started to stand with the aid of the couch, but instead of rising to her full height, she brought herself forward and connected her lips to his. Her lower lip moved slightly, but for the first moment they were both frozen like that, as the reality of the moment slowly took hold. She stood awkwardly, bent to meet his face with her own as he sat on the couch, her hands making their way to either side of his face and guiding it as her lips began to move, opening and finding their way to each part of his.

Her mouth was warm and wet, and all at once she smelled like fresh daffodils in a way he hadn't noticed until that moment. His hands moved as if by their own fruition, finding their way to the small of her back and gently pulling her in. She moved a knee to either side of him on the couch and guided his head to stay with her, her thumbs barely caressing the arch of his ears.

Her tongue -- a small pink thing like an attempt at blowing bubble-gum -- was in his mouth as she unbuttoned the clasps of her blouse, that small sound of release she made as it made its way off her shoulders becoming his guiding light as he slide his hands down the bare flesh of her back and cupped her firmly.

She broke off their kiss and kept his head in her hands, those same thumbs tracing the scant scars of his rough-hewn face. Her hair was everywhere around him until the room they were in disappeared, his world becoming a sea of red curls with her face in its centre, smiling at him with that same knowing smile she had a moment ago.

She nodded, and he lifted her. She pushed her lips forward into his with force even as he brought her through the open doors and into the suite's bedroom.

CHAPTER TWENTY-TWO

Shiro woke up on the floor, the burned ash copies of *The Great Gatsby* all around him.

"That's a fine mess you've made for yourself," Krystal said. She was leaning against the wall on the far side of the room, on the opposite side of a beam of light that was somehow making its way in past the blackout curtains. She was holding a cup of coffee by her side and it wafted up thick curls of steam around her, caressing her and clinging to her like smoke.

He winced and looked away from her, slowly making his way to his feet with the help of his chair.

Xander sat on the edge of the down bed, feeling the way it curved and contorted to the shape of his buttocks even here. He had one sock on and was rolling the other into a small circle when he heard Megan raise her head off her pillow for the first time since the sun had risen, propping it against her wrist and letting her hair tumble onto her bare pale shoulder, much in the way it had the night before.

"Good morning." She smiled as she watched the way the light from the window curved around the tense muscles of his back. "There's spare socks in the suitcase, if you want some."

He turned over his shoulder and nodded at her, even as he started to peel off the sock he'd already applied. "Morning," he said, his voice haggard and tired, then leaned over and kissed her again. The smell of daffodils surrounded him again as the kiss continued, until she finally lay a hand gently against his chest and, applying the barest amount of pressure, backed him away. He grinned at her, and she back at him, the two of them holding back the laugh at the end of a joke that only they were in on, and then he turned back away to her suitcase.

"Top pocket," she said, her head falling down and her red curls splashing out onto the solid white pillow. "How'd you sleep?"

He winced, even as he unzipped the pocket and pried it open. A pair of black socks stared back at him, rolled into a small plump sausage of fabric, and he took it out. It smelled like lavender; everything in her suitcase did. "Well, I think. I stayed up a while after you fell... I couldn't get the case off my mind." He turned and cocked his head toward the bed. "But that thing took me eventually."

She laughed, spreading her arms and legs as though making a snow-angel with the sheets. "It's the softest thing you've ever been on, right?" She hummed, then sat up, bringing the sheets with her around her unclothed form.

Despite all his best intentions, he found himself watching her. She got up and started to get dressed, and after a moment he shook his head clear of whatever spell he was under and found his jeans.

He turned to her again when she was buttoning her blouse, this one another shade of blue, though not quite the same as the one that was still on the living room floor. It was closer to purple, existing on the edge between the two... but it was still firm across the shoulders, constraining her. When the blazer was added, it would restrict her movement even more, and the sound she'd made when clasping the last button -- the sound that had made him turn back toward her as he pulled on his own shirt -- was somehow an inverse of the one she'd made the night before.

She had two selves too, he realized. And while the sounds she made while going from one to the other were much more subtle than his, they were still there.

Before his eyes, Megan transformed from the woman who had left a subtle pink mark in the soft flesh where his chin met his neck, back into the lawyer. She stood straighter with her shoulders broader.

She turned to him and watched him watching her, and then a wry grin grew on one side of her face, showing that the woman he'd known last night wasn't gone, only disguised.

"How long do you think the trial will go on for?" he asked, stepping out of the bedroom to find his shoes.

She paused, leaned out of the doorway to watch him, but straightened before he could turn to see. "If it goes to trial? Months. I'm trying not to let that happen though... This kind of thing, it's best to stomp it flat before a jury gets involved." She found a skirt in her case, judged it for a moment, then started to step into it. "All that stuff with the Nazi symbol and the rest... it's too much to sort out with a jury. Juries muddy waters too much as it is, and anything with hate-groups comes pre-muddied."

He stepped back around the corner just as her skirt was rising up her leg, the milky white of her calve exposed to him one last time before being hidden away.

She caught where his gaze had gone and smirked to him, but continued with what she'd been saying. "When you get political ideologies and that mixed in, jurors lie during selection. That's never fun, and you might as well throw the whole case away, because the jury will come out hung. They went in knowing what they thought was the answer, nothing you say will change it: they'll come out hung."

She turned to him; his brow was furrowed.

"Do you think he's guilty?" she asked, finally.

"I'm not sure," he admitted, moving his head from side to side. "I wasn't involved in that part of the case back when... I'm just biased towards Horton. I just... I don't know."

"If you don't know, he should walk," Megan said, extending a palm-up hand in his direction as though it were a scale. "That's the way our justice system works."

He nodded. "You?"

She paused, thought on it, then clicked her tongue against the back of her teeth. "I think he's innocent. I know I'm supposed to say that --"

"But it's me."

"Exactly. I do think so, though. I'm not one hundred percent sure... but sure enough. More than reasonable doubt sure, put it that way." She stepped across the room until she was in the living room with him. Now that they stood face to face, without her heels on, she was a good half-foot shorter than he was. He hadn't noticed the night before... everyone was the same height in bed.

She took him by the chin and pulled his face down to hers even as she raised herself up onto her toes to meet his lips with her own. His hands rose up around her, coming together atop either shoulder and holding them gently. She broke off the kiss, then followed it with a second, shorter one and smiled wide, showing her teeth. "No matter what happens, find your way back into this bed tonight," she said. It was firm and decisive, removing the last shreds of lingering doubt that came with any unplanned morning after.

He nodded, and she moved in to kiss him again.

CHAPTER TWENTY-THREE

The morgue at LAPD12 was cold, always. It was the only place Duncan had found to be consistently cold since he moved to Los Angeles, and he found it to be a disconcerting transition every time he descended the west stairwell of the building and entered it. Every floor, every step became more and more chilled until, just before the metal door that cut the morgue hallway off from the rest of the stairwell came into view, he started to see his own breath.

Los Angeles was a hot city, with the sort of dry oppressive heat that he had thought would drive him mad when he'd first arrived. It was relentless and overpowering: never giving up, even during brief bursts of rain. Even the rain was warm, sometimes even hot, and was always dry in an instant after its fall ceased. It played tricks on his mind and made him wonder if it had been there at all.

Every time he felt as though he was starting to get used to the burning sun of the city, Duncan was pulled back down into the LAPD12 morgue and felt again what true, damp cold comfort felt like: moisture in the air that

clung to the hair on your arm as you walked past it, clouds
of breath making their way into your eyes and then dis-
persing like a magician revealing their prestigious mas-
terpiece.

He was standing outside the door to the autopsy studio where Dr. Travis Moore did the bulk of his work.

Janet stepped up beside him, popping the gum in her
mouth. When it snapped, it released its scent into the atmosphere. It was overpowering, the mint so strong that it
was closer to disinfectant. "Why you out here?"

"Because it's an autopsy."

"No, I mean, why aren't you in there."

He paused. "Nothing."

She held up a stick of the gum. He eyed it for a second,
then turned back to the window without saying a word.

"It helps with nausea."

Duncan breathed deeply, in through his nose and then
out through his mouth with one palm resting against the
chilled steel of the door, then finally took a deep breath
and pushed himself in.

Travis looked up suddenly when the door opened, his
prosthetic eye still sagging downward toward the body of
Laura Bennett on the table in front of him.

She was naked but for a sheet that had been folded
down to just above her knees. Her eyes were open, staring past Travis up to the ceiling with milky pools and
swamp-water. The entire tableau sent an uncomfortable
shiver down Duncan's spine as he approached the table,
each new detail making the experience more and more
upsetting. Janet stepped up with her hands resting in the
big pockets of her bomber jacket, and managed to keep

her eyes trained on Travis even as she walked up.

Duncan had been to sixty-five autopsies during his tenure with the FBI, and he had learned to adjust to some things. It had taken a full five autopsies for him to be able to engage in the experience without taking breaks outside the room every ten minutes. It had been fifteen before he had been able to be present in the room while the actual dissection was taking place... he had conquered almost all of these phobias and unwanted responses, but there were still some that made him balk.

"You're late," Travis said, glaring at him through his one good eye.

"You can't start without me, so I wasn't late. You were just very early," Duncan snapped.

Travis's frown deepened and he worked his jaw from side to side. He turned and cocked his head toward Janet. "You're here, too?"

"He's here in case it's a federal case," Janet clarified, sticking a thumb toward Duncan. "I'm here if it's local." She paused. "Unless you want to do this twice."

Travis shook his head, then turned back to the body in front of him, his head finally lining back up with his glass eye so that they both faced the same direction again. He reached to the tray to his right and turned on the recorder that rested there. "Adult female, age thirty-six, weight one-hundred and twenty-five pound. Laura Bennett file number --"

"Can we skip the technical crap?" Duncan snapped suddenly.

Janet turned and snapped her head towards him, surprised by his outburst. His cheeks were white, she noticed.

Travis narrowed his eyes. "No."

"We need it for records," Janet whispered, through clenched teeth. "Chain of custody."

"Yeah, but it's digital now; can you add in that shit after the fact?"

"You think after Raymond Coup that's a good idea?"

Travis continued to stare at him, unmoving expect for the jitter of his fake eye attempting to right itself in its socket.

"Fine," Duncan said finally, and Travis continued. Despite himself, Duncan found the body taunting his peripheral vision. The pit in his stomach moved when an unwanted thought came to him, and he made himself promise that he would not vomit.

Janet glanced over at him several times as Travis continued with the needed formatting, noticing that his eyes kept dancing over the nudity in front of him and getting whiter and whiter.

He was brought back to the moment by Travis testing the motor on his handheld saw. The sharp buzz cutting through the drone of pedantic factifying of the past few moments made Duncan jump. Though both Travis and Janet noticed it, neither commented on it. Travis may have found this man detestable, but making someone feel shame for their discomfort in the morgue was not something he did under any circumstances.

"We're going to separate the scalp," he repeated, without giving any hint that it was repetition. "Ultrasound shows evidence that the cause of death was the blow to the head, but we need to be sure."

Duncan nodded, holding his breath as Travis turned on the saw again and lowered it to the thin line that existed less than an inch below where Laura's hairline ended. Her eyes remained open during the whole of it, not fluttering or fluctuating as the saw hiccupped on uneven stretches of calcium as Duncan's did. When it was over, the top of her skull and hair came off like a bowl, exposing itself face-up on the table behind her like some obscure phrenology prop.

Duncan urged but masked it with a cough. "What do you have?" he asked impatiently.

Janet shot him a look, leaving forward and seeing the marks alongside the inner ridge of her scalp. "Lots."

Using a half-moon shaped tool with a long handle, Travis removed Laura's brain from the base of her scalp and placed it gently in a bowl atop the tray next to him. With both hands he maneuvered it until the gangly, Cthulhu-like flesh at the bottom of the organ was facing upwards. He lowered a magnifier on a long pole and positioned it between he and it, squinting at the mass of tissue for what felt to Duncan to be an eternity.

"Right there," Travis said, pointing with his gloved pinky finger and barely caressing the flesh of the brain. There was an indent there that led into a small cavity, hollow and almost perfectly circular except for a few splayed edges. The flesh around it was distorted and creamy, not the pale pink mess of wires that described the remainder of it.

Janet leaned in and watched where Travis was pointing with a handkerchief over his mouth.

"What it is?" Duncan asked. He had actually drawn

closer, the ability to focus on the skull an excuse to take his mind off the rest of her.

Janet squinted. She saw what Travis was pointing to, but would not have recognized it as an anomaly without him marking it.

"There was a massive impact there. Massive," Travis stressed. "I'd be shocked she lived long enough to feel the damage on her neck."

While Duncan was leaning in, Travis pressed his pinky finger into the hole, his tongue finding its way out of his mouth with concentration as he worked. Duncan lurched back and feigned a cough again and thought his streak of avoiding sickness was about to come to an end before the turbulence in his gut subsided.

Travis pulled the finger out. "The damaged tissue is about the size of a golf ball; I'll have to run a check to be sure. I'll do a scope and send the results up to trace for you."

Duncan nodded, then paused. He was pale again.

Janet watched him, turned back to the body, then understood. "Hey," she said, in an authoritative, respectful tone.

Travis turned, one eyebrow raised in silent question.

She gestured to Laura's de-scalpified body. "Can we cover her up a little first?" She said it as though it were a request of solidarity, trying to hide her knowledge of the source of Duncan's discomfort.

Travis stared at her for a long moment, then nodded. He reached and pulled up the white sheet that covered her legs until it covered all but the area above her meager cleavage.

Satisfied, Duncan let out a long breath he hadn't been

aware he had been holding. He stepped up to Janet and motioned towards his mouth silently. She withdrew the previously offered stick of gum and he took it. Mint filled him when he put it into his mouth, but this time he didn't mind.

Travis moved to Laura's neck and motioned across it with his pinky finger, and Janet followed. "She bled out from here, no doubt. Even if the blow to the head did her in -- this seems like it was done to send a message. She bled a lot, but the slice was peri-mortem. No bruising around the ridges." He pushed the ruptured flesh back, revealing black masses of clotted blood.

Duncan's mouth went dry and he stared at the gloved pinky-finger making the motion again and again across the slice. His face somehow lost even more of its colour.

Janet turned to him, finally unable to hide her corner. "What is it?"

"Something... it's ah... familiar."

"Familiar how?"

He licked at his lips with a dry tongue, then shook his head. Colour returned to his cheeks, though with a sickly shade of green imbued. "I'll deal with it. I'll... check it, before I say anything. Keep going."

She stared at him.

Travis nodded. "These were hesitant cuts... see here, where there's one slice, then another connected to it and continuing? That kind of start-and-stop... you don't get that with experienced killers."

"We think this is the Shane Killer," Duncan drawled. "If eleven bodies isn't experienced, I don't know what is."

Travis shrugged. "I call it like I see it. There were some

foreign obstructions in the wound; I swabbed and sent it up to trace. We'll see if anything comes back." He motioned to the bumps in the sheet that were Laura's knees. "This is where we get some insight." He started to pull the sheet back down, saw some of the color drain from Duncan's cheeks, then pulled the sheet up from her feet instead.

Her shins, from knees to ankles, were a long series of gashes and scrapes and ripped flesh. Some were small and superficial, others the checkered pattern of road rash... some were deep, cleaving away the flesh clear to the bone. Like the slice across her neck, there was little bruising around them.

Duncan felt the stone in his gut move again and had to turn away.

"She was dragged quite a distance," Travis said, motioning to the wounds.

"You don't fucking say."

Janet tisked at him. "This is more than the yard to the street -- she was dragged to the yard and left there. That's why there was so little blood at the scene." Travis nodded at her. She turned to Duncan. "That's odd for the Shane Killer, right?"

Duncan squinted. "Very."

Travis continued to explain the pattern of the scrapes and how they implied repetitive, differing dragging attempts. Janet listened and nodded and took notes, but Duncan's mind was already turning to new possibilities, his head slowly turning up toward Laura's chalky white face and the bright red smear across her neck.

CHAPTER TWENTY-FOUR

There were more guards in the courtroom today, a result of Xander's escapade the day before. There was a guard at every entrance, as well as three at equal intervals up the space between the dual rows of seats. There were ten in total now, enough that they formed a mosaic of Los Angeles' equal rights hiring policies. Each of them turned and looked at Xander and Megan as they walked up the hall toward the front of the courtroom, as he got closer and closer to the front -- where the attention would be -- and with all eyes behind him, an anxiety built in the centre of his chest, pushing against his ribs.

"Are you sure this is okay?" he said, under his breath.

She smiled professionally but did not turn to look at him when she spoke. Her client was already at the head of the room, sitting as comfortably as he could while fastened to his chair. "Ninety percent of human recognition is context. Yesterday you walked into the back and skulked there alone... Today you're walking up to the front with me. They won't even give you a second glance."

As if on cue, one of the guards turned at their approach, regarding them both, then smiled and nodded politely and turned back away to continue scanning the crowd.

"I should bring you on stakeouts," Xander grumbled, continuing to watch the guard as they passed, looking for some hint of recognition in him and finding none.

"Magicians learned that trick all the way back in the eighteen hundreds -- there's no disguise quite like a beautiful woman."

He laughed despite himself, a real laugh that would have drawn attention to them in any other situation.

They were at the end of the hall now and about to enter into the mouth of the courtroom. Megan turned to him and they both smiled politely, even as they spoke through clenched teeth. "Did you see him?" she asked, glancing at the crowd through her peripheral vision, but keeping her face turned to Xander.

Victor Murdock turned to them in his chair. He was unable to turn all the way around until Megan arrived and the guards unlatched him, but he could turn enough to see her out of the side of his eye.

"I didn't," Xander admitted, turning fully away from Megan and looking over the crowd that was amassing. "But if he's here, he definitely sees me."

She frowned, then nodded. There was dust on his shoulder, and she reached up absently and brushed it off with one quick, deft motion.

Victor narrowed his eyes as he watched this, then turned back in his seat to face the judiciary.

"If something starts, try and take it outside?" She met his eye. "There's only so much mess a pre-trial can take."

He nodded, then turned and found his way to a seat a row back from the front.

The hour was filled with motions, although neither attorney moved from their seat much. There was a motion to suppress, a motion to suppress witnesses, a motion to alter charges. It became a debate, like watching verbal ping-pong, with one side landing a motion that would hurt the other, and then that side retaliating with a motion to inflict damage on the first -- each of them were chipping away at each other, until one would have nothing left to their case.

Shiro watched this from the middle-right row of the seating area, not far from where he'd sat the previous day. It was away from the churn of the fans, the swirls of air they created somehow avoiding him, as though he were in a vacuum. He felt weightless, observing the thrusts and parries of the trial from beyond it all.

"Do you think she'll get him off?" Krystal asked, leaning in close to his shoulder but making no effort to lower her voice.

He frowned. "I'm not sure," he whispered. He craned his head to Murdock, who was watching the back and forth between the lawyers with a kind of surreal, detached fascination, his gaze moving from side to side, always facing right, with each change in speaker.

Krystal watched, her gaze following Shiro's, as Megan began a motion regarding the evidence that had been processed by Raymond Coup. Just behind her in the seats was a man with dark hair, sitting far cloistered and taking up as little room as possible.

"Is that--"

"It is," Shiro answered, before she had a chance to finish her question. Xander turned his head slightly to see some of the crowd, and Shiro slinked back.

"We should *go*," Krystal warned.

Shiro sat with dry, pursed lips, watching the way the man's head tilted to eye the crowd. He was sitting closer to the Defense today than he had yesterday -- closer by far. By Shiro's estimation, he was as close as he could be without being in striking distance, a full arm's length away in all directions. As much as the man's vision was turning to keep a sly eye on the crowd... some part of it was always trained on the defense table, keeping it safely within his peripheral vision.

Shiro's brow furrowed into a stern glare.

"We should go," Krystal said again, touching his shoulder when she gave emphasis.

"Yes," Shiro agreed, rising quietly to his feet and apologizing his way through the row on onlookers. He made his way to the hall between seats, still lined with guards, and then excused himself as he made his way to the door at the back of the room. It opened with the barest pressure from his hand, and with one foot through it, he turned and looked back toward the front of the courtroom.

The proceedings were still happening -- Cross was offering a rebuttal to Megan's last point... but the man with the dark hair had turned fully around in his seat now, his fiery pale gaze locked on Shiro.

They remained like that for a long moment, frozen in a bubble of time even though time continued all around them, arguments and counterarguments, murmurs and calls for silence.

Xander stood, put his foot on the chair he'd been on, then hesitated.

Shiro smirked and made his way out of the courtroom, even as Xander was making his way to the end of his row.

The hall was as empty as it ever was by the time Xander made his way out of the courtroom and into it, his footfalls echoing off the walls and floors until each one was heard a dozen or more times.

"Sir?" said the guard by the door, taking a step towards him.

"Shut up," Xander snapped, pointing a stern finger back at him without looking in his direction. "Wait, no." He turned. "Did you see where the other guy went? The one that just came through this door?"

"Sir, is everything okay?"

"Rah," he growled with frustration, turning back out in the direction of the street, where the hot Los Angeles sun blazed down. He swallowed, checking every vacant doorway and inlet in the architecture as he put one foot in front of the other, the side of his foot first so as to make as slight a footfall as possible.

The hall was bare and white, and he could hear the murmur of voices behind each wall and through each and every door. They were all trials and hearings and suits, he realized, all going on at once: although the building was busy, the hallway was bare.

"I know you're still here," he said finally, his tone

firm and authoritative. "You wouldn't leave... any more than I would." He paused. There was no answer. Xander reached deep into his pants pocket, retrieved something, and continued forward. "That's the trick with us... right? You can't give up and neither can I. Unstoppable force meets immoveable object, and all that."

He paused and waited for a response, then turned to made sure Shiro had not ducked out of some alcove behind him. He licked his lips, cleared his throat, then walked slowly over to a waiting chair by the far wall of the room.

"What was it for you?" he asked into the void again, conversationally. "Nobody starts out fucked up -- not as fucked up as we are, anyway. For me it was a girl... and then another girl, if we're being honest. And then I lost someone young... what was it for you?" He paused. "Was it the wife and kid? Because I read about that... or was it something else that made you snap and do that?"

He stepped up onto the chair suddenly, raised his hand high until it was next to the sprinkler on the wall, then flicked his lighter.

"And does this still fuck you up?"

Water gushed out from the sprinklers in rapid succession, travelling from the one Xander had ignited to the next in both directions down the hall as the release signal reached each one. There were screams of shock and surprise as the signal reached the extinguishers in the courtrooms and their own sprinklers shot to life, raining down freezing cold water on everyone. The alarm sounded, and in the indent in the wall next to Xander, steam shot out and accompanied the anguished scream that came with it.

Shiro stepped from the steam that seemed to gush from him in rolling cascades, his skin pink with the heat he was expelling. He was glaring at Xander, his eyes bright and flickering with orange flame.

"Hello, beautiful," Xander smirked, hopping down from his chair with a self-satisfied smirk on his face.

Shiro screamed, pummeling forward and connecting with Xander's midsection, pushing them both back through a double set of doors that led to an empty courtroom just as the water gushing from the walls was making the inhabitants of each of the others empty out into the halls. There were screams and wails, the sort of sounds humans made when being doused with cold water.

Nobody noticed the scream Xander made when Shiro Gilbert wrapped his red-hot fingers around his neck and let the heat of his rage flow through them.

Megan ran to the side of the courtroom as a guard rushed to secure Murdock, shoving her papers into her briefcase as she went. "Fuck fuck fuck," she said, finally able to turn her back on the court to see that Xander was gone.

Hiding from the reach of the sprinklers, she put both those facts together. "*Fuck.*"

Xander brought both his knees up between he and Shiro and pushed back, hard, forcing distance between the two and he scrambled to his feet. His throat wasn't bleeding... that would have been a benefit. As it was, boil-ing-hot blood surged from the four charred finger-lengths that ran along his neck, finding its way up to his brain and out into the organs of his torso. It made everything twitch as it reached it, losing thermal as it went but passing it on to everything around it and making it react.

"Fucker," he cursed, keeping his eye on Shiro. Xander was between Shiro and the door and maneuvered himself to keep it that way as the taller man shifted.

His voice was harsh, with the cadence of vocal chords that looked like well-done steaks. "You do not speak of my wife," Shiro snapped, pointing a finger to the ground as if to mark territory. "You do not *ever* speak of my wife! You understand me?"

"Yeah, got it, wives are off limits," Xander said with forced levity. "If we're making demands, how about you -- you know -- stop killing people, and stuff. Just a thought."

Shiro paused, fuming. The sprinklers were settling down, but steam still rose from his hot flesh when the wa-ter touched them, and from his feet that stood in the pools of it that had yet to drain. "Murdock... that's what this is about? You were there when Horton found him, why are you defending him now?"

"Probably because that same day I was getting hot-and-bothered with you just like I am now while you were trying to kill the last motherfucker Horton had pegged for this crime," Xander said. "What exactly would be your position if I hadn't stopped you then, if you'd killed Le-onel... hm? Murdock would probably still be out there, and now you're trying to stop him from being released by due process. You see how you're a little confused?"

Shiro growled and pushed forward, connecting with Xander yet again, and both men fell back into the water that lined the floor of the courtroom.

Xander sprouted his claws with a burst of blood from his fingertips and brought them across Shiro's face.

Shiro screamed, the water around his knees bubbling with excitement, as he forced both hands onto Xander's face. Pain seared through him as Shiro's thumbs sank into his flesh beneath his eyes, the bones of his cheeks bending in under the force of the applied heat.

'Fuck!' he tried to scream, but failed to. His voice wouldn't work, nothing would work, and darkness was ebbing at the corners of his eyes again.

"There are only two things in this world that can make a difference, boy," Shiro hissed, bending close as his hands sank millimeter by millimeter further into Xander's flesh. "Shadows and flame. Blissfully, I am both."

Xander's cheek erupted in a geyser of black blood, squirting up as if bursting and striking Shiro in the face and mouth.

Shiro screamed and fell back spitting, that taste like cigarette ash and bile baking into the heat of the flesh of his mouth. When he turned back to Xander, his face was covered in it and it was spreading, gushing from the hole he'd put in the younger man's cheek and clinging as it went, making its way down and over his body. It covered his eyes, but as Shiro looked on in terror, new eyes formed out of the tar: red slits formed their way down from the centre of his face as though drawn on by a sick artist, then opening into large cat-like slits that glowed a bright red that put his own to shame.

"What in heaven?" Shiro gasped, stumbling backwards.

"Black Womb lives," Xander coughed, scrambling to his feet and chocking up more blood, both red and black. He ran his hand back over his hair, which was matted down by the black tar that was still coming out of him, defying gravity in its attempts to cover him wholly. "Guess we both have a few secrets, huh?"

Blackness continued to ebb its way into the corners of Xander's vision even more, tunneling it again and making it hard to see anything except Shiro, even with the extra peripheral vision that the red Womb-eyes allotted him.

The red of his eyes blinked, began to shine a greenish-blue tint of aquamarine, then faded back to red again as the pain tried to take him.

Shiro made his way to his feet and stepped around, giving Xander a wide berth as he found the door.

"Hold on," Xander said, the gruff of the Womb leaving his tone already.

Shiro kept his eyes trained on him, turning to walk backwards as he found his way out of the room and into the crowds of the hall.

"Fuck," Xander cursed, clasping his hand into a fist and resting it in the water. The darkness was still trying to ebb its way over his body, and he fought, concentrating and taking deep, haggard breaths in through his nose and back out through his mouth. He felt air escape through the hole Shiro had made in his cheek and get trapped between his flesh and the black tar-flesh of the Black Womb, causing pressure and discomfort.

"Fuck off," he said, low in his throat. "This isn't going to happen again. Not now, not here. So fuck right off."

The ascent of the dark flesh halted, wavering, and with it pain returned to his cheek anew. All at once the black blood coating Xander seemed to lose its consistency all at once, hanging from his skin like snot until finally slipping as one and splashing to the puddle of water that was slowly finding its way to the drains at the four corners of the courtroom, now the weight of milk.

He reached up to find the blood that had been left behind, the membrane that formed between his skin and the black flesh of the Womb, and felt that there was none there but the barest scraps of flesh. He coughed, spitting up the last of the black that had been making its way up his throat, then turned and let himself fall onto the floor, facing the stone-white ceiling of the room. He took seven long, strained breaths before they started to feel natural again, reached up to touch the tender skin of his cheek, then quickly thought better of it.

"My life is so fucked up," he said grimly, before forcing himself to his feet.

CHAPTER TWENTY-FIVE

Duncan shuffled awkwardly from foot to foot as the last of them came in from the meager kitchen into the living room. In his time in Los Angeles, the kitchens had been the most disappointing thing to him: the heat had been as advertised, the skin had been as advertised, and the smog had been as advertised... But every sitcom he'd ever seen based in California had had massive, expansive kitchens, and every one he'd actually stepped into had been small and cramped and shunted off into its own tiny wing of the house to vent the heat it produced. It disappointed him to no end to see people wedging themselves between tables and cabinets to get in and out of rooms that -- thanks to the absence of a fourth wall -- he'd been taught were going to be the size of his first apartment.

Janet was sitting with an old woman at the kitchen table who sobbing into the hem of her shirt. In that moment he remembered that he wasn't peering into just any kitchen, it was the kitchen Laura Bennett had had in life, and suddenly he felt a strange sort of guilt from ruminating on its smallness. A flash of her on the autopsy table, exposed and pale, flashed through his mind and he felt his stomach warble slightly and threaten to betray him again.

There were five of Laura's loved ones in her living room with him now, with one in a plaid shirt and a bushy scowl. He had pointed an accusing finger out at Duncan several times, while electing to stay inside with Laura's mother and Janet. They were all at least a decade younger than he, although looking from one to the other and trying to find a friendly, welcoming face to latch onto, it felt much more like a hundred-year age gap to him.

There were three on a flower-print couch in the far corner, not one of them older than twenty-five. One had purple hair and her hands were covered in rings, but none of them cost more than a dollar each. They were all those smooth stone rings that were sold as impulse-buys at corner-stores, and all of hers were black. Her lipstick was a shade of purple that Duncan was sure had matched her hair when she'd dyed it, although it had since faded to a slightly less-extreme tint. She was chewing gum and hadn't cried; the cleanness of her mascara betrayed that.

Next to her was a Puerto Rican woman wearing a green tank top and had large, frizzy hair. She cried profusely and was leaning forward with her elbows resting on her knees, letting drops fall straight from their ducts onto the shag carpet. The was a lanky boy in a lime tank top next to her doing the same, though he was sitting on the arm of the couch with his feet next to her.

On the smaller couch were two men, both of them closer to Laura (and Duncan's) age. One sat on the couch proper and took up almost the whole of it, the other leaned on its arm with one butt-cheek and stood with the rest of his weight. They were buff, their pecs peeking out of polo shirts that looked to barely contain them. The seated one had a beard and the other was clean-shaven to the point that Duncan couldn't even see the stubble.

"Thank you all for coming," Duncan said. He nodded with pursed lips and took a deep breath, then tapped the legal pad he had made his notes on that he held in front of him like a teenager trying to disguise an erection. He made eye contact with each of them and got only blank stares back at best and contempt at worst. "I know this must be hard for all of you, but Miss Bennett --" he motioned to the woman crying in the kitchen with his paper "-- she says that the five, six," he motioned again to the kitchen, this time to the man who'd elected to stay in it, "of you were Laura's closest friends. Now this is... this is hard, I know, but I need help here. I need to know about her, and I need to know the things I can't learn in this." He held up Laura's HR file from Shane and waved it.

The youngest of them, the boy in the lime-green tank top, snorted. "You can't learn anything from that, if it's anything like the ones where I work."

Duncan looked at the file, dropped it back onto the coffee table, then nodded to the boy. "Seth, right?"

Seth nodded.

"Where you working to, Seth?"

Seth smirked, wiped a tear with the back of his hand defiantly, then smirked again. "Government," he said.

"Oh? What branch?"

He laughed. "Naw, sorry. *Unemployment*, I meant. Inside joke, sorry. I used to work at a call centre though, doing political calls for republicans. Hated it. But those files," he pointed at the file, "those files are whack. They're just -- you're late once, and they put down that you're someone who comes in late so that when it's time to give out raises they can give you five cents instead of ten. I'm telling you, you can't get anything of what a person was like from those things."

Duncan nodded appreciatively. "And in essence, that's why you're here. I need context, I need clues." He paused. Nobody but Seth would meet his eye, and even he was mostly focused on the blurry inkjet picture of Laura that stood out from the top page of the file. "Look, I know this is fucked up. It is, well and truly. Usually I'd have you all in separately, bring you down to a local station or something... but honestly, none of you are suspects, so it just made more sense to do this like a talking session, because you might jog each other's memories. But I need something."

"Funny how a fed comes down for Laura and not for Fabian," said the man in the kitchen. He stood with anger and intent, hands semi-clenched, and walked over to stand in the doorway to join the rest of them.

"I'm not working the Fabian Mitchells case," Duncan apologized, then checked his notes. "Carlos."

Carlos rolled his eyes. "Of course not, Fabian was just some little -- Fabian was just nobody." He faltered. "Fuck Fabian, right?" He turned to the others. "Fuck 'em. But someone who works for the big company gets killed, they send down a fed, right? Shows what you care about, right? Same death, but one has your corporate masters yanking your chain." He cocked a head at Duncan, his unibrow clenched.

"Stop it," the Puerto Rican woman, Freah, snapped stressfully. "This isn't going to help."

Carlos let air pass through his lips, then let his arms fall to his sides. "Yeah... yeah damn right it won't."

"You could say I'm here from that angle," Janet said, doing her best interpretation of a calm voice. Her hand was on the old woman's hand, and when Carlos turned in the direction of her voice, he couldn't help but see them both and softened. "I knew the detective that worked that case. He's retired."

"Fucking bullshit case is what it is," Carlos huffed. "Fucking pigs don't know what goes on."

"Dead, actually," she clarified.

He stopped, set his jaw, and remained silent.

"Laura *does* link two cases," Duncan said, raising two hands to illustrate. "One of them was already a Federal case, that's why I'm here. That's why I'm *allowed* to be here." He looked at Carlos, then to the rest of them, with his eyebrows up in his best impression of pleading. "I'm not trying to hide that. I'm just trying to catch whoever did this to her... if that means my case gets solved at the same time, all the better. But I'm here for *her*," he stressed, then motioned to the Shane insignia on the file. "Not for *them*."

The large bearded man, Craig, shifted uncomfortably in his seat, drawing Duncan's gaze. Finally, with great reluctance, he spoke: "He's just angry. Our community has taken a lot of hits these last few months."

"*Craig*," said the man standing next to him, in an intonation that Duncan recognized as meaning 'shut up.'

Craig waved him off. "Stop it, El."

Carlos huffed and receded back into the kitchen slightly.

"What community?" Duncan asked, cocking his chin forward.

Craig frowned, motioned to the crowd of Laura's friends gathered in a broad gesture, then shrugged. "This community, I guess. Flexes in the shadow of the Heavenly Father."

Duncan's brow creased. "You're all part of that church?"

"Were, past tense," Raven, the girl with the purple hair, stressed.

"Speak for yourself," El huffed, and Carlos nodded appreciatively.

Raven rolled her eyes at them. "Self-haters I swear." She met Duncan's eye with something besides contempt for the first time. "Those of us with sense left when Leo did."

"Leo..." Duncan trailed, consulting his pad again. He turned the page from his notes on Shane and Laura to those he'd made on the death of Fabian Mitchells and Thomas Horton. "Is that... Leonel Brooks?"

"Raven," Carlos said, with stress, from the kitchen.

Raven nodded. "He left about two weeks after I did."

"Wait, he... wasn't a part of the church when he was arrested?" Duncan frowned, flipping back and forth between the pages. "Sorry, wasn't my case, my notes must be wrong."

"He wasn't, no. No, I got him to leave. It was all too... restrictive. Leo, he was a confused kid. Did you meet him?"

Duncan shook his head.

"Okay well, his parents were real pieces of work. White supremacist fucktards. I met them once, in passing, and they were just... they were sick. They spit on him and called him --" She paused. "They called him names when they saw us in the streets. If you have a list of people *not* to meet in your life, you put those people at the top post haste."

Duncan nodded, then made a mental note to do exactly the opposite.

"Anyway, after growing up with that... regular life was kink. Like, after growing up with fucking Neo-Nazis, just being a regular blissfully ignorant white alter-boy was revolutionary. He was the odd-man out even when he was trying to fit in: the rest of us started in the church and rebelled our way out of it --"

"Ahem," Carlos harrumphed angrily again.

"But Leo," Raven continued, "Leo got into the church as a part of his rebellion. He's part of the reason I stayed as long as I did -- I had to get him out."

Duncan nodded, wrote a star next to his scribble of Leonel's name, then cleared his throat. "So, Laura was a part of this little... this Church Brigade... and she worked for Shane. There's some question as to whether Fabian was a part of the parish when he was killed --"

"He was," Carlos snapped, stepping back into the room. His eyes were wet. "He was." Janet stepped up to check on him, and he nodded.

Duncan saluted him without malice or sarcasm. "Okay, so Fabian was, Leonel wasn't, Murdock was... was Laura? Was she still -- you know -- with it?"

Raven frowned out of one corner of her mouth, even as Freah started to tear up even more.

"I'm sorry," Duncan sighed, trying to meet Freah's eye and being avoided. "I don't... I don't get what I'm missing here."

Raven looked out the window, clicked the piercing of her tongue against the roof of her mouth, then turned back to him. "Laura was still in the church when she died, yeah. She could have these blinders on, where she couldn't see how restrictive it was. She could make excuses for things in a way we..." She minded a glance from Carlos, "In a way that *I* couldn't."

"Give me an example."

She sighed.

"My parents joined the church right around the time I turned ten," Seth said, his hands clasped in front of him. He would not turn to address Duncan. "They'd gone to a few different Non-Doms."

Duncan raised an eyebrow.

"Non-Denominational Churches," Carlos clarified.

"Yeah, they'd gone to a few," Seth continued. "They'd used to be Catholic, but there was a huge sex scandal at the time... not the first time, but one of the flare ups, and the church was just kind of... hiding it. I was in Catholic school. It was rough. I was never attacked... but the aftermath of it was rough. We all split up, went to different schools, different churches. A lot of people said goodbye to religion altogether, some just left the Catholic church."

"That was your parents," Duncan said, pointing his pen at the boy.

He nodded. "Like I said, they tried a few different

churches, then they see Reverend Trask... he was younger then, but he liked to go on TV then, too. That was where they saw him, I think, yelling on TV about the perverts that the Catholics had let in and how horrible what they'd done was... which was true. It echoed what they were thinking, and I think that's what drew them in." He wiped a tear from his cheek with the back of his hand again, then used the sleeve of the same hand and dragged it across his nose. "I think... I think Laura maybe bought into that harder. I'm not --" he paused, glancing toward the kitchen, where Laura's mother still sat sobbing. He lowered his voice. "I'm not sure why. I could guess, but it'd be a guess."

Janet stiffened, narrowing her eyes at Seth in deep thought.

Duncan nodded solemnly. He flipped back through his files. "The rest then... the assault victims that came before Fabian was murdered... they were all the same. You guys," he motioned to them. "You knew them all?"

They nodded.

"Bob Odin, David Chipman, Daryn Pine..."

They nodded. Seth's lip trembled at the mention of Daryn Pine. Janet watched this.

"Some of them had left the church," Raven volunteered. "They weren't all... I mean, we knew them. We knew Daryn, we knew Omar... we knew Kinney." She smiled out of the corner of her mouth, then it faded. "Kinney and Daryn hadn't left the church, not yet anyway. They were thinking on it, I think. Campbell and David and Bob, they'd all left the church."

Duncan winced, looking back at his notes: some who

had left the church, some who hadn't. Some who were a part of this clique, some that weren't. And then there was Thomas Horton... and Laura Bennett, who was clean as a whistle and worked for Shane Industries and the only things in her HR jacket were reports she'd made about unwanted advances from a co-worker. There had been not a single complaint against her, not one, not even from the co-worker. Duncan rolled his tongue, reading, as the six of Laura's friends waited for him.

"This is an attack on our community," Carlos said again, his voice hot with barely concealed rage.

"Yeah," Duncan nodded honestly, his eyebrows bobbing with his head. "Yeah, that appears to be the case."

They stared at him blankly for a moment, before Freah broke down into fresh tears.

Victor sat in his new cell, the light from the afternoon warm on his back. It was tanning the back of his neck a bright red, but he found he didn't care. The warmth of it was enough.

Reverend Trask reached out, put a gentle hand on Victor's, and squeezed reassuringly.

Duncan slammed the door to his car, paused, then let out a long, frustrated sound. He leaned back in his seat and ran his hands through his hair. He took the yellow legal pad he'd been making his notes on and threw it in the back, atop a growing pile.

Janet got into the car next to him. "That was hard."

"If I never have to do another sympathy call for the rest of my life, it'll be too soon," he cursed.

She turned back to the house, squinting at it. "Did you see the way some of them choked up at some names, and not others?"

He started his engine and cranked the air conditioner to fight the mid-afternoon heat. When music started to play over the radio, he jabbed at the dial and turned it off. He closed his eyes and leaned his seat back as far as it could go, then rubbed his eyelids for several minutes until the growing tension behind them started to waylay.

"Did you?"

"I did not."

"It was telling. It was... it was something."

"Different people mean different things to different people." He paused. "You talk to me about my uncle dying, I will not give a fuck. You talk to me about his wife dying, I'll barely be able to breathe through the grief."

She narrowed her eyes. "Either of those people exist?"

"Not really." He sighed, opened his eyes, then looked back at the stack of paper in the middle of his back seat. His notes had landed atop a green folder, upon which the name 'Fabian Mitchells' had been scribbled in Thomas Horton's hand.

Janet looked at it, remembering those thin F's that were not upper-case F's the way they were supposed to be in cursive, but just lower-case F's enlarged to the height of one. The way the loops of the L's intersected one another, creating a lopsided Venn-diagram. For some reason those specific quirks made her breath catch in her throat, and she did her best to turn and hide it from Duncan.

Duncan slid it out and started thumbing through the pages, passing by crime scene photos which were eerily like those taken of Horton's own murder scene, finally stopping on a full-page glossy photo of a hardcover book that had been found inside Leonel Brooks' apartment. It was an aged copy of *Mein Kampf*, the autobiography of Adolf Hitler. There was a yellow sticky note attached to the photo, upon which was scrawled the simple notation: 'something.'

He turned the page and found several illustrative photos from the inside of the text, where were large sections crossed out with a red marker, its ink so wet that it had bled into the page at the hesitation lines and made much of the text unreadable.

The last image was of the first chapter, from which a single, small sentence had been circled, not struck: *His goal was achieved; but no one in the village could remember the little boy of former days, and to him the village had grown strange.*

"What the fuck is going on with these people?" he asked aloud, both to her and to the open air.

She paused, pursed her lips, then turned back to the house and reiterated Horton's only analysis: "Something."

He frowned. "I think it's time I got some outside help with this."

"Where we going?"

He shook his head. "Not this part. Sorry. This part... it's beyond your pay grade."

She turned to him to object, then saw something in

him she did not expect. It was not condescension or pos-turing or boorishness: it was shame. She stopped herself mid-snap and turned forward towards the road, as if that was what she had meant to do from the start.

Duncan squinted down at the glossy photo and the text left unstruck, then pulled his seat back up and put his car into gear. He pulled into traffic, deep in thought.

CHAPTER TWENTY-SIX

Judge Mandis sat behind a large oak desk in his chambers. There were two identical seats in front of him, the sort of tall, pleather, mauve monstrosities that every law office seemed to have somewhere, even if they were mothballed into some back corner away from public view. Their backs went up far too high, peaking with headrests that were too vertical to be used.

Megan sat in the chair to Mandis' right, Cross to his left.

"Apologies for the recess," Mandis said, stifling a stiff cough. He had ordered them back after the fire team had concluded that there was no cause for alarm, but there was still significant flooding in his preferred courtroom, so he had elected not to involve the public.

Megan shifted uncomfortably in her chair, trying to make the motion not noticeable. Her skirt was still damp and was sticking to the fake leather of the chair.

Mandis stroked the sides of his mouth with his thumb and forefinger. He had removed his robe -- it too had gotten drenched when the sprinklers had come on -- and was wearing a suit. He cleared his throat a second time as he examined the pages of motions in front of him, then turned to Cross: "Have you got anything else?"

Cross opened his mouth to respond, hesitated, then closed it again. "I do not, your honor. Nothing but the solve rate of one of the best detectives in LAPD history."

Mandis nodded.

"There was another murder in the Fabian Mitchells style," Megan said, making a note in her agenda and then putting it down on her lap. "Just so you know. They found it yesterday, but they suspect it was from the night before. She was found with a blow to the back of her --"

"That will be enough, Miss Greene," Mandis said dry-ly, interrupting her.

"Your Honor, with all due respect I have the right to represent --"

"It will not be necessary as I am granting your mo-tion for dismissal." He turned and made eye contact with her as he spoke. He lingered, made sure his words were understood, then turned to Cross. "Thomas Horton was a good many things, a good detective among them. I knew him -- well. There were parts of this job he was the best in the world at... bringing a case to a trial win was not one of them. He followed a case until he was sure of the outcome, and he considered the rest a loss for the District Attorney." He paused and motioned to Cross. "A loss for you. I don't see it that way, but I can't let the legacy of a good officer stand in the way of a man's right to personal justice. The case is being dropped, without prejudice."

Megan smiled.

Cross stood, buttoned his blazer, then collected his

briefcase. "Thank you, your Honor," he said, nodding to Mandis. He turned and extended a hand to Megan. "Well fought."

"As well," she smiled, taking his hand and standing herself.

"Your client is free, with the apologies of the court," Mandis said, then tapped the gavel he kept on the corner of his desk.

Shiro sat in the hall outside The Market, his back to one wall and the flats of his feet pressed against the opposite wall. Even in the late afternoon, crowds bustled around him, but none ventured down the small enclave he was stretched across. The hall he was blocking led to an all-use bathroom and a seldom-utilized janitor's closet. Several who had stepped towards it had seen Shiro sitting there, reconsidered, then turned away.

"You scare them," Krystal said, squatting down until she was at eyelevel with him. She was on the hall side of him, blocked from the rest of The Market by the poor blockade his body made. She was staring past him, looking up and out of the gap in the wall he was protecting and staring at the masses as they moved from one shop to another. Most were blissfully unaware that he was there... but every so often one would get too close, see the pink flesh and swelling that surrounded his eyes and that coated his hands... and they would falter.

"They should be scared," he said, staring straight into the wall in front of him. "It is a myth that fear makes men weak. Fear, in the end, is all a man has. Every man, when stripped down to his barest -- still has his fear. It is the last companion we walk our final mile with."

"Are you scared?" she asked, craning her head to see around the corner but seeing nothing. "Of him?"

Shiro reached up and touched the scratch on his cheek that the Womb had made. It had been cauterized and was already crusted over, taking on the same dried appearance of the rest of his flesh. "No."

In the background, the dulcet tones of the *LaMire at Night* audio began to play over the speakers of The Market.

LaMire at Night was an evening call-in program that aired on stations local to Los Angeles six evenings a week. As in the morning, Kendra LaMire was a blonde woman that still perpetually wore blue pantsuits. The set was made up of blue and yellow hues, accomplished by pulling a blue sheet of vinyl down over the painted-on orange of the morning show. Though one aired in the evening and the other in the morning, they filmed back to back, with *At Night* being the live variant.

"Thanks, Tom," Kendra said, beaming with her too-perfect smile. It was too straight and too white, lending itself to an uncanny-valley-like affect. She said 'Thanks, Tom' even though she hadn't heard from the man in question, the twenty-second delay between air and program meaning she had to fabricate her interaction with her lead-in program, *Tom Talk*. "Following up on a story from earlier in the week, Los Angeles native Victor Murdock has been released from his stay with the Los Angeles penal system, with their apologies. The revelation comes after a heartfelt defense from Maine's own superstar lawyer Megan Greene, who argued a significant lack of evidence to proceed with trial. Greene says that justice was done when escorting her client into a town car after the verdict, but what do you think? We'll be taking your calls, now."

Kendra paused as an ad played, taking her eye off the camera for a moment as someone hurried over to fluff her hair. They scurried back off-camera as quickly as they'd come, and she turned back to camera 2's teleprompter.

"We're talking about the release of Victor Murdock in the death of Fabian Mitchells and we have community member Carlos Bone on the line, a community organizer from the very region Mitchells was killed in. Tell me, Carlos, did you know the victim?"

There was a deep, rustling sound on the line not unlike heavy breathing as the mic picked up a deep exhale from Carlos' nostrils.

"You are on the air, Mr. Bone," Kendra smiled, laying one hand atop the other on the arm of her chair.

"I knew Fabian, yes. He was a good... he was good. Everyone loved him, everyone." Although the words were sorrowful, there was a twinge of barely concealed rage masking them that made Kendra shift uncomfortably. "Everyone... everyone loved him."

"Well, if you can judge a man by his friends, then that's --"

"Everyone loved Laura Bennett, too," Carlos interrupted, his voice breaking from rage and cracking like a teenager whose voice was changing. "And Leonel Brooks. Nobody's allowed to talk about Leonel Brooks but we loved him, too. And Jack Kinney, and Omar Frits... these attacks are a systematic attack on my community. If they're not killing us, then they're attacking us and driving us away or they're arresting us. This is a *pattern* of systematic abuse and... and... and *horror*."

Kendra nodded along with her perfectly practiced smile, transforming it into an equally practiced look of sympathy when he was done. "Yes, we had Father Trask on, and he spoke at length about his parish being under atta--"

"Not him," Carlos interjected again. "Not... not that. This is all fucked up." The curse was censored by the twenty-second delay. "If it wasn't Murdock that's fine, but it was *someone*. Either that LAPD just let a killer go or they've been focusing on the wrong man for months and letting a killer walk free. I'm not happy with either answer. It speaks to the priorities of our police force that my community can be attacked and nothing be done about it: we are invisible people, those of us in the shadows of the Church. The Church... the Church has done us no favors."

There was a sound in the background that was not unlike a woman crying, and before he could continue, the connection was broken.

"Thank you for your call, Carlos Bone. We wish your community safety and a speedy recovery. Our next caller is a professor at Harvard Law who would like to speak on the matter. Dr. Spiegel, you're on."

CHAPTER TWENTY-SEVEN

Megan sat on the edge of her bed with her palms planted squarely on the comforter to either side of her. Her phone was next to her, its ringer turned up as loudly as it could go, yet no sound had come from it since the end of the trial. There were no calls of congratulations, no remarks from friends or family... and no word. She was still in the blazer and skirt she'd put on that morning no more than a foot away from where she now sat. The television was on and casting her in an artificial blue glow that was like moonlight but moved like water as characters moved across the screen, but the volume was muted. She had poured herself two fingers of scotch but had yet to take any of it.

There was a knock at the door, faint yet sharp, three in a row. She got up after the first knock and headed for the door, unlatched the deadbolt, and swung it open without checking the peephole to see who it was.

Xander leaned against her hotel's doorframe, his hair matted and wet even though it was dry outside. His flesh was gaunt and chalky, and when he moved to make eye contact with her, she saw that there was a deep, craterous wound beneath his right eye. "Can I come in?" he said hoarsely.

"Oh my God!" she said, stepping aside and letting him in quickly. She looked out into the hallway briefly before she closed the door. When she turned around, he was already slumping onto her couch. She moved quickly toward him, then stopped short when she was a foot away, afraid to touch him. "Is it... I mean, I don't want to hurt you."

"It's fine," he said, motioning to the damaged area of his face with a four-fingered wave. He accidentally struck the concave cheek and winced back from his own hand, making a liar of himself.

Her eyebrows curved up empathetically, and she leaned forward to gently pull his hand away so that she could see. She frowned, then touched the healthy flesh lower on his cheek and pulled it back, stretching it to reveal that beneath the mass of redness the still-healing hole connected the area just under his right ocular orbit to his mouth via a complex, connective burn.

"Jesus," she breathed. The power escaped her legs and she sat next to him, unable to look away from the wound.

"It looks worse than it is," he said unconvincingly.

"It would have to." She got up and walked into the bathroom. A moment later she emerged with a pack of cotton squares, tape, and a bottle of hydrogen peroxide. She straddled him with a knee on either side of him just as she had the previous night, soaked one of the squares with peroxide, then slowly began to clean away the blood and baked flesh around the wound.

He winced. His phone chimed and he reached for it. Megan raised her leg to let him get his phone, then gently rested it back where it had been. He checked the screen. "It's a message from Duncan," he said. He paused. "A Fed that's been working with Tim and I. He wants me to meet him there tomorrow morning." He checked the side of his phone, then frowned. "The ringer is melted into the ON position."

She tisked. "Too bad."

He shrugged. "It's a burner."

She nodded, then laid a gentle hand on either side of his head and leaned it back against the backrest of the couch, his wound pointing up. She continued to clean, using her nail through the shield of the cotton to remove the last of a large charred mess, revealing pink and yellow flesh underneath. "It is healing," she said, absently. "It looks bad... could this have killed you?"

His eyes turned toward her, maintained contact for a long moment, then turned away.

She sighed, then went back to her work.

"I'm sorry about the sprinklers," he said after several moments, as she brushed some of his discarded flesh from the chest of his shirt. "Hope it didn't cause the case trouble."

"It soaked me to the bone," she said with a smirk, which he returned. "But I won the case, so I can't complain too much." She ran her nails through his hair, dislodging debris and sending it to the floor.

He sat up straighter, turning toward her. "The case is over?"

She nodded.

"Are you... leaving?" he asked, tentatively.

She smirked at him, her hair falling over her shoulder just as it had the night before. She shook her head. "No time soon, I don't think. It depends on the work... but no, I don't think I'm going anywhere anytime soon."

His hands lingered on her hips near the ends of her blouse, the strands tickling the edges of them. With a nod from her, he rose them up, bringing the shirt with them until it was over her head and onto the floor, her hair spilling over the petite, milky mounds of her breasts.

She took his face in her hands gently and guided his mouth to her own.

There was a phone booth in the back alley behind The Market, one of the last on the block. Shiro stood at it with a phonebook page he'd ripped out of the Yellow Pages in front of him, going through the page H for Hotels one after another. There had been eight pages of Hotels for the area, he had taken the one with the most mid-to-high end names on it.

"Hello," he said when someone picked up, trying to disguise his accent and failing. He glanced at the sheet again, it was the fourth number down. "Yes, I'm looking to be connected with Megan Greene's room, if you please."

CHAPTER TWENTY-EIGHT

"This shouldn't take long," Xander said. He raised a hand to hail a taxi as he and Megan stepped out from under the hotel's awning. The LA morning sun was hot on their faces.

"What are you doing after?" Megan asked, shielding her eyes from the bright as it came off the top of the cab.

He eyed the cabbie. "Getting some Thai food, checking my emails, securing my --" He got in the car and the driver closed the window between them and started to drive. "Figuring out the Horton case," he said, not even bothering to finish his facade sentence.

She nodded and smiled, even as she took out her phone and started to scroll through her email. "Thai food sounds good," she said, absently.

His eyebrows raised. She turned and gave him a wry smile.

"Yeah?" he asked.

"Yes," she smiled, then leaned over and kissed him.

Across from the awning in the car park, Shiro stood between two smoking drivers in the shadow of a large van. He watched Xander and Megan's cab pull away, then raised a hand and hailed his own.

Reverend Trask sat in a pew midway up the left side of the Church of the Holy Heavenly Father, his arms crossed before him. There were scrapes along his knuckles and a slice working its way up his sleeve. He was smiling to himself as he fiddled with it, the pinky of his opposite hand worming through the gap and coming out the other side.

The fake candles at the front of the church were all flickering this morning. He had lit all of them. The only wicks that remained darkened were the real candles in the first row.

"It's good to have you back," Trask smiled, speaking loud enough that his voice echoed off the walls. He turned around and rested one arm on the back of the pew.

Victor Murdock stood just inside the entrance of the church, quietly closing the door behind him.

Trask's smile broadened, and he moved to stand.

"I hope I'm not interrupting you," Victor said. He stepped up the hall between the pews, one hand holding its opposite arm sheepishly.

Trask spread his arms wide as he reached the hall and met him. "Not at all," he said. He motioned for Victor to walk with him deeper into the church. "Come with me, please. I have something for you."

Victor smiled and followed.

"Stop here," Shiro said, tapping on the glass that separated himself from his driver. They were four houses back from the home Xander and Megan's cab had stopped in front of. He watched Xander get out and start to circle around before Megan got out. They spoke, briefly, as Megan paid the driver, then they both started toward the house.

"You want I should keep going?" the driver asked.

"No," Shiro said, never taking his eyes off the two of them. He reached into his pocket, pulled out several bills, and slid them into the window without looking at them.

He got out of the car and the sun immediately started to burn his flesh. He winced, then stepped into the shade alongside the house he'd stopped next to, crossing over into the alley behind it and counting along until he was at the back of the house he'd seen Xander and Megan enter into. It had a large, secluded balcony. Frowning, he made his way around until he could see inside.

There was a man standing with brown hair, taking off his coat and laying it over the feet of another man, who was in bed despite the room not being a bedroom. The standing man had a gun holster strapped to him over both his shoulders, in the style that looked like suspenders.

Megan slowly came into view from over the block of the bed.

"Tim," Megan said, her smile broad and wide, showing off the whole of her top row of teeth and some of her gum as well. She walked to him with confidence, stopped next to his bed, then leaned over and hugged him.

"Megan?" he said, surprised.

She kissed him on the forehead, leaned back, then used

her thumb to wipe the mark of her lipstick from him.

Duncan turned to Xander as he took off his sneakers. He lowered his eyes, worked his mouth back and forth, then crossed his arms. He tisked, then stepped away over to the couch near the printer, cocking his head for Xander to follow.

Xander raised an eyebrow, finished removing his shoes, then stepped over.

"What are you doing here?" Tim smiled, straining his eyes to keep her in his field of view.

She obliged him by stepping to the left. "Xander was helping me with the case." She paused, resting a hand on his arm that was perpetually propped up onto his mouse. "I'm sorry about... this. I should have come when I heard."

"It's fine," Tim said. "I understand, really. There's no card for this. It's hard to process... even when you're living it, believe me."

"You wanted to talk?" Xander said, stepping over next to Duncan.

Duncan took him by the arm and pulled him over to the couch. There was a folder there that he scooped up, started to open, then pressed forward into Xander's chest instead.

"What's this?"

Megan caught the motion of the shoved folder out of the corner of her eye and watched it for a moment as she listened to Tim.

"Laura Bennett," Duncan said. He poked at the file's centre -- and Xander's chest beyond it -- with two fingers, aggressively. "Did you tell anyone else about my plan to leak shit?"

Xander furrowed his brow. "What are you talking about?"

Duncan frowned, grabbed back the folder, then flipped it open to a shot of Laura's body that showed the disjointed cuts across her neck, stretching from just under one ear to just under the other. "You see this?"

Xander squinted. "That's new."

"Yeah, yeah no shit that's new," Duncan said, stabbing at the picture with his fingertip again. "That's *mine*."

Xander shot him a confused look.

"I told you -- I told you *days ago* -- that I was thinking about leaking to the press that some of the Shane victims had their throats slit, to see if we could shake out the killer. Get him active again so that I can nail his ass. Now this," he sliced his finger along the track of the slice across Laura's neck. He turned and pointed those same fingers and pressed them into Xander's pectoral muscle.

"Hey," Megan barked, loud enough for all the men to hear.

Duncan turned to her. Xander moved between glaring at Duncan and looking at the file, balanced precariously on the back of the couch.

"What's happening?" Tim asked, his brow furrowed.

Duncan scooped up the folder and stomped over to Tim's bedside. He wedged it open to the page he'd shown Xander against Tim's monitor, like a book, shaking the monitor from its aligned position as he did. He pointed at the cut, bringing his finger from one edge to the other.

"Jesus," Megan said, bringing a hand to her mouth.

"Not even close," Duncan snapped. He was chewing

the inside of his mouth again. "That's Laura Bennett. We found her not three blocks from Powell's Convenience, and she belongs to that same damn hippie-dippie church as the rest of the people in your case."

She stared at it openly, the color draining from her cheeks. "Um..." she stammered, then righted herself. "That's not... that wasn't the MO of my case. Of whoever the killer was in my case."

"Yeah, no shit, then we find out she works for Shane too, which messes this whole thing up. But the thing is, the throat-slitting doesn't fit Shane either... but it does fit a false leak I was planning on planting *about* the Shane case." He threw a hand towards Xander. "Which I told to this fucker."

Xander stepped into view of the monitors, and the file. His brow was still clenched tight as he tried to make sense of it.

In his pocket on the bed, Duncan's phone let out a single vibration.

Megan turned to Xander. "He was with me last night and the night before."

Tim raised his eyebrows and looked toward the both of them.

"This was before that," Duncan cursed, placing both hands on his hips and pacing. "Fuck," he said, then pointed at Xander again. "You saying you don't know anything about this? You didn't tell anybody about this?"

Xander shook his head.

"Fuck me, fuck. That means there's like, three people that know about this thing, and they're all in with the LAPD. This is going to get messy and fucking sin, I don't have to tell you."

Xander nodded.

Duncan's phone vibrated again.

Tim's computer made a chime. He ignored it, pulling up files and arranging the windows around the file Duncan had propped up which he was unable to move from obstruction. One was the Shane file on Laura Bennett, the other the Fabian Mitchells file. "Xander," he said, cautiously.

Duncan ran his hands through his hair, pushing much of it asunder. "Do you have any idea the shit this will cause after Raymond Coup? You know." He motioned to Megan. She nodded apprehensively. "This precinct, I swear it seems squeaky, but it is just... it's fucked, it's all kind of fucked."

"Xander," Tim said again, his voice sterner. His computer pinged again.

Xander turned to him, pushing between Megan and the monitor.

Duncan's coat vibrated again. He cursed and picked it up, rustling through the pockets to find his phone.

"You seeing this?" Tim said, his voice more hushed. He pulled the windows around so that they were unimpeded by the file. "Fits the MO of Mitchells and Horton..." He motioned his mouse curser around a blow to the back of the head mentioned in the autopsy report. "Fits the Shane profile as far as we know, and fits Duncan's imaginary profile." He left his mouse pointer on the slice that ran across Laura's neck.

Xander squinted. "That's impossible." He frowned. "Statistically, I mean."

Tim met his eye.

"A city as big as LA, to have two murders cross over like that, and it happen to be the two we're working is... that's..."

"Incalculable," Megan breathed.

"Yes," Xander nodded. "That."

"So it stands to reason, then," Tim continued through gritted teeth. "That the link is something that connects the two cases. One of Homicide12... or one of us."

Duncan found his phone, turned on the screen, then turned to them. "Wait, what are you saying?"

"Duncan, I need a minute with Xander," Tim said. He turned his gaze to Megan.

"You can say whatever in front of her," Xander said. "What do you mean by--"

"Have you been *out* lately?" Tim asked, putting extreme stress on the syllables.

Xander paused, standing straighter. "What? No, I... no. You know that. We --"

"Guys," Duncan said in a loud voice, as he scrolled through his messages. "Someone found footage and leaked it to Channel Two."

Tim frowned. "Footage of what?"

Duncan held up his phone screen to them. "Laura Bennett's murder."

Tim's cheeks flushed as he turned his attention back to his screen and opened his inbox, just as it pinged again. There were three messages in his email, each one a frantic plea to look at the footage the email linked to. He glanced to Xander, then to Megan, and pressed play.

The audio was scratchy and nasally, with the sort of

whines and interruptions that usually came over dollar-store two-way radios. The shot was from security footage and was a wide view of a hallway. There were cars parked along one side of the screen, and along the other was a solid wall of concrete. The Shane logo was stenciled along the far edge of the wall.

Duncan came around the side of the bed opposite Xander and Megan to watch.

For a long moment there was nothing in the frame, the only evidence that the video hadn't paused to scrub the continuing progress bar at the end. It was already a quarter of the way through the clip. Whatever was going to happen was going to happen quickly.

Suddenly there was a snap of the frame and the time-stamp in the lower right moved five seconds forward. A woman appeared on the screen in the doorway at the far right of the frame, walking forward towards the camera. Her shoes clicked along the pavement as she made her way along the row of cars, closer and closer to the camera.

"That's her," Duncan said when she got close enough that he could be sure. He glanced at the file folder photo of her, still propped up against the adjacent screen as if to be sure, then looked back. "That is her."

"Oh no," Megan said.

There was nothing else in the frame and she was half-way to the camera, the video halfway through completion. Suddenly, a part of the shadow between cars reached out and found her, striking her in the back of the head.

Megan hissed when she saw the way Laura hit that hard concrete.

The shadow raised, dark and black and looming. It was fully black, as if the dark noise at the edges of the video had come to life and was haunting their feed. It stood above her, watching Laura as she moved.

She was still moving, half of her just out of frame as she writhed, trying to find the leverage to get back up. Her knee kept slipping, blood already making its way past her hairline and into her face and disorienting her.

The shadow creature bent like a cat, its sharp hands grabbing Laura and forcing her around, its feet on either side of her, pinning her. There was a scream when she was spun around to face it. It was so sharp and sudden after the quiet of most of the video that it cut through the air of Tim's apartment like a blade.

"Tim," Xander said, his eyes widening.

The shadow creature grabbed her and shook her, slamming the back of her head against the pavement again and again until she stopped making sounds and stopped moving.

It brought its hand up to her slender neck and pulled, each of its four fingers making a separate slice that combined to form one long cut that ran from ear to ear.

"Tim..." Xander said again, his voice hoarse.

Blood spilled out as her head leaned back, growing in a steady pool that leaked back into the frame, making its way toward the drain that the floors all sloped towards.

The creature tilted back its head to reveal two large, cat-like red eyes. It opened its mouth and revealed it to be full of massive serrated teeth.

Megan's hand went to her mouth, her eyes wide.

The creature grabbed Laura by either side of her shirt,

thrust back its head, and bellowed: "Black Womb lives."

Tim turned his attention from the video feed to Xander, who had lost all the color in his face.

The video played again, its last few seconds looped into slow motion. Once again, the creature pushed back its head, opened its mighty jaws, and screamed "Black Womb lives," so loudly that the sound distorted when coming in over Tim's speakers.

CHAPTER TWENTY-NINE

The sound of glass shattered filled the room and suddenly everything was hot. A wave of heat hit Xander with such force that it sent him back against the wall where it pinned him, wedged in the corner between the wall and the floor.

"Jesus!" Duncan screamed, fumbling for his gun even as he turned. Glass showered him, and Megan threw herself forward over Tim to shield him. Shards bounced off and were caught in her curls as she clutched his face into her breast to protect it.

"It's always you!" Shiro bellowed from the balcony. His voice had the roar and cadence of a fire furnace revving to life. Both his hands were outstretched and glowed white hot, the flesh on them peeling back painfully but he did not stop. He stepped into Tim's house and closer to Xander.

Xander looked up and gritted his teeth but made no effort to move. He clenched his fists, barred himself against the coming dark that was working its way through his vision, and felt it pound through him. The nearly healed hole in his cheek bubbled and cracked back, blood bubbling up and charring upon contact with the superheated air.

In his right side, the Womb sputtered to startled life and forced its way into him... then reached junction after junction that was boiling off and cauterizing itself shut and was forced to stop.

"I can superheat your skull," Shiro said, stepping forward. "I can finally end your hell."

Something inside Xander's ear whined and then made a distinct popping sound, and all of a sudden he went from smelling nothing but charred flesh to smelling everything at once. Strawberries, hay, pavement, and fresh plastic. His boiling brain fired neurons randomly from one place to the next, and before he knew it, he was seeing and hearing things as well.

Megan turned away from Tim and saw Xander's eye go cloudy. Her hair was singeing, curling back away from the heat at the tips. "Stop it," she said hoarsely, her throat as dry as the air in the room. She turned to Duncan. "Stop him!"

Duncan pulled his gun, aimed it level with Shiro's head, then bellowed "Freeze!" loud enough to be heard above the roaring flame sound that seemed to come from nowhere.

Shiro turned, his teeth barred, and aimed one glowing hand at Duncan. The gun glowed bright orange almost immediately, and Duncan dropped it to the floor. It went off, the gunpowder in the casing superheating.

"Fuck!" Duncan yelled, as both he and Megan stepped to be out of its path. It went off again, then a third time.

Shiro stepped forward, now past Tim's bed, both glowing hot hands aimed back at Xander.

Xander tongue swelled and the random bursts from his frying, stroking brain started to take the form of not only sensations but entire memories.

"Run!" Mike yelled, as he forced Cathy ahead of him. The creature landed on all fours on the sidewalk. His glossy eyes studied their movements, how they ran. The way Mike still veered left after his injury months ago. The way Cathy's right leg still limped a little at its base. They'd both been... damaged. It moved quickly, like a jaguar, leaping to the sidewalk and then onto two legs to pursue them.

"Keep... going..." Mike encouraged Cathy, holding his side. They were almost to her house. But they'd both danced this dance before. He wasn't about to make the same mistakes twice. He cut through an old alley, hoping to run across the backyards of the complexes until reaching her back door. They could see the house now.

"Mike..." Cathy pleaded, grasping at the stitch in her side. "It hurts."

There was an audible pop from inside his own skull. He bent down, braced himself, then turned up to face Shiro once more. "Do it," he mouthed, all the moisture gone from his throat. "Bloody do it."

Sara's lips twitched as they turned blue, her body struggling to suck in air as she fought for life. An inaudible word passed through her lips. She cringed. Her body went limp as Genblade breathed her in. His jagged teeth rattled as he brought his lips to her face, his breath smelling like the sole of an old shoe.

"You taste like strawberries," he said finally, letting her fall to the floor.

She looked up at him, and he could feel the terror on her face. Blood oozed from her lips as she mouthed one final plea, then fell to the ground, her blonde hair waving behind her as she did. He felt the restraints around him loosen, and his limbs slipped from the loops. For a moment he was in free fall, the ground coming up on him fast. He stretched his arms and legs out in front of him, landing on all fours like a cat. He pounced almost instantly, pushing off of the floor with both feet. He sprang into a dive, extending his arms and catching her even before she hit the ground.

"Stop this!" Megan screamed. She tried to bolt forward between Xander and Shiro, but the wall of heat stopped her. The instinct to back away from something so hot overrode her will to do so and she backed away despite her own volition. "Stop it, you're killing him!"

Crowley and Lisa are crying. Lisa holds a child covered with blood. Tears are streaming down her face. Xander tries to reach out to her, but his hands are knives. He keeps trying to reach out, to help her... hold her... but just keeps cutting her, stabbing at her until... eventually... they both die. Eventually all three are dead in a pool of blood at his feet, and all he can do about it is to keep reaching out...

Megan steeled herself and forced herself forward into the path of the heat, and suddenly Shiro stopped, steam rising from his skull and from the sockets of his eyes.

"Get out of my way," he said, his voice thick with malice.

The Womb blood made its way into Xander's brain and he could feel the healing process start. Slowly his senses returned to him, but with everything dialed to eleven: he could hear every sound, smell every scent, for blocks at a time.

Tom Petty, blaring on a loudspeaker. Too loud. Burning air. Pop tarts. Red. Blood red. Red. Red hair. Hurt. Pain. Hurt pain. Scream: too loud! Shattered. To ground. Look up. Smell of cream. Touch. Hair. Cheek. Grinding teeth. Death Death! DEATH!

"Get out of my way!" Shiro yelled again, thrusting his head forward as he screamed.

"Calm the fuck down," Duncan said, pointing his secondary at Shiro's head. "You so much as twist a knuckle this time and I'll fire."

"Calm down," Tim stressed. His screens were out, the computers that ran them having overheated. He tried desperately to bring them back online so that he could see what was out of his field of vision, to no avail.

"He deserves death," Shiro hissed through clenched, glowing teeth. "He brings it with him everywhere. Everything he does -- it's all him. All this, it's him."

"Heasa poin," Xander tried to say, his tongue swollen but shrinking as he made his way to his feet.

"It doesn't matter," Megan said, stressing the point with a gaze leveled first at Xander and then at Shiro.

"It's all that matters," Shiro said.

"It doesn't matter because this," Megan motioned back to the non-functioning screens that surrounded Tim. "This means that it was a copycat that killed Laura... and Horton."

Xander winced.

She turned back to Shiro. "Which means the main point that got Victor Murdock off isn't true."

Shiro narrowed his eyes, then lowered his hands as

they ceased to glow. The flesh on them was a glossy, hurt pink.

She knelt and squat next to Xander, tilting his face up toward her. His cheek was like jelly, threatening to shake loose from its connection to his skull if jostled too hard. His eyes had black rings around them and were milky white. They didn't follow her gaze. "Oh my God," she said wetly, her eyes brimming with moisture.

"I'm okay," he said hoarsely. His left cheek warbled with the vibration of his voice and threatened to shake loose. "You're right. We need to find Murdock."

The room was red, from dual lights on either side that faced each other across the brief void of the room's width. It was the red of a photo-developing chamber, the red of neon and blood and valentines. There was a single table in the centre of the room, less than a foot in width but four in length. On it were an assortment of stones: some porous, some smooth. Some were large, hulking masses, others were small, the size of stones one would skip across the water as a child.

The bright, overpowering redness of the room made all colors bow to its will. Everything but the shadows were red. Once one stepped into the room the world became monochrome: the world was either red, or a deep, carbon black. The black was so black that it skewed perception, changing the way objects looked under the shall of it.

Victor stepped up to the table, a smile spreading over his thin lips. "This is a lovely collection," he said, his voice wet with anticipation.

He turned his head up toward the wall beyond the barrier of the table. The floor was raised, becoming almost a stage, equal to the height of the table a foot beyond it. Atop the table, Carlos Bone lay hunched over uncomfortably, his hands cuffed around a hot water pipe running up the wall behind him. He was staring out at Victor with wide eyes that were somehow sleepy and unable to focus simultaneously. There was blood running down his face in long trails, and he was shivering.

Victor picked up a stone, feeling the weight of it in his grasp. His smile broadened. "So, you shall stone him to death because he has sought to seduce you from the Lord your God."

CHAPTER THIRTY

Duncan slammed his foot against the gas pedal, his cruiser's engine revving and thrusting them forward as he pulled to the left and into oncoming traffic, passed the car in front of them, then quickly pulled back in as they rode the dividing line across the turnpike.

"Jesus!" Megan said in the passenger seat, gripping the handle to stop the inertia from hurtling her into the foot-well. "At least put on your flashers!"

"Feds don't have flashers," Duncan said, keeping his eyes glued to the road. His jaw was clenched tight and his knuckles were taut and white as they gripped the wheel.

"Why the fuck not?"

"Wondering that at the moment myself," he said, even as he pulled out onto the curb, passed his car in the space between pedestrians and a tractor trailer, then pulled back onto the street. Without turning away, he grabbed at his radio, pressed the trigger on its side, then pulled it close to his face. "Do we have response on All Points Bulletin for Murdock, Victor?"

The static sound of snow-crash filled the car, almost

drowning out the whine of the engine, until finally a voice responded: "That's a negative, he's not at the house."

"Fuck," Duncan cursed.

"He's at church, the," Xander said. He and Shiro at in the back seat, Xander on the left and Shiro across from him. The gap between them was as wide as it could be. "He's definitely the at church."

"Oh, you're some expert now?" Duncan snapped, glancing at him briefly in the rearview mirror. He then jolted the car to one side to avoid connecting with the bumper in front of them and reminded himself not to do so.

Xander winced, ground his teeth, then brought his hand up to his eyes. His brain was still firing random signals from one area to the next as it tried, desperately, to heal itself. His skull was weak, and the bones of his nose felt soft and malleable when he touched them, as though he might end up with a vastly different look when this was over if he wasn't careful. His jaw snapped into place and shot pain through the left side of his skull, though after a moment it blended with the steady sear that was floating around his mind like an agonized specter.

Crowley and Lisa are crying. Lisa holds a child covered with blood. Tears are streaming down her face. Xander tries to reach out to her, but his hands are knives. He keeps trying to reach out, to help her... hold her... but just keeps cutting her, stabbing at her until... eventually... they both die. Eventually all three are dead in a pool of blood at his feet, and all he can do about it is to keep reaching out...

Tom Petty, blaring on a loudspeaker. Too loud. Burning air. Pop tarts. Red. Blood red. Red. Red hair. Hurt. Pain. Hurt pain. Scream: too loud! Shattered. To ground. Look up. Smell of cream. Touch. Hair. Cheek. Grinding teeth. Death Death! DEATH!

Megan turned to look at him, concern waving over her face. She turned to Shiro. "What did you do to him?"

Shiro opened his mouth to speak.

Xander cut him off. "Fried my brain. Fried it..." he winced, collected himself, then made several forced swallows of the spit and bile and blood that had made its way up into his throat. He turned to glare at Shiro. "He figured out a way to kill me. Superheat my skull and it fries my brain -- healing factor doesn't know what to do with itself. It... it still isn't sure what to do with itself."

Despite himself, Duncan glanced into the rearview mirror once again.

Megan reached out and touched Xander's leg.

Shiro squinted.

"Are you going to be all right?" she asked, plaintively.

Xander snorted back, balked, then thrust forward and threw up. What came up was mostly blood, but some of his last meal was present as well. "Rose oil," he gasped. "Sorry, the car we passed, the woman was drenched in rose oil." He turned to Megan, his eyes bloodshot. "I have no idea. Everything keeps turning up to eleven... it doesn't know how to react to this kind of threat so it's just throwing everything at the wall to see what sticks, I think."

"That's not what I meant," she said, even as she checked the windshield and the proximity of their car to the van in front of them, just as Duncan smashed them to the left of the car to avoid it. There were honks and yells, but they were in the distance within seconds.

Xander stared at her for a long moment, maintaining her gaze despite the thrusting of the vehicle. "No," he said finally. "And I don't think I will be."

Shiro glared at him side-on, then moved his jaw back and forth and turned towards the window.

Megan turned back around, wincing as Duncan narrowly missed a flagpole as he passed a police cruiser on the right-hand side.

Without taking his eyes off the road, Duncan reached into his breast pocket, withdrew his backup pistol, and handed it across the passenger side.

Megan turned to him, shocked "What's this about?"

"If it gets rough," he said simply, then turned quickly. He took a deep breath, not blinking or looking at her. "If it gets rough, with any of them, use it."

She opened her mouth to protest, but for the first time in years could find no argument that she could convincingly make, and took the gun.

A large, oval stone connected with Carlos' clavicle, causing him to yelp out in pain. The pitch of the expression was so high that it echoed off the stone walls and became a distorted thing, like the yelp of a dog.

The stone hit off the wall an instant later, cracking and cackling to the floor with a skittering, dimming din.

Carlos breathed heavily, sweat lining both his cheeks and making them shimmer red.

Victor smiled and picked up another stone, bobbing it in his hand. "Did you think about this -- when you started down this life of sin?" he asked, his voice calm but for the end, when it raised up, like a question.

Carlos steadied his quivering lip and lowered his eyes angrily. "Nothing sinful here 'cept you."

Victor smiled again, then threw the stone. It connected full force with Carlos' gut, threatening to fold him in half from the impact.

Carlos lost his breath, fell to one knee, but was caught by the length of his restraints. He took a shuddering, deep breath, then looked up to make eye contact with Victor.

There was a gun on the table behind him, glimmering dimly in the red light of the room. Carlos' vision found it and focused on it, then pried itself away to maintain his standoff with Victor Murdock.

CHAPTER THIRTY-ONE

There was a time, many, many years ago, when his flesh never went more than a day without touching her auburn hair. She would turn to him every morning with sparkling blue eyes that caught to sunrise, the thin flatness of her hair tickling the inner curve of his elbow. He awoke to her smile and they spent their morning minutes together all days but one.

Her name was Krystal. Krystal Anita Gilbert.

They married when he was thirty and she was thirty-one, and not long after they had had their first and only child, Cameron. The three of them lived in a small home just outside the boundaries of Pittsburgh, Pennsylvania. Krystal worked for an accounting firm from an office in their basement, and Shiro whittled wood for sale by a local art dealer. Though he was not yet of age, they had long since decided that Cameron would be home schooled... they simply could not bear to be apart. As a point of fact, there were only three hours in any given week when they were apart: on Sunday morning, Krystal took Cameron on a one-hour commute into the city for mass at the church she'd grown up in.

He had taken her name, but not her religion.

He'd taken her name because he'd been keenly aware of its connotations in Western culture... of the issues he'd had at airport terminals and on job applications. He could not shelter his son from the heredity of his almond-shaped eyes or his black mop of hair, but he could shelter him from the simple, every day and almost invisible racism that came part and parcel with the name he'd been born with.

She moved forward and kissed him, her hips sweet and wet against his. She braced herself against him, rising to her feet, clinging their loose sheet around her as she rose. She moved to their closet, opened it, and started to move through her clothing options.

"It's Sunday then," he said, leaning his full head of hair back on the pillow. He could hear Cameron stirring in his room with a father's preternatural hearing. He wasn't fully awake yet, was simply rustling and exploring his crib.

"It is," she grinned out one side of her mouth at him, picking out a black tunic with a white collar and laying it out on their bed. She let their sheet fall to the floor -- she did this as a way of making sure he did not sleep the day away -- and removed her flannel top.

He stretched both his arms out to their fullest, then placed both hands behind his head as he watched her dress, a wry smile on his face. "Stay with me," he said, plaintively.

She shot him a droll look, which changed and morphed into something approaching concern. She stressed forward and touched her hand to his chest's central plexus, where there was a patch of dried and reddened skin. They were small circles, banded close together until they formed the rough shape of the old USSR. She tisked. There were similar patterns in the crooks of both his arms, she now realized, and she brought her hand to those as well. "Do these hurt?"

He shook his head, craning his head to see them. "I wouldn't have known they were there if you hadn't told me."

She touched the patch on his left arm gingerly. A flake of skin broke off and fluttered to the ground, revealing bright pink new flesh beneath. "I'll get a cream from the June Market while I'm in town."

"Don't change the subject," he said, touching her arm gently. "Stay with me."

She smiled. "I do not question your lack of faith, Shiro. Please do not question mine."

He frowned, then sat up in bed and let go of her hand. He watched her continue to dress, pulling on black cotton pants she only wore on Sundays. He had considered burning them during many a laundry load. He had come to associate them with time spent away from her. Slowly, his gaze shifted towards the hall, where he could hear Cameron patting against the wall of his crib. His expression became slack, vacant. "How do the other children treat him?"

She stopped buttoning her pants in mid-snap and looked up at him. She turned and looked toward Cameron's room, as though he could have been standing in their doorway, then turned back. "They're children, Shy. They don't have those prejudices yet... and growing up around someone different will only help."

"Children are cruel," he said. He stated it as fact. "Those prejudices run deep, they're inherited from family faster than jewels." He turned to her. "There's been nothing?"

Her jaw moved from side to side, her mouth warbling with it. "There was one incident, weeks back. It wasn't a big deal, not worth mentioning."

"What happened?"

"It was Cliff Warbuck's son. He called Cameron a slur."

Shiro looked at her pensively.

"He's a child, Shy. He didn't even know what it meant. He said it to the other children... those whispers children do. It was nothing. One of the teachers heard it and spoke to him and told the parent and told me. It was nothing."

"Whoever he heard it from knew what it meant," he said, matter-of-factly. "What was the slur?"

A small amount of color fell from her cheeks, and she turned a degree away from him to continue fastening her clothes.

"Ah," he said, nodding. "*That* slur."

"It was nothing," she said again, but quieter now, more to herself.

"We should take him out of that church."

She shot him an annoyed look.

"We're teaching him about the world at home, we can teach him about faith at home as well."

"You don't have any faith," she corrected, grinning. She was trying to take the tension from the situation, but he would have none of it.

"I have faith in you. That is enough."

"Almost every person in this world believes that there is some God or greater being or better thing out there that cares for them and loves them. Can so many people be wrong?"

"I have seen hundreds of sheep be led to slaughter by one wild dog. I see no difference."

She frowned at him.

He sighed, turning his attention back toward the hall. "...Consider switching congregations, at least. To one that's more... inclusive."

"I grew up in that congregation."

"If you had grown up in a time before the smallpox vaccine, would you insist on him having the same as well?"

She furrowed her brow, then finished getting ready in silence. When she was finishing tying her shoes, she looked at him again, and at the oddly shaped patch of red on his chest. "I'll consider it," she said, finally. "Please get that checked." She leaned forward and kissed him again, then left their room to collect their son.

The house was instantly vacant without her in it, and that vacancy began as soon as he knew he couldn't convince her to stay. Once she left the room and the choice was made his missing of her began, a hole that was only filled by her returning.

When he was young, he hadn't had many friends. At the time he hadn't understood why, but now he attributed it mostly to cultural differences. None of the children he'd gone to primary with had been preoccupied with race or ethnicity -- this was evidenced by their having added Krystal to social media when the boom of it began, just to stay in contact, and the type and frequency of their posts. It hadn't been race that had kept him separate as a child, but culture. Children existed through a lens of easily understood options, everything black and white, and he brought different values and options to the table that none of them shared.

It wasn't until double-digit grades that he had begun to experience true, unwavering hate, of the sort his father had always warned him was out there but that he'd never quite believed. He had a scar along his right jawline from one such lesson outside a club he'd been walking past one evening.

Krystal had enjoyed running her thumb over that line of malformed flesh while they'd been dating, the both of them occupying the same seat of his father's pickup truck. There had been parts of the American experience he had thoroughly enjoyed, and one of them was indeed pickup trucks. He had never used it to haul a single item, but the pan of it was the perfect bed for lovers on starlit nights.

"You stay away from that girl, Shiro," his father had said once, his voice coming to him now as clear as if he were hiding behind the headboard. "Like should stay with like, as they say."

He was shocked. He had heard such racism before, not the least of which from slack-jawed men who had given him bruises and kept him out of clubs, but he would have never expected anything of the like from his own father. He said as much, in unkind words that he would regret later in life.

His father had tutted and shaken his steady head. "It's not the girl, or you, or the two of you... but if it should work, it's the child. A beautiful child that would exist between boxes, in a world that loves to put things in boxes above all else."

That had made Shiro's lip tighten, and he hadn't spoken to his father for the remainder of the day, as often happened when the two came to a philosophical impasse.

A hum reached his ears, and he sat up in bed. It had the cadence and rhythm of speech, in tones too low to be coming from Krystal or Cameron. He couldn't make out the words. They had the sound of something distorted through several layers of cloth. He got up out of bed and pulled on his jeans, then made his way to the window. There was no one there, so he started out into the hall.

The rash on his central plexus began to get warmer and warmer, and his hand raised and started to scratch at it without noticing that he was doing it.

"It's not the girl, or you, or the two of you... but if it should work, it's the child. A beautiful child that would exist between boxes, in a world that loves to put things in boxes above all else."

He entered Cameron's room, the walls light pink and blue in alternation. The sound was louder here, the slow heat rising up from his middle growing stronger. He made his way slowly to the far side of the room and parted the canary-yellow curtains that covered his son's bedroom window.

Krystal was outside, holding Cameron over her shoulder and rocking him in the way she did when she was trying to burp him. He was fussing and trying to turn around and see the other people. There were five other people standing in front of his house, the truck they'd come in parked lengthways across his driveway and blocking Krystal in. Four of the men were between the truck and his.

Apart from the others and nearest Krystal was Cliff Warbuck.

The heat radiating up from Shiro's middle reached a fever pitch, but he was no longer scratching at it. His focus -- both conscious and unconscious -- was on the scene playing out below him. His hands both pressed against the glass, and condensation stretched out from where he touched, framing the action below between his thumbs.

Cameron turned his eyes up toward him, from his place nestled against the nape of his mother's neck.

Cliff pointed at Krystal, saliva flying from his mouth in tiny arcs.

The heat in Shiro's chest became so hot that it hurt, fighting with the confrontation below for his attention.

Krystal extended a hand, palm up, the way he'd often seen her do when making a reasoned argument. She continued to bob Cameron, who continued to stare at Shiro.

Cliff grabbed the extended wrist and pushed it aside. The jolt jostled Krystal, and Cameron fell roughly to the ground. He screamed almost instantly, the way only small children could scream.

The heat in Shiro's middle exploded in a wave of white light, and he could see nothing for a long time.

When he woke up several hours later, he was lying on what had been the foundation of his home. The remainder of its studs were burning around him, turning themselves to cinders.

He strained to focus, the evening sun hot and painful against his flaking flesh. He turned to look where Krystal and Cameron had been when last he saw them, and saw only two smoldering piles of ash and bone.

"Shiro," Krystal said, as his mind let go of reality.

"Shiro!" Xander said, and suddenly Shiro turned, his mind back in the car that was speeding towards the Church of the Holy Heavenly Father.

He stopped, licking his parched lips with an equally parched tongue.

Xander squinted at him. "You with us?"

Shiro shook. On the empty seat between them, Krystal sat staring at him. She nodded slowly. "Yes," he said hoarsely. "Yes, I'm with you."

A large, oval stone connected with Carlos' clavicle, causing him to yelp out in pain. The pitch of the expression was so high that it echoed off the stone walls and became a distorted thing, like the yelp of a dog.

The stone hit off the wall an instant later, cracking and cackling to the floor with a skittering, dimming din.

Carlos breathed heavily, sweat lining both his cheeks and making them shimmer red.

Victor smiled and picked up another stone, bobbing it in his hand. "Did you think about this -- when you started down this life of sin?" he asked, his voice calm but for the end, when it raised up, like a question.

Carlos steadied his quivering lip and lowered his eyes angrily. "Nothing sinful here 'cept you."

Victor smiled again, then threw the stone. It connected full force with Carlos' gut, threatening to fold him in half from the impact.

Carlos lost his breath, fell to one knee, but was caught by the length of his restraints. He took a shuddering, deep breath, then looked up to make eye contact with Victor.

There was a gun on the table behind him, glimmering dimly in the red light of the room. Carlos' vision found it and focused on it, then pried itself away to maintain his standoff with Victor Murdock.

CHAPTER THIRTY-TWO

"Is this the place?" Megan asked, stepping up to the door of the Holy Heavenly Father church.

"This is it, yes," Shiro said under in breath.

Xander turned and squinted at him.

"Got it, yes," Duncan said, speaking into his cellphone and then hanging it up briskly. "That was local PD. There's no sign of him at his house, his ex-girlfriend's house, his previous employer or any known haunts. This is it, there's backup on the way."

Xander nodded, then stepped toward the door and opened it.

The church was vacant of worshippers, as it had been the last time they were there. The hallway sprawled along either side of the rows of pews until it reached the glowing light of the faux candles, their light framing the only other person in the hall. Reverend Trask stood in front of the candles, turning away from lighting the last of the genuine ones, and faced them. "Hello," he said, his voice dull and calm.

"Don't move," Duncan said, his voice clipped and authoritative. He stalked ahead of the others, stepping toward Trask. "Where is he?"

Megan turned and saw the dim light of the stained-glass. She stepped back from the others as they proceeded forward and walked over to it.

"Where is who?" Trask smiled.

"Cut the crap. Cut it all, right now," Duncan sneered, pointing an accusing finger at Trask. "I have had a long, weird day and I do not know what's up with most of it, so don't try me, just tell me where Murdock is."

Xander stopped three pews back from Trask, and when Shiro saw this he followed suit.

"I haven't seen him, I'm sorry," Trask repeated.

Duncan turned to Xander, who was looking around the room.

"He's been here," Xander said.

"Fuck this," Duncan huffed. He produced a pair of handcuffs from around his belt. He stepped up to Trask. "I'm placing you under arrest."

"For what?" Trask demanded.

"I'll figure it out," he replied under his breath, even as he snapped the first metal clasp shut.

From the wall, Megan raised an eyebrow. "You know that'll never stand up, right? Like, I could have argued that in law school."

Duncan led Trask to a nearby pew and looped the handcuffs around one of the artful gaps in its railing before closing the second clasp around his opposite hand. "I'll deal with that when I deal with it," he said, frowning. "Fan out, he's here."

Shiro raised his hands as Xander and Megan opened the door to Trask's office. He felt the heat radiate from along the tips of his fingers, ready to pour out, just as it had that day many years ago.

As he watched, waiting to see if Murdock was on the other side of the door, he noticed Megan's hand touch Xander's shoulder-blade gingerly. He turned to her and stopped what he was doing for a moment, before continuing.

The door opened suddenly and Shiro felt the heat crackle and bubble his fingernails. The room was empty, small, and narrow. He felt the heat in his hands subside slightly.

"Dammit," Xander cursed under his breath. Then he turned toward Duncan, who was on his phone and checking another room but keeping Trask in eyesight, and spoke louder: "Clear."

The two of them moved into the room, cautiously. Shiro followed. When he turned the scant corner, Krystal was sitting on what was assuredly Trask's desk, with her feet on his chair. She smiled at him with a lopsided grin and was wearing the sort of spaghetti-strap top she had typically worn when they met, but hadn't often in her last few years.

"They care about each other," she said, turning and watching as Xander and Megan searched the drawers and shelves they passed, looking for some hint of where Murdock might be. Krystal smiled at them. "She knows it's not his fault, what happened."

"It is his fault," Shiro said under his breath.

Xander turned to him. "Trask? Yeah, seems like." He started moving items on Trask's desk, looking for something that was hidden under a weighted object. There were no computers in the room, nor even a phone or ethernet option where one could have connected from. He grabbed toward an iron cross to move it, paused, then let his hand fall away.

Megan rolled her eyes at him, then stepped forward and moved the stand. There was nothing underneath.

"He believes," Krystal said, nodding her head in Xander's direction. "He might not carry it with him all the time, but he believes. That's what gets him through this... this shit. That's what keeps him on the right path. Faith, it isn't useful because society has gotten too easy. But for people who are tested -- people like you, and like him -- faith is needed to keep you on the right path."

He glared, through cracked eyelids, out at where Trask sat. "Look at the wonders faith has led him to do."

Xander turned to him but did not say anything.

"Shy," Krystal said, plaintively. "You know this is true... because I'm not here. You're talking to yourself."

He turned back around, and suddenly it was only Xander and Megan in the room with him. He sighed, long and heavy.

"There's nothing here," Xander said under his breath. He clenched his fists, relaxed them, then turned quickly and knocked everything off of Trask's desk -- cross included. "There's nothing fucking here!" he barked.

Megan raised a hand to help him, then pulled it back.

"It's going to be okay. We'll find him, just like you found Genblade and god only knows how many others. We'll find him."

Xander took a deep breath, resting both sets of knuckles on the desk. "This is on me. *Again.* Bennett, Murdock getting out... Horton. This is me. I thought the Jekyl-Hyde thing was done... but what if it isn't? What if it never was?" He turned to face her. "What if LA is so big a place that things have been happening without my notice?"

She reached out again, but his shoulders heaved as her touch neared, and she pulled back away. "I don't have an answer for that. I deal in legal absolutes, not moral ones. I can tell you that Murdock is not your fault, it's mine. It would have taken longer, but I would have gotten him off. It was the Raymond Coup chain of custody argument; the prosecution's case couldn't withstand it. What you did... what the Womb did... it expedited matters; it didn't create them."

His nose twitched as he fought a sneer.

"This belongs to all of us," she said, touching her chest with one hand while finally reaching out and connecting with him with the other. "This is on me and my arguments, you and your personality disorder, and his," she gestured to Shiro, "fucked up rationales. We did this, the three of us, and we have to make it right."

Xander's lip curled, his barred knuckles turning white.

"She's right," Shiro said, stepping forward into the room fully. He had been bisecting the doorframe ever since they had gained entry into the room, but now came fully in. "This is on all of us and none of us. We all have different selves... demons, ghosts, loved ones... that haunt and affect who we are today."

Megan stepped back from Xander, giving Shiro room to enter the narrow quarters.

Xander grimaced. "The last thing I need is a pep talk from you, honestly. You can say what you want about my other half, but I've never killed." He thumped his chest. "Not me, not intentionally."

Shiro nodded. "I suppose drunks aren't responsible for those they kill under the influence, either."

Megan winced, but Xander's face fell. He heard the words in every part of himself, and she turned and stepped out of the room. Duncan was leaving to put Trask in the back of his car, already on the phone with the oncoming backup. She looked back at the two of them -- Shiro and Xander -- and exited the room fully, making her way down the length of the church along its far wall.

Shiro stepped forward and picked up the cross Xander had knocked over, placing it back on its perch on the desk. "Things are not as black and white as most of me thought," he said, almost to himself. "Like ash, most of it is gray."

Xander squinted, looking from the cross to Shiro and then back again. "I didn't take you for the religious sort."

"I'm not. My wife was, and I suppose my child would have been. They had something I didn't... a faith that the world was more than random. But their deaths... their deaths were random. Fanatics came to our home, of the sort that didn't care for race mixing." He turned to Xander. "You've met the type."

Xander nodded.

"They came to keep them out of their church, they didn't want different people there... they said they wanted their faith to include all, but that was a lie they told themselves. They shunned everyone who was different out and then told themselves that what remained was all there was. They wanted the same for my wife and son, and they grabbed at her, and he fell." He raised his hand, palm up, steam rising from his pores. "And then this happened for the first time."

Xander narrowed his eyes, then nodded. "I thought you killed your family."

"I did kill my family."

"That's not what I --"

"I know what you meant," he said coldly, turning his palm around. The steam subsided. "The point is, I think that she was right... somehow. This black and white, all-or-nothing thinking... it doesn't honor her or avenge her, it disgraces her." He pursed his lips. When they relaxed, he turned in the direction Megan had gone. "By all rights she should hate what we are, just as my Krystal would hate what we are. She believes in the law the way Krystal believed in the Lord. Wholly. And yet neither hates us. They both set a path that rejects violence and are the better for it." He turned to Xander. "What does that make us?"

In the red room, Victor stood on the stage with Carlos, his feet wading in a shallow pool of blood. His eyes were wide in a way they'd never been while Megan had interviewed him, bulging and lidless with unobscured pupils. He stared at the door with his hand pressed tight to Carlos' mouth, pressing so hard into his jaw that blood squeezed from between them like an orange.

CHAPTER THIRTY-THREE

Megan straddled the space between the wall and the pews, stepping carefully along the scant space between the two. Her hand moved along the edge of the wall, feeling to folds and ebbs of the damp brick that made up that entire side of the structure.

She passed a stained-glass image of Jesus healing a beggar. At least that's what she thought it was... it could have been anything. It had yellow glass panels splaying out from where Jesus' hand touched the man, but that could have been anything. For all she knew the man could have been firing yellow laser-beams at him.

The area between the stained-glass windows was dark, her eyes taking a moment to adjust to each lapse into darkness. It wasn't warm like natural light... it was coloured, even the parts that came through the plain, clear glass. It had the greenish din of fluorescent lighting. The next image was of an angry bearded man, whose arm was outstretched and pointing away, beyond the viewer. She leaned back until she could see the inscription: "And then I will declare to them, 'I never knew you; DEPART FROM

ME, YOU WHO PRACTICE LAWLESSNESS. - Matthew 7:23."

She squinted, feeling the cold light that came from behind the glass on her face. She turned to see if Xander or Shiro had left Trask's office yet. Neither had. She regarded the glass again, and stepped back as far as she could, her back leaning against the rail of the pew behind her.

All at once, her first conversation with Victor Murdock came to her.

Victor's head turned to one side, and that small smile of his broadened just a little. "Thank you. There's something so nice about natural light... light that comes from a place farther away than our grasp of things. We can't step behind natural light, can't see it from the other side. It's... real."

She clicked her tongue against the roof of her mouth, then reached out and ran her hand along the left edge of the frame. A foot from the bottom her finger caught on something and the stained-glass swung forward on a hinge, opening like a door to reveal a light on either side of the wall behind it -- and beyond that, a hallway that stretched deeper into the church.

She turned back toward Trask's office, swallowed, then reached for Duncan's gun and raised it. She raised her leg high and stepped over the ledge of the lights and into the hidden hall, which bent to run perpendicular to the length of the church.

She turned back toward where Xander and Shiro were, not wanting to call out. "Pssst," she hissed through gritted teeth, turning back down the secret hall after she did to make sure there was no one poking their head out around. "Psst!"

Nobody came. She cursed in her head but said nothing out loud, then started back towards them.

There was a moan from deep in the bowels of the hallway. It was low at first, then grew. It grew end over end, like rising notes, then fell sharply again. In all her years Megan had never heard a sound like it, and yet something evolutionary -- something instinctual -- inside her knew what it was. It was the sound of pain nearing death.

She bit her lip, checked the gun, then turned back toward the source of the sound.

Ahead of her, near the end of the hall, was a room from which red light bled. She swallowed and stepped forward on the sides of her feet, sliding with her back as close to the wall as she could get it without making a sound. Her palm was sweating around the butt of Duncan's gun, and her lips were parched. Somewhere she could hear a radio playing classic rock, the slow hum of only the bass making it through the walls of the extension.

There were two open doors between her and the red room. The first was across from her, and she peered in. It was an office with a cluttered desk, a mirror-image almost of Trask's office from the church's main hall... except that this one looked used, devoid of the dust and settlement that had been there. The room was lit with its own stained-glass visage, this one showing a different bearded man, this one holding a stone as more behind him gathered more.

The inscription read: "If a man lies with a male as with a woman, both of them have committed an abomination; they shall surely be put to death; their blood is upon them. - Leviticus 20:13." The light that came through it was a putrid green, changing the bearded man from the sort of pale mischaracterization from Da Vinci to something craven and lizard-like. The shapes of the glass fingers around the stone were sharp, making them look like claws.

She craned her head into the room, saw nothing alive, then continued forward. The next room was filled with books, aged and dusty. The entrance had no door on it; the only thing separating it was the difference in tile and that the glut and clutter of red-leather-bound books seemed to stop dead at the door. There were red silk bookmarks sticking out of some of them, their edges flopped over impotently.

She continued along the arch of the hall, trying to find some moisture in her mouth as she got closer and closer to the glowing, humming red room at the end of the hall. As she moved, more and more of the room came into view, like a camera panning slowly across a set. Eventually the view of the doorway found its way to Carlos Bone, who sat bleeding and alone on a slight rise.

"Oh my god," she gasped, moving into the room quickly and making her way past the table displaying the long row of rocks. She hit it with her hip when she passed, rocking it and sending several rolling to the floor. Her eyes went bad in the red light of the room that turned everything monochrome. She laid down her weapon, then took Carlos' head in her hands and lifted it. "Can you hear me?"

Carlos' head lolled, his eyes moving about his head independent from one another. "Un," he said, blood running from his mouth when he tried to speak.

"Thank god," she said, and immediately reached for

the chain that was binding him. "We've got to get you out of here. We get you out first, we'll deal with whoever did this. I've brought --"

"*Run*," he repeated, forcing the word out.

She stopped, her eyes wide, and locked her gaze with his. She turned and reached for her borrowed weapon, only to find it was not where she had left it.

Victor Murdock stepped closer to the table that divided the two of them, and lowered Duncan's gun toward her.

There was a scream, and then a shot.

"Fuck!" Xander yelled, his head shooting up from the file he was looking through. Shiro was already on his feet when Xander crossed the threshold of Trask's office back out into the church proper. He turned, found the half-open faux glass door, and started toward it. He could already hear the changes in the sound of the room: the soft din of radio rock that was filtering in from the building next door into the new part of the church, and then out into the main hall and the pews. "No, no, no," he said over and over, as he sprinted for the glass door and bolted through it, hopping over the gap.

He ignored the two rooms along the right-hand side of the hall, sprinting for the red room at the back.

"Hey!" Shiro shouted, following.

Xander ignored him, plowing forward with one leg in front of the other, until he eventually turned the corner.

Megan was slumped between the table and the stage, Carlos Bone unconscious and stretched against the confines of his chains behind her. At first, he wasn't sure what was happening, until he saw the steadily growing puddle of black that was ebbing its way from Megan's feet, slowly making its way out across the floor.

"No no no NO!" Xander yelled, pushing forward. He lifted her by her shoulders and pushed her back against the stage, revealing the long, gurgling gunshot wound in her central plexus. He could hear the blood forcing its way out to the beat of a Tom Petty song that was droning through the walls of the church.

He tries not to hear her. Hearing her means knowing.

"Iiiiii," she said, her eyes already refusing to focus. She didn't move her hands. Couldn't. "Iiiiii."

"It's okay," he said, his mouth distorting. "I know."

The air all around him was burning. That combined with the scent of blood and her perfume was activated the Womb senses. Suddenly, he could smell what Carlos had had for breakfast that morning. Pop tarts. Red, strawberry Pop Tarts. Red like blood. Red like Megan's hair. It hurt him so to see her like this. To see her in so much pain. Hurt and pain. He looked up. The shampoo she used smelled like strawberries and cream, and he leaned in and got his lungs full of it one final time, hearing her grind her teeth against the pain in her chest with the last ebb of strength she had.

A second shot rang out just as Shiro was coming around the corner, and a large chunk of Xander's shoulder splayed up and out, spattering against the far wall. He turned, his face low and distorted by rage, to see Victor Murdock against the far wall, Duncan's gun extended and smoking.

"Murderer," he growled, stepping forward and crossing the distance between them in two steps. Murdock fired again, removing a second chunk of flesh. Xander did not break stride. He grabbed the gun and forced it from Murdock's hand, then grabbed him by the throat and pinned him against the back wall.

"I saw you," Victor sneered, his mouth twisting in contempt. "Don't think I didn't see you touched her, the way she touched you. You practice lawlessness. These are wicked things, as wicked as when man lay with man, and must be stoned."

Shiro balked, stiffening. He recalled similar words said by himself. Not the same, but too similar.

"She was going to stand in the way of the Justice and it had to be stopped."

Xander turned and looked over his shoulder at Carlos slumped against his chains, the marks along his head, and the line of stones great and small along the table between them. Fighting the darkness that edged along the side of his vision, he turned back to Murdock and tightened his grip around his neck.

"You have to stop him!" yelled Krystal from somewhere behind Shiro. "You know what this does to someone... you know this won't solve anything!"

Shiro narrowed his eyes.

Xander ground his teeth together as Murdock's lips began to turn blue.

"Stop this," Shiro said. His voice was low at first, then he spoke again and raised it: "Stop this."

Xander did not turn or make any indication he'd heard him at first, then slowly he released his grip and Murdock fell gasping to the floor. Xander worked his jaw back and forth, made a growling sound deep in his throat, then turned around and slammed both knuckles into the table and barred them there.

"She believed in the law," Shiro said. He took a single step closer to Xander, but still kept a good distance between them. "Just as my wife believed in the lord. My wife wouldn't have approved of the path I'd taken... any more than she would approve of you going down the same path. And you know -- you *know* -- that if you kill him, you become him." He paused, then brought a hand to his chest. "You'll go down a path where everything burns -- like me. But I believe I can turn that around, that I can honor those I've loved by living as they would have wanted. That I can change."

Xander's lips pursed tight and wrinkling his chin. "I think you can, too," he said finally, after a long pause. "And you should." He unwound his knuckles, raised his left hand, and let his right fall onto a pointed stone the size of his head. He turned to Shiro, met his eye, and nodded once. "I have better things to do."

He turned, too quickly for Shiro to react, and whipped the stone around, connecting it with the side of Murdock's head. His head slammed to the left so quick that his neck strained, slamming into the far wall and then toppling to the ground, the flesh of it turned and aligned wrong. Blood rose to the surface where Murdock had been struck, formed a bruised bubble, then gushed forth, mingling with Megan's blood as it made its way across the floor.

"No!" Krystal yelled. Shiro remained silent.

Xander raised the stone and brought it down again. And then a third time. And then a fourth. He continued until after Shiro had turned and left, after Murdock's putrid breath had stopped wheezing out into the secret halls of his church, and even after the part of his skull he was striking had been reduced to a maw of blood and brain matter.

He stayed there, breathing deep of the stench of copper and bile that filled the room, until he heard the sirens come.

EPILOGUE

Duncan Taggart walked into Tim White's bungalow apartment just after three in the morning. His hair was ravaged and stuck high with sweat and he had more than a day's scruff along the edges of his face.

He took off his coat as though it ached just to do it, let out a long, strained sigh, then laid it over Tim's legs.

Tim stared at him, his lips held tight.

Duncan stared back for a long moment, his exhaustion evident. "Tell me. Everything."

Xander watched Martha Horton from the shadows outside her home, hidden from the light of the rising sun by the large bushes on either side of her driveway. He stepped to the porch steps, his feet resting comfortably on the third. There was still enough width to the steps that a second man could have stood there next to him, and again he remembered when Horton had.

He started to step forward into the kitchen, toward Martha, mouth open to say something. He hung there for a moment, waiting for words, or for tears, or screams -- waiting for *something* to happen.

Once again, he turned after a moment's hesitation. He left Martha alone and decided that he always would.

The funeral at Coral Beach had been small. Only a few residents had come, close friends, really. Megan hadn't had any relatives, and her ex had been too busy to come out for the funeral. It was raining again, and the minister finished the ceremony under an umbrella held by one of his orderlies.

"Ashes to ashes, and dust to dust..."

Cathy Kennessy did not cry as she looked onward, staring blankly at the gravestone before her. She wanted to, but somehow couldn't. She'd buried so many friends, she guessed that she had shielded her heart to that kind of pain by now, if that were even possible.

As the casket was lowered, she couldn't help but think of the news report about the Black Womb and wonder. She wasn't wondering about whether or not Xander was responsible or not, that much wasn't really important at this point. No, she kept her eyes on the forest surrounding the graveyard and wondered: Will he be here?

Eventually, the crown thinned. Many people left right away because of the rain, but Cathy stayed a long time, even after nightfall.

Xander stood in the rubble of Joucastle, the heat of the setting Los Angeles sun against his back. In front of him was a large stone, blocking the way down the stairs that led beneath the grounds.

He picked up his sledgehammer, raised it high, then brought it down against the stone slab. He did this three times in quick succession. On the third he screamed, long and loud, and brought the hammer down as hard as he could.

It shattered against the stone slab, the wooden handle breaking and splintering into bits.

He fell forward without a pause to consider the shattered tool, digging his nails into the edges of the rock and pulling at it. It slipped from his grasp three times before he dug his nails in deep, fighting back the urge for the true womb to produce his claws. They got solid purchase and he pulled, leaning his whole body back for momentum.

He yelled so loud it echoed off the buildings around, and when he slipped free this time, the boulder kept his nails. He skidded across the gravel, clutching the bloody tips of each finger and holding them to his chest, each one stripped of its shield.

He gasped. "I'm sorry."

At the sound of his own voice, red color returned to his cheeks and he clenched his hands into fists, slamming at the boulder that blocked the entrance to Joucastle. He slammed it again and again with white knuckles, ignoring every lesson about how to throw a punch he'd ever learned. Skin split, then splayed, and then healed itself again for the next blow.

Eventually, he broke away enough of the boulder.

And found himself deep in the centre of the dark hole it guarded.

Alone.

AFTERWORD

This book went through a number of drafts. Despite being the sixteenth book published starring Xander Drew, I wrote its first draft fifth. The time between its first draft and last was fully nineteen years.

This novel is very different than it started, but there are some plot points that had to remain for the larger narrative of the series, and where we're taking it. Books that come after this one are already written, so some things couldn't be avoided... as much as I might have wanted to. I'm assuming nobody is reading this page first, so I'll say it bluntly: the deaths of Thomas Horton and Megan Greene.

On a practical level, I don't like the idea of Megan Greene being 'fridged,' and I tried hard to avoid that reading. But it's there. There were many conversations with my writing partner Ellen Curtis and my editor Erin Vance about how to mitigate this reality, but it's hard. It's a plot point that was conceived and built upon when I was much younger, and now I'm forced to contend with it. If you're going to miss Megan Greene -- know that I'm right there with you.

A key component of the 'fridged women' trope, to my understanding, is that the death motivates the male main character into action. I've tried to avoid that, but there's definitely an easy way to read it that way. If you're offended or upset about this plot point despite my efforts to mitigate that reading, know that I am sorry. I am aware of these issues and I tried very, very hard to fix it while staying true to the grander series narrative.

On a thematic level, both Thomas and Megan die for the same reason. Stories featuring Xander Drew exist in two worlds -- his stories are as dual natured as he is -- on one level visceral, violent horror novels and on another slow, contemplate crime thrillers. We've lived in the latter for some time now, and so has Xander Drew -- and he's gotten as complacent as we have.

In simpler terms: he forgot what book series he was in. He thought that he had things under control and that normal people could get involved in his orbit and not be hurt by it, and he let his guard down. So did we -- I got attached to these characters and almost forgot where this was all headed.

Xander Drew will always be a character who lives on the knife's edge, and when he forgets that, it's never him that pays the price. Maybe this time he's learned. I hope so.

The next novel is called *First Aid*, and will explore this more fully. Without giving away too much: it is our first full crossover with the *Infinity* series, because Xander has finally reached the point that he needs to be taken down.

I'd like to thank my editor Erin Vance for all her help on this text; her input to the Engen Universe has been invaluable.

This book is dedicated to my partner, Ellen Curtis, who makes me a better writer. Every day.

Matthew LeDrew
May 14, 2020
St. John's, Newfoundland

ENGEN TIMELINE

With over twenty novels spread over three different series by many different authors, the Engen Universe of titles is growing every day and into genres we couldn't have imagined! From the original ten book *Black Womb* thriller series, its crime novel sequel series *Xander Drew*, our flagship adventure title *Infinity*, or single-novels like *Jacobi Street* or *light|dark*, there's something in the Engen Universe for everyone with more books by more authors on the way soon!

...But how do the events relate to one another, chronologically? While some astute readers have guessed at the potential timeline (some accurately, some not), we're going to finally set the question of the Engen Timeline to rest.

Turn the page for an up-to-date guide of the ever-widening world of Engen, featuring the works of Ali House, Ellen Curtis, Andrea Hackett, Sarah Thompson, Jay Paulin, and Matthew LeDrew!

In the 10 Years Prior Black September

"Reptilia" by Matthew LeDrew
published in *light | dark*.
Danger descends on a small secluded town in the form of a deadly virus with fantastic and terrible side-effects. Can a small group of doctors escape alive?

Compendium by Ellen Curtis
Three short stories forming the basis for the Engen Universe's ties to suspense, genetic engeneering, and the supernatural. Features the stories "The Tourniquet Revival," "Falling into Fire" and "At Midnight, the Dawn."

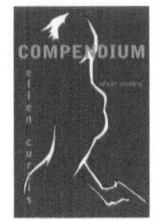

"The Theogony" by Matthew LeDrew
published in *light | dark*.
A tale of young Theo Flaherty of the *Infinity* series and his time admitted against his will to the Black Springs hospital, where he learns to paint, and seeks out his father.

Black September

"Revving Engen" by Matthew LeDrew
published in *light | dark*.
A direct lead-in to both *Infinity* and *Black Womb*, Tasha travels to Coral Beach, Maine on a hot tip about a recently discovered young man with incredible abilities.

Infinity by Ellen Curtis & Matthew LeDrew
Faced with a destiny he's uncertain of, the enigmatic Victor must bring together four unique people with very special abilities… or face the tasks ahead alone. Guaranteed to excite!

Black Womb by Matthew LeDrew
Fifteen years ago, something happened in Coral Beach, Maine that resulted in the present death of a seventeen-year-old boy. Now four high-school students must try to solve the mystery... before the killer picks them off.

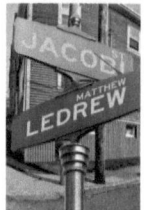

Jacobi Street by Matthew LeDrew
When a mysterious painting shows up at an art gallery he works at, Bob must work with Eddie and Sloan to track down its sinister origins and convince the people living on Jacobi Street of them, before its too late!

Transformations in Pain by Matthew LeDrew
When two girls are assaulted and one is hospitalized, the residents of Coral Beach must put their shared tragedies behind them and stop the man responsible, as well as unlock the secrets behind the true nature of the Womb...

Year One: October

Smoke and Mirrors by Matthew LeDrew
The approaching trial of Genblade brings closure to the people of Coral Beach, until people start showing up dead in the same manner they did when he was at large.

"Scarlett" by Andrea Hackett
published in *light | dark*.
Introducing Scarlett, the slightly damaged hunter on a mission to save others from the monsters from her past.

"The Inevitable" by Ali House
published in *The Lightbulb Forest*
A young woman must contend with the
emergence of a frightening new power alongside
the emotional high of a first date.

The Tourniquet Reprisal by Curtis & LeDrew
A man lives in Atlanta, Georgia that people
don't talk about, but everyone knows he's there.
He arrived a year ago and turned a gaggle
of uneducated youth into something new,
something to fear.

Roulette by Matthew LeDrew
As the teen suicide rate in Coral Beach starts to
climb astronomically fast, Xander travels to Los
Angeles to fight his most terrifying adversary
yet… and learns that the only thing worse than
looking for release… is finding it.

Year One: November

Exodus of Angels by Curtis & LeDrew
Victor's enigmatic past is illuminated when
Jaycee accompanies him to visit a new friend
in the paliative care ward of the Black Springs
hospital, where Theo also happens to be
searching for a cure for Leigh.

Ghosts of the Past by Matthew LeDrew
Coral Beach faces its most awesome threat when
one of Engen's past mistakes is unleashed upon
the unsuspecting populous. Friends and enemies
unite to fight a common enemy… but will even
that be enough?

Touch Your Nose by Matthew LeDrew
Simon Monk must infiltrate the San Fransico branch of Shane Industries, a massive company with deep ties to the Engen Universe. Where do his true loyalties lie? And can he get out without causing harm?

Ignorance is Bliss by Matthew LeDrew
After being set through the ringer one too many times, Xander decides that his life with Julie needs a little more attention… which is bad news because a new villain has come to town with his sights set on Adam Genblade.

"Gristle While You Work" by Jay Paulin published in *light | dark*.
A short story centering around the rise of a new, and possibly cannibalistic, serial killer in the Engen Universe.

Becoming by Matthew LeDrew
For months Xander Drew has been doing his level best to keep the streets of Coral Beach clean, which means it's time for the forces of darkness to strike back… all at once.

Inner Child by Matthew LeDrew
Julie is hospitalized with life-threatening wounds to both body and soul. But the real threat comes from the hospital walls themselves, as a demonic presence makes itself known to Xander and his friends.

End of Year One

Gang War by Matthew LeDrew
The Tees, a homicidal gang of evil men, has finally been taken down by Xander Drew. But his victory is short lived, as retired Tees are mysteriously killed. With a town of suspects, anyone can be the culprit… including one of their own.

Chains by Matthew LeDrew
Sociopath Derek Smith has been freed from prison and is praying on the weak; and none are weaker than August Styles: a pregnant girl with Down Syndrome who has run away from home.

"Omega" by Ellen Curtis
published in *light | dark*.
A sinister division of Engen begins a series of experiments on pregnant women in a fashion eerily similar to those that created the original Black Womb project.

The Long Road by Matthew LeDrew
Xander meets the American people — and realizes that the world is harsh and wicked, but can also be soft and gentle, even loving. Xander Drew comes of age on the road, and sets his new direction.

Year Two

Cinders by Matthew LeDrew
Detective Horton enters a violent and dangerous world he didn't know existed beneath the veneer of order and structure that he has based his entire deductive method around.

Sinister Intent by Matthew LeDrew
One of the killers Detective Horton could not catch has resurfaced: a serial killer who flaunts his sinister intent in front of the Los Angeles Police Department, making it so that no one is safe.

Faith by Matthew LeDrew
Xander's mysterious and troublesome past returns to haunt him on the streets of Los Angeles; a place where even more people can get caught in the crossfire of the games of death and deceit that makes up his life.

Flickers in the Night by Matthew LeDrew
Lisa Rowdan is hunted by her haunting -- and powerful -- ex-boyfriend Ryan through a lonely city street. Can she escape him?
One of over twenty great sprine-tingling short stories!

Family Values by Matthew LeDrew
Xander and his new friends Crowley, Lisa, and Tim investigate a series of kidnappings and murders that stretch back decades, all of which have the same similar twist: victims being found after years of being missing.

The Future

Fate's Shadow by Matthew LeDrew
When one of Xander's old cases comes up for trial, Megan Greene returns with it. The former friends are led into conflict regarding her client's innocence. However, they put their difference aside when they both become targets of the vigilante known as Shiro Gilbert.

The Future

"Remers" by Sarah Thompson
published in *light|dark*.
In the not-too-distant future of the Engen
Universe, young athletes are the targets of a
scouting program to create the next stage of super
soldier with cybernetic enhancements.

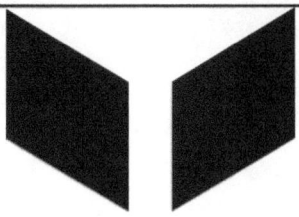

THE XANDER DREW SERIES

Prologue: The Long Road (May 2014)

Book One: Cinders (April 2015)
Book Two: Sinister Intent (November 2015)
Book Thee: Faith (December 2017)
Book Four: Family Values (December 2018)
Book Five: Fate's Shadow (May 2020)
Book Six: First Aid (forthcoming)

COMING SOON FROM ENGEN BOOKS:

FIRST AID

When Xander takes his feud with mob boss Stephen Fields to
the streets, his attracts the attention of the *Infinity* team of Tash,
Nick, Kelly, and Iseult. Before the arrive, he'll have pushed the
mob boss into an all out gang war, the likes of which the city
will never recover from.

The early years of **Xander Drew** as he struggles with the evils of his small rural hometown of Coral Beach, Maine. Cursed with the heart of the Womb and the gift of seeing the world around him for what it really is, Xander must learn the hard lessons about the nature of humanity to traverse the minefield of criminals, gangs, and abusers that stand between him and ultimate happiness -- but most of all that **sometimes it takes a monster, to catch a monster.**

"THE WRITING OF ITS GENERATION-- VISUAL, TO-THE-POINT AND IN-THE-MOMENT."

- The Northeast Avalon Times

The Coral Beach Casefiles series by Matthew LeDrew:

Book One: Black Womb (October 2007)
Book Two: Transformations in Pain (April 2008)
Book Three: Smoke and Mirrors (February 2009)
Book Four: Roulette (October 2009)
Book Five: Ghosts of the Past (April 2010)
Book Six: Ignorance is Bliss (October 2010)
Book Seven: Becoming (April 2011)
Book Eight: Inner Child (November 2011)
Book Nine: Gang War (April 2012)
Book Ten: Chains (April 2013)

Epilogue: The Long Road (May 2014)

For more information, please visit

www.engenbooks.com

infinity

The world is changing, and we have to change with it. That was the one thing that Victor was really sure of when he started looking for special people: people who could change the possibilities of the future from something certainly grim... to something *infinitely* positive.

Now four unsuspecting people from different backgrounds and walks of life have been thrown into the mix together, and nothing will ever be the same. But there's a difference between hoping for a better world and actually having one, and there will always be resistance to change.

Book One:	Infinity (October 2010)
Book Two:	The Tourniquet Reprisal (October 2012)
Book Three:	Exodus of Angels (April 2016)
Book Four:	Garden of the 8th Circle

Related Books:

> Compendium (October 2009)
> light|dark (April 2012)
> Roulette (October 2009)
> The Long Road (May 2014)
> Touch Your Nose (May 2018)

Written by the superstar author team of Ellen Curtis (*Compendium*) and Matthew LeDrew (the *Xander Drew* series).

Destiny doesn't wait for anyone.

ABOUT THE AUTHOR

Matthew LeDrew holds an Honours Degree in English from the Memorial University of Newfoundland with a minor in Anthropology, and studied Journalism at College of the North Atlantic in Stephenville, Newfoundland. He was honoured to be a jury member of both the 2018 NLBA awards and the 2020 Arts and Letters Awards

He has written twenty other novels for Engen Books: the ten book Coral Beach Casefiles series, *The Long Road, Cinders, Sinister Intent, Faith, Family Values, Jacobi Street, Touch Your Nose, Infinity, The Tourniquet Reprisal,* and *Exodus of Angels* the latter three of which with co-author Ellen Curtis.

He lives in St. John's, Newfoundland.